Also by Macy Beckett

The Dumont Bachelors Series
Make You Blush (a novella)
Make You Mine

The Sultry Springs Series
Sultry with a Twist
A Shot of Sultry
Surrender to Sultry

MAKE YOU REMEMBER

THE DUMONT BACHELORS

Macy Beckett

A SIGNET ECLIPSE BOOK

SIGNET ECLIPSE
Published by the Penguin Group
Penguin Group (USA) LLC, 375 Hudson Street,
New York, New York 10014

USA | Canada | UK | Ireland | Australia | New Zealand | India | South Africa | China
penguin.com
A Penguin Random House Company

First published by Signet Eclipse, an imprint of New American Library,
a division of Penguin Group (USA) LLC

First Printing, November 2014

ISBN 978-0-451-46534-4

Printed in the United States of America
10 9 8 7 6 5 4 3 2 1

Chapter 1

Devyn Mauvais looked at the gratitude in her client's rheumy eyes and said the most expensive words in recent history. "Now, don't you worry about my fee, hon. Your happiness is payment enough." Then she helped the old woman tuck a folded twenty back into the pocket of her tattered housedress, along with the talisman she'd just "bought."

"Thank you, child." The woman wrapped her bony arms around Devyn's waist, bringing with her the scent of arthritis cream. "You do your mama proud, God rest her."

No, not really. Mama would spin in her grave if she knew her oldest daughter was peddling sacred oils and ritual kits out of her living room. The first rule she'd taught Devyn was that it's bad juju to profit from helping others. Out of habit, Devyn crossed herself while patting her client's back.

After walking the woman to her car, Devyn returned to her sagging front porch, where her gaze landed on the brand-new sign affixed near the screen door. In odd contrast to the faded aluminum siding, the sign announced: EFFECTIVE IMMEDIATELY, A FEE OF $20 PER HOUR WILL BE CHARGED FOR ALL SPIRITUAL CONSULTATIONS. POTION, SPELLS, AND CANDLE PRICES ARE AVAILABLE UPON REQUEST. INQUIRE WITHIN OR BOOK AN APPOINTMENT AT MAUVAISVOODOO.COM.

God, she had a Web site. Could she possibly sink any lower?

She threw open the front door and tried to ignore the prickle of shame tugging at her stomach. A month ago, she never would have accepted a cent for reading the bones. Funny how quickly life could spiral out of control when you lived paycheck to paycheck. Since she'd lost her temp job at the Lord of the Springs mattress store, bad juju was the least of Devyn's worries.

The rent was overdue, her cupboards were bare, and for the past week, she'd parked her Honda behind a Dumpster a few blocks away in a game of hide-and-seek with the repo man. She'd even resorted to "borrowing" wireless Internet from the trailer park across the street, something no twenty-seven-year-old woman should ever have to do.

But not even *she* was desperate enough to take grocery money from little old ladies.

"Yet," she muttered.

Checking her cell phone, Devyn noted she had five minutes before her last appointment of the day, some out-of-towner named Warren Larabee who'd prepaid online via credit card. In preparation, she lit a stick of incense, then mixed a satchel of herbs, coins, and ancestral soil from Memère's tomb for a Good Fortune charm. Nine times out of ten, that was what men wanted. The other was "natural male enhancement," which she couldn't provide. If the flag wouldn't fly, there was something wrong with the pole, and that was a job for the doctor.

She was a Mauvais, not a magician.

At six o'clock on the button, a gentle rapping sounded at her door, and she ushered a middle-aged man with a thick salt-and-pepper crew cut into her living room. He wore a business suit and an easy smile that told Devyn he wasn't a true believer in voodoo. With his relaxed posture, both hands tucked loosely inside his pockets, it looked like he'd come here to bring the word of the Lord. Not that she needed it. A devout Catholic, she'd chaired the Saint Mary's fish fry six years running.

In any case, it was obvious that Warren Larabee hadn't come here for a reading. Devyn's eyes found the Louisville Slugger she kept propped in the corner. The man seemed harmless, but creepers came in all sorts of packaging.

"Mr. Larabee?" She swept a hand toward the sofa while taking the opposite chair. "What brings you in?"

He ignored her question and smiled while assessing her strapless red minidress and black stiletto pumps. "You're not what I expected."

Devyn laughed when she imagined what he must be thinking: that for an extra fee, she would offer spiritual *and* sexual healing. "Trust me, I don't usually wear this to meet clients. My ten-year high school reunion is tonight." And if she wanted to make it in time for the complimentary open bar—which she did—she'd have to rush out the door as soon as this appointment ended.

"Well, you look lovely," Warren said. "I'm sure you'll make your classmates green with envy."

"Isn't that what we all want?" Joking aside, she folded both hands in her lap and got down to business. "You're not here for a charm, are you?"

"Very perceptive." He nodded his approval like a proud parent. "No, I'm here to offer you an opportunity."

Visions of sales pitches danced in Devyn's head, but she suppressed an eye roll. "You paid for an hour. How you use it is your prerogative."

"I own Larabee Amusements," he said. "Maybe you've heard of it?"

Devyn shook her head.

"We sell sightseeing packages in cities all over the country." He shifted forward to rest both elbows on his knees. "Celebrity mansion tours in Hollywood, honky-tonk pub crawls in Nashville, boat trips in the Everglades, that sort of thing."

"And let me guess," Devyn said. "You're branching out in New Orleans?"

"No, that market's already saturated. We're opening a franchise right here in Cedar Bayou." He lifted a shoulder. "It's only twenty minutes away, and the town has a rich history. I can't believe nobody's capitalized on it yet."

"If you're looking for investors, I can't help you." Devyn had already depleted her nest egg by helping her sister get the Sweet Spot bakery off the ground. Several years later, they were finally breaking even, but not doing well enough to keep Devyn from assembling lunches from free samples at the grocery store.

"That's not why I'm here," he assured her with a lifted palm. "I'd like to hire you."

She perked up. Now he had her attention. "To do what?"

"You're Devyn Mauvais," he said as if that fact had slipped her mind. "Direct descendant of Juliette Mauvais, the most feared voodoo queen in Louisiana history. From what I hear, the locals are still afraid to speak her name." Warren pointed to Memère's portrait on the wall, where Juliette looked down her nose at them, her full lips curved in a smirk. With her smooth olive skin and exotic eyes, she'd been the most beautiful woman in the bayou, but anyone who trifled with her did so at their own peril. There was a local family—the Dumonts— who knew it firsthand, even after a hundred years.

"You look like her," Warren said.

Devyn gave a dismissive laugh. "Not as much as my sister. Those two are the living spit."

"But enough that you could pass for Juliette if you wore traditional period clothing and a headdress." Warren paused as if for dramatic effect, then made jazz hands. "Just imagine how chilling a haunted cemetery tour would be if you were the one leading it."

Devyn's stomach sank. This wasn't the kind of opportunity she'd hoped for. She would rather spend all day asking *You want fries with that?* than lead gawking tourists to her great-great-grandmother's resting place so they could pose for cheesy pictures in front of her tomb.

"There's more," Warren added when she didn't respond. "I'll set you up in a shop near the cemetery so you can sell"—he thumbed at the rows of dressed candles on display—"your little trinkets when the tour is over."

"Wait just a minute." She held up an index finger. "Little *trinkets*? This is my heritage you're talking about, not some Tupperware party."

Warren's eyes flew wide. "Of course. I didn't mean to offend."

"Well, you did."

"But in addition to a generous salary, you'd make tips from the—"

"No, thank you." Devyn reminded herself that she'd earned twenty dollars listening to this drivel, which would make a small dent in the electric bill. But that was a bargain for this man, and she'd had enough. "Not even for tips."

Warren fell silent, taking in the peeling paint on the walls as if to ask *Seriously, lady? Don't you need the cash?* "If the salary is an issue, we can negotiate."

"Do you need spiritual guidance, Mr. Larabee?" When he lowered his brows in confusion and shook his head, she added, "Then I'm afraid our appointment is over."

To his credit, Warren didn't push. He fished a business card from his shirt pocket and set it on the coffee table. He then stood up and offered his palm. "I'll be in town until Halloween, so take a few weeks to think about it. I hope you'll change your mind."

Devyn shook his hand and walked him to the door, but that was as far as her courtesy extended. Warren gave a final wave, then strode to the sleek Mercedes parked at the curb. Seconds later, he was gone, taking his job offer with him.

Devyn blew out a breath and told herself she'd made the right choice. Selling a few satchels of gris-gris during a time of need was one thing, but cashing in on her heritage was another. No amount of money was worth her dignity.

So why was she still on the porch, watching his Mercedes fade into the distance?

She shook her head to clear it and went back into the house for a quick lipstick touch-up. There was free booze awaiting her in the Cedar Bayou High gymnasium, and she was overdue for a good time.

Devyn parked her Honda behind a Salvation Army clothing receptacle at the rear of the school, then locked the doors and paused to admire her reflection in the driver's-side window.

She had originally planned to skip the reunion, but that was before she'd found this amazeballs Gucci dress for thirty dollars at a thrift store in New Orleans. Fire-engine red and so short it barely covered her butt, it hugged her curves like it was hand-stitched for her—by angels. The only thing wrong with it was a tiny spot of ink on the side hem, but who cared?

It was Gucci!

This dress almost made her forget how far she'd fallen. Maybe she didn't have a job or a family of her own, but her body was still bitchin'—if she did say so herself—and one out of three wasn't bad.

Devyn clicked across the parking lot and through the school's back door, her peep-toe stilettos echoing in the narrow hallway. She had a sway in her hips tonight, the kind only a custom-fitted designer dress could inspire. Even Jenny Hore—appropriately pronounced *whore*—would eat her heart out. The one girl in school unfazed by the last name Mauvais, Jenny had made it her unholy mission to steal everything that mattered to Devyn: her lunch money, her project ideas, her spot on the varsity cheer squad—even her junior-year boyfriend, Slade Summers, may they both rot in hell.

With any luck, Jenny and Slade had aged horribly and grown miserable in each other's company. The prospect put an extra pep in Devyn's step as she approached the sign-in station.

The table was unmanned, so she scanned the rows of name-tag stickers for her own. When she didn't find it, she picked up the attendance clipboard and ran her fingernail down the class roster.

"Excuse me, Miss," said a familiar baritone voice before its owner plucked the clipboard from Devyn's hands. "That's mine."

Instantly, her jaw clenched. She slid a glare toward

the voice, which brought her eye-level to a gray polo stretched tight over the broadest chest in Cedar Bayou. She would know. From there, she craned her neck toward the ceiling and met a pair of arrogant green eyes smiling beneath a thatch of auburn hair. Mirrored sunglasses were pushed atop his head, despite the fact that the sun had set an hour ago. His name tag said HELLO, MY NAME IS INIGO MONTOYA, but she knew better. This overgrown muscle head was Beau Dumont: high school football star, ex-marine, class demigod, and a constant pain in her ass since the day he'd returned to town a few months ago.

"I was hoping you'd stay home," she said. "But then, who would the idiot masses have to worship?"

His gaze took a leisurely stroll up and down her body. "With you in that dress, nobody's going to notice little ol' me."

The compliment didn't touch her. She'd learned a long time ago that Beau's pretty words carried no weight. She sneered at his clipboard. "Who put you in charge?"

"Why wouldn't I be in charge? I was voted Most Likely to Succeed."

"What's that?" She leaned in, cupping an ear. "Most Likely a Sleaze? I'd say that sounds about right."

Beau chuckled low and deep, then lifted a dark curl from her shoulder. He rubbed it between his thumb and index finger before using the end to tickle her cheek. "You didn't always think I was sleazy, Dev."

Devyn's knees softened, and she discreetly grasped

the folding table for support. "That was before you—" *said you loved me and disappeared for almost a decade.* "Left me on the hook for what we did after graduation."

His lips slid into a crooked grin that used to make her panties fall off, back when she'd naïvely thought she could break the curse that had turned all Dumont men into liars, cheats, and runners. Now that cocky grin made her palm itch to smack him upside the head.

"Best night of my life," he said.

She narrowed her eyes. "That's because you weren't the one who got arrested."

"Aw, now. I said I was sorry for that." He pulled her name tag from his pocket and began scanning her dress for a place to stick it. "Besides, I heard the charges were dropped."

Devyn snatched the name tag from him. "Bite me."

"Any time you want." Beau tipped her chin, leaning close enough to fill the space between them with the scents of shaving cream and male body heat. "I still remember all the delicious places you like to be nibbled, Kitten."

Kitten.

The casual use of her old nickname sent fire rushing through Devyn's veins. She batted away his hand. "In your dreams. The only thing giving you a good time tonight is your hand. It's a match made in heaven. Not even *you* can ruin that relationship." She whirled toward the gymnasium and strutted away, shaking her moneymaker to give him a sweet view of what he was missing—what he had abandoned ten years ago.

Screw Beau Dumont and his big, gorgeous chest. She was *so* over him.

She reminded herself of that as she strode into the gym, where the bleachers were folded against the walls and the basketball hoops were cranked toward the ceiling. The decorating committee had covered several rows of cafeteria lunch tables with white linen and a scattering of balloon clusters, transporting her back to a time when her greatest worry was which outfit would make a boy's jaw drop.

Aside from her financial woes, it would seem she'd come full circle.

Streamers crisscrossed the dimly lit room, and Snoop Dogg's "Drop It Like It's Hot" played from someone's iPod docking station in the corner. It was like prom night all over again, except for the standing bar erected near the floor mats. She made a beeline for the booze, and once she had a lemon drop martini in hand, she scanned the room for a familiar face.

"Dev!"

A woman's shout drew Devyn's attention to a small group gathered on the opposite side of the gym. She squinted in the dim lighting and recognized Margo and some of the other cheerleaders who'd moved away from the bayou after graduation. When Devyn waved, Margo bounced with excitement, then cringed and cradled her pregnant belly between both hands.

"Hey," Devyn said, joining Margo with outstretched arms.

After a long hug, Margo pulled back to look at

Devyn. "You're stunning. I hate you." But her warm smile promised the opposite.

"Oh, please." Devyn flapped a hand and patted her friend's swollen tummy. "You're absolutely glowing. Congratulations! Is this your first?"

"Our third," Margo said and introduced her husband. One by one, each woman in the group did the same until they glanced at Devyn and paused expectantly.

She held up her naked left hand. "Still single." The girls followed with a chorus of *Good for you* and *Nothing wrong with that*, but a shadow of pity softened their tone. "My sister, Allie, got married, though," Devyn said, shamelessly deflecting. "Just a couple of months ago, to Marc Dumont."

That made eyebrows rise. Until recently, no Dumont man had made it to the altar since the day Memère jinxed their line. Few people believed in the curse, but firsthand experience had shown Devyn it was like thunder—impossible to see, but very real. She still didn't know how Marc had broken the hex, but for her sister's sake, she was glad that he did. Allie's feet hadn't touched the ground since their Vegas wedding.

"Maybe Beau's next," said Margo with a teasing elbow nudge. She nodded toward the gym doors. "He's been watching you since you walked into the room."

Devyn glanced over her shoulder and saw him standing there, the top of his head barely clearing the doorway as he leaned against the jamb and folded his muscled arms. He winked at her, and she turned back to Margo with an eye roll. "Don't hold your breath."

From there, the discussion turned to careers. Devyn learned that her old cheer squad had gone on to become Web designers, freelance writers, and stay-at-home moms. When her turn came to share, Devyn played it off with a carefree shrug. "I haven't quite decided what I want to be when I grow up."

Everyone laughed and Devyn was able to unclench her shoulders. Margo had just pulled out her iPhone to show everyone pictures of her children when she glanced across the room and squealed in delight. "Jenny's here! And Slade!"

Devyn smoothed the front of her dress, sucked in her tummy, and turned slowly toward the gym entrance to catch a glimpse of her nemesis. Would Jenny's eyes have grown dull, darkened by circles of exhaustion? Had her golden hair faded with time and too much chemical processing? Would Slade have lost half his hair and gained a hundred pounds?

As it turned out, no.

The pair strutted into view looking better than ever, damn it.

Jenny tossed a curtain of glossy blond hair over one shoulder, rocking a designer halter dress paired with knee-high stiletto boots. Even in the dim lighting, a set of obscenely large diamond studs winked from her earlobes, and she made sure everyone spotted the quilted Chanel bag on her shoulder. Slade was dressed more like a Greek billionaire than the soccer stud that Devyn remembered. Whatever the pair had been up to these past ten years, they had clearly made more money than the Rockefellers.

Those bastards.

After a round of hugs and hellos, Jenny pinned Devyn with a critical gaze. "Well, if it isn't Devyn Mauvais. Bless your little heart."

Whatever. Every Southern girl knew that was code for "Go die in a fire."

Devyn smiled sweetly. "Well, if it isn't my favorite *Hore*."

"Actually, it's Summers now." Jenny thrust forward her left hand to display a diamond approximately the size of the moon.

Devyn quietly sipped her martini, but her lack of enthusiasm didn't stop Jenny from launching into a story about her sunset wedding ceremony on a private beach just outside Cabo San Lucas. For the next ten minutes, she spun a tale of nauseating excess that had the whole group transfixed. Even Beau Dumont had ambled over to hear the details.

Devyn had long since tuned out the prattle, so she was caught off guard when Jenny abruptly stopped and pointed at her.

"What?" Devyn asked.

Jenny covered her mouth to stifle a giggle. "Nice dress, Dev."

Devyn stood a bit straighter and smiled. "Thanks. I picked it up for a steal."

"I know," Jenny said. "From the Tulane Avenue Goodwill, right? That's where I donated it." She leaned down to inspect the side hem. "Yep. There's the stain I never could get out."

opened her mouth to dig herself a deeper hole, Beau crossed through the center of the group and stood by her side.

Slipping an arm around her waist, Beau pulled her hard against him and announced, "It's me. I'm Dev's boyfriend—*and* her boss."

Chapter 2

Beau kept going and hoped like hell no one realized he was talking out of his ass.

"That's why we had to keep it quiet," he said. "Dev's managing the education center on my riverboat, and I didn't want anyone thinking she earned the job on those pretty little knees." He delivered a hard smack to her bottom. "Isn't that right, Kitten?"

Devyn squeaked at the physical contact, fisting her martini glass almost hard enough to shatter it. When she swiveled her ice-blue gaze to his, he couldn't tell whether she wanted to kiss him or drive one of those pretty little knees between his legs.

"Mmm-hmm," she forced out. "Plus, there's all that bad blood between our families."

"A hundred years' worth," he agreed. "But now that Marc and Allie have tied the knot, why not go public?"

Margo bounced on her toes, pointing a wild finger at them. "I knew it! I could tell from the way you were watching her!"

Beau playfully ruffled Devyn's curls. "What can I say? The flame never died. I got back to town and we picked up right where we left off," he said as he waggled his eyebrows. "Except it's a thousand times hotter. I can't keep her off me—she's an animal in the sack."

The corners of Devyn's mouth tightened. "I'm just making up for lost time, Sugar Dumplin'. You know, that whole decade we missed out on."

He ignored the jab and lifted his Sam Adams toward that bitch, Jenny Hore. "I don't care where her dress came from, it's going to look great on my bedroom floor tonight." Then he tipped back his bottle for a deep pull.

Dev pinched his back hard enough to make him yelp. "I can't wait," she said. "Did you remember to take your little blue pill?"

Beau coughed and sputtered beer into his fist. She knew damn well he didn't have any performance issues, and that shit was hitting below the belt. "Come on, baby," he said as he set down their drinks and nodded toward the dance floor. "They're playing our song."

Slade Summers wrinkled his forehead. "Your song is 'Bump n' Grind'?"

"Yeah." Beau thumbed at Devyn. "It's her stripper jam. She loves to dance for me."

"Lucky bastard."

"You said it, man." Beau went in for a fist bump, but Devyn tugged him away before it connected.

"That's enough, honey," she said. "Nobody wants to hear what I have to do to get your Magic Stick to stand—"

"Great seeing you again," Beau boomed while ushering Dev away from the group. When they were out of earshot, he whispered, "What the hell? I'm trying to help you."

"My stripper jam?" she hissed. "You had to go there?"

"What about that Viagra comment?" He pulled her into a dance, his hands sliding around her waist while she reluctantly locked both wrists around his neck. "I don't need a pill to get my Magic Stick standing, which I'm sure you remember all too well."

She shot him a smile full of poison. "Methinks the gentleman doth protest too much."

"Yeah?" he asked. "Methinks you weren't protesting all those times I had you wide open on the riverbank begging for my—"

"Bless your heart, Beau Dumont," she interrupted, eyes cold enough to freeze the balls off a brass monkey. "Bless it right out of your chest."

He chuckled to himself. "I don't think you really mean that."

"Then maybe you're even more stupid than I thought."

Ouch. It seemed Kitten had her claws out tonight.

Beau remembered a time when Devyn talked sweetly to him—in the months before graduation, when they were young and head over heels in lust. She had spent countless hours wrapped around him, all softness and light. They'd hiked and fished and skinny-dipped before making love in the tall grass and walking home with chigger bites in some really interesting places.

Those were the best days of his life; so naturally, he'd bolted.

For the first time since leading Devyn to the dance floor, he became aware of her nearness, the way their fused bodies moved in an effortless, synchronized rhythm. It had always been like this with her. They'd had their fair share of problems, but rhythm wasn't one of them. Of their own volition, his hands slid from her waist to find their favorite resting spot at the base of her spine, right where the curve of her ass began. With her heated skin pressed so close, he realized she still smelled the same, like honeysuckle and sex. He'd missed that scent.

He'd missed *her*.

Devyn seemed to sense the shift in his mood, because she peered up at him and lifted one eyebrow in warning. "Listen," she began, then hesitated. "About what happened with Jenny . . ."

"I think the words you're looking for," he said, dipping his mouth an inch from hers, "are *Thank you, Beau. You're my hero.*"

She pushed him back. "Whatever. Thank you."

"You're welcome."

Devyn's icy mask faltered as she studied him beneath a fringe of thick lashes. "Why'd you do it?"

Beau shrugged. "Jenny's an asshole. Back in high school, she came on to me in the boys' locker room, and when I shot her down, she spread an ugly rumor about my mama."

"Oh, yeah." Dev sucked a sympathetic breath through her teeth, and for a moment, they were friends again. "I remember that. Nobody believed her, you know."

"Good." Beau was used to folks flapping their gums about his daddy. The old dirty bastard had six sons by five different women, including a baby due in December. But Beau's mama was innocent in the whole mess. The only mistake she'd made was loving the wrong man. "Still pissed me off, though."

"Not to change the subject," Dev said, "but when are we going to break up? I need to quit that fake job, too."

"Whoa, now. Not so fast." He really did need an educational director for the next cruise. Devyn wasn't a certified teacher, but she'd spent some time in college training as one. Plus, now that her sister had married Beau's brother, they were practically family. She would fit right in with the rest of the crew. "You can dump me any time you want, but the job's not fake. You start next week."

"Excuse me?" She pulled back and cocked her head. "You can't be serious."

"Careful, Kitten," he said, nodding toward the group. "We're supposed to be madly in love, remember?"

With an exasperated sigh, she rested her cheek on his chest. The affectionate gesture did nothing to soften the acid in her voice, and in the blink of an eye, their temporary friendship came to an end. "I'm not setting foot aboard that floating garbage heap. Especially not with you."

"Watch it," he warned. Trashing the *Belle* was almost as bad as talking smack about his mama. "I saved your hide back there, and you're going to repay the favor. Our director's on maternity leave. I only need you for a couple of weeks."

"Not happening."

"What's the problem?" Beau asked. "Allie told me you lost your job. The salary for this position is more than what your old temp agency paid." Once again, Devyn should be thanking him, not digging in her heels.

"Maybe I don't want to work under you." Then she emphasized, "Or *be* under you."

An automatic grin formed on his lips. It sounded an awful lot like she didn't trust herself around him. To test his theory, Beau lowered his mouth to her right ear, which he recalled was more sensitive than the left. "Afraid you won't be able to keep your hands off me?"

She shivered in his arms and said, "You wish," but her breath hitched, rendering the words powerless.

Beau brushed his lips over her earlobe before taking it gently between his teeth. In response, Devyn released a sigh that sent a jolt of lust straight to his Jockeys. "Then you have no reason to worry," he murmured. "I'll see you first thing Monday morning . . . unless you want to admit to your friends that we lied."

The song ended, and they ceased their lazy sway.

Devyn looked up at him, her blue eyes charged with a mingling of desire and loathing, mostly the latter. "All right," she said. "But only for two weeks, then consider us even."

"See, that wasn't so hard, was it?" he said, noting that his Magic Stick certainly was. That soldier was all too happy to be back in Dev's company. Beau gave a slight nod toward her friends. "We can go over there if you want. But I'm warning you, any more mentions of little blue pills and I'll tell them about your recent spanking fetish."

"Forget it," she said, her shoulders sagging in defeat. "I'm just going home to burn this dress."

Beau couldn't blame her. For show, he settled a hand at her lower back. "Come on. I'll walk you to your car."

She shifted a glare at him. "Not necessary."

"What kind of boyfriend would I be if I didn't walk you out?"

"Fine." She sighed, kicking off her high heels and handing them over. "A good boyfriend would hold my stilettos."

They reached her table and she shoved her purse at him. "And my bag."

Beau grumbled under his breath. This fake boyfriend thing was for the birds. Here he was holding a purse, and he wasn't even getting fake lucky tonight. As long as she didn't ask him to buy a box of tampons. That was where he drew the line.

After a round of good-byes to their old friends, Devyn and Beau walked out the back door and crossed the parking lot. He didn't know where she was leading him, though. Once they made it to the rear of the lot, it became clear there were no cars out there.

"Oh, no," Devyn moaned, jogging a full rotation around a Dumpster-sized clothing donation bin before stopping and hanging her head. "It's gone. He must have followed me here when I left the house."

"Who followed you?" Beau glanced around the parking lot. Years of military training kicked his senses into high gear as he checked the grounds for any visible threat. The area looked secure. "Did someone steal your car?"

Instead of answering him, Devyn crouched into a ball and wrapped both arms around her knees.

"Do I need to call the police?" he said.

"No. Nobody stole my car. And don't mention this to my sister. I mean it—not a word."

She looked so small and broken curled up like that, vulnerable in a way Beau hadn't seen since his return to town. The new Devyn allowed nothing to chip her cold facade. Strange as it seemed, he was kind of relieved to see a flash of weakness from her. It proved she was still human under all that armor. But when he rested a comforting hand on her shoulder, she shrugged it off.

"Are you going to tell me what's happening here?" he asked.

She stood and brushed off her hands, and just like that, her icy shields went up. "Here's what's happening, Dumont. You're going to be a good boyfriend and drive me home. But first, you're going to pick up a bottle of Bacardi from the grocery. And a box of Tampax."

Monday morning, Beau awoke with the sun. He poured his coffee into a thermos and rolled down the windows in his old Chevy Tahoe while driving to the *Belle*'s docking station in downtown New Orleans.

Autumn had mercifully stolen half the humidity from the air, so he enjoyed the cool breeze while it lasted. Around here, crisp oxygen was a delicacy. He felt around the front seat for his sunglasses before realizing they were resting on top of his head. Squinting against the windshield's glare, he pushed his glasses into place and wondered how his fake girlfriend planned on getting to work today.

He had finally gotten Dev to admit that her car had been repossessed, a tidbit he'd promised to keep under wraps. Out of the kindness of his fake boyfriend heart, he'd offered to pick her up, but Devyn had scoffed and claimed she didn't want "any kind of ride" from him. Never mind that her gaze had flickered to his lap when she'd said it.

As long as she arrived with the rest of the staff, let the stubborn minx find her own way into the city. If he didn't see her curly head aboard the *Belle* by nine thirty, he would personally drive back to her house and haul her in over his shoulder. He caught himself grinning at the mental image.

This was going to be a fun couple of weeks.

When he pulled into the dock parking lot, he cut the

MAKE YOU REMEMBER 27

Chevy's engine and took a few minutes to gaze at the *Belle* through fresh eyes—the eyes of a soon-to-be co-owner. When Daddy had retired, he'd made Marc captain and deeded over the boat, which was the sensible thing to do at the time. There was no resentment for it on Beau's part. He had left the family business for a military enlistment, followed by half a decade of private contract work that had earned him a nice six-figure nest egg. All the while, Marc had stayed in Cedar Bayou and busted his ass to keep the *Belle* thriving. Marc had deserved the reins their daddy had handed him.

But things were different now.

Ten years living in crowded barracks and dusty hovels had shown Beau where he belonged, and it was right here in the bayou with the half brothers he'd left behind. He was looking to put down roots, and as it happened, Marc was seeking an investor to share the burden so he could spend more time with his new bride. Beau had the money and the inclination. It was a win-win.

Assuming they could get along . . .

Like most brothers, Beau and Marc had a tendency to bust each other's balls. Add the fact that their daddy had bounced back and forth between their mamas' beds for decades, and it was a wonder any of the Dumont brood had survived the animosity of their teenage years. But they were older and wiser now, and the *Belle* was a really big boat. With four expansive decks and hundreds of interior suites, she was larger than some motels. And if that wasn't enough room for two brothers' egos, they had worse problems than sibling rivalry.

Beau crossed the ramp onto the main deck, his shoes clattering over the metal grates until every bird within earshot startled and took flight. That sound used to make his chest tight, back when summers aboard this boat had felt more like a prison sentence than a seasonal job. It had taken ten years of dodging bullets overseas for him to realize how good he'd had it right here. Today he found himself smiling as he jogged up the steps to the second-floor dining room, where the scents of freshly cleaned carpet and touch-up paint greeted him.

Today the *Belle* felt like home.

The family meeting was already under way, four Dumonts gathered in their usual spot near the executive bar. Marc occupied the chair at the head of the table, but the real boss of this operation was the curly-headed pastry chef in his lap, Allie Mauvais-Dumont. The pair had thwarted a hundred-year curse with "perfect faith" in their love, and as corny as that sounded, it was mighty sweet to see them together. In fact, Marc was so busy rubbing his wife's back that he didn't notice Beau moving up behind him.

Beau kissed his sister-in-law on the cheek and took the seat beside her. Then he tugged a lock of his brother's idiotically long, wavy hair and dispensed some well-deserved ribbing. "Sorry, Captain. Now that Allie's around, you're not the prettiest girl on board any-more."

Marc laughed, not even bothering to raise his middle finger. That was a man in love, right there. "It's all right," he said. "Because next to you, I still look like a million bucks." He extended a hand, palm up. "And speaking of money . . ."

Beau pulled a cashier's check from his wallet and slid it toward his little brother while Alex and Nicky leaned across the table to gawk at it. Their blond brows lifted in perfect synchronization, the word *whoa* forming on their lips. Identical twins, they were the only Dumont brothers who shared the same mama, a Swedish beauty who had caught their daddy's eye for the better part of a year. Unlike the rest of the tawny-skinned clan, Alex and Nick's looks favored their mother's, with light hair, blue eyes, and a perpetual sunburn.

"I'm in the wrong business," Nick said, shaking his head in envy.

"No shit," Alex agreed. "If the marines pay that well, then sign me up."

The money Beau had invested wasn't even half of his savings, but in Alex and Nick's eyes, because they were fresh out of college and subsisting on ramen noodles and Milwaukee's Best, it probably seemed like a fortune.

"Hate to break it to you, but you wouldn't make much as enlisted men," he told his brothers. "The real money's in contract work, and you'll have to earn every last cent of it." To prove it, he lifted his T-shirt to show them the shrapnel scar from a dirty bomb he'd had the misfortune of encountering during one of his tours.

That's when Marc's half sister, Ella-Claire, happened to join them. "It's not even five o'clock, and Beau's already busting out a six pack?" She teasingly wolf whistled at his exposed abs and took the chair on the other side of her brother.

Marc shot daggers at Beau. "Put down your damn shirt." Even though Ella-Claire didn't share a drop of blood with the other Dumonts, they were all expected to treat her like family. Which they did. But try telling that to Marc, who thought everyone was out to defile her. Alex must have known it all too well. He scooted his chair a few inches away from Ella, lest he brush her leg and incur the captain's wrath.

"Let's get the meeting started," Marc said. He launched into a status report—everything from the functionality of the train linkage to the new staff members he had hired. He said that Worm, their kid brother, couldn't work the upcoming trip due to school, but he'd bus tables on the weekend dinner cruises. "Allie's agreed to stay on as pastry chef," Marc said and paused to kiss his wife's hand. "And I managed to sweet-talk Chef Therein on board to replace Beau in the galley." He nodded at Beau. "The money our brother invested will update the state suites and fix the plumbing issues from last season's possum invasion."

"And we'll add a few upgrades to the casino," Beau

said. "Which I'll be managing, along with general security. I can even pilot the boat if I have to."

"That reminds me." Marc pointed a ballpoint pen at
Alex and Nick. "Make sure the staff knows that Beau's
co-owner now. What he says goes. We eventually want
to get to the point where he and I can seamlessly switch
off as captain."

"You got it," the twins said in unison.

"Speaking of which," Beau said, "there's something
I should mention. My first act as co-owner was hiring
someone to fill in managing the education center."

A flash of annoyance passed over Marc's features,
but he recovered quickly and took a silent moment—
probably to unclench his ass cheeks. "Oh, yeah? Anyone I know?"

Beau leaned back to assume a casual pose in hopes that
his body language might soften the inevitable shit storm
to come. "Devyn," he muttered and took a sip of coffee.

"Devyn . . ." Marc trailed off, waiting for a last name.

"You know." Beau raised his thermos toward the
woman who could almost pass for Dev's twin. "Allie's
sister."

Allie's eyes nearly bugged out of her head while everyone else at the table drew a collective breath. Marc's
voice sounded half strangled when he clarified, "Devyn
Mauvais?"

Beau played it cool. "Does your wife have another
sister named Devyn?"

"The same girl who threw a drink in your face at the
wedding reception?" Alex asked.

Laughing, Nicky elbowed his twin. "That shit was priceless."

Beau shot his brothers a glare. "Okay, so she's not my biggest fan right now." And in all honesty, Beau had come on too strong at the reception. "But I know she can—"

"She kind of scares me," Ella-Claire interrupted.

"Hell, she scares everyone," Marc said, staring at Beau as if he'd sprouted horns. "Devyn Mauvais sends her exes to urgent care, and you want her working with the passengers' kids?"

"That was a coincidence," Allie piped up. "All six times."

"But still!"

"Look," Beau said. "I know Dev's a little . . . intense. But you don't know her like I do. She used to tutor little kids after school, and she had a way of explaining things that made sense to them." He had faith that the old Devyn was still alive—maybe buried deep, but still in there somewhere. "I'm sure she'll do a good job."

Marc shared a concerned glance with his wife. "I get where you're coming from," he said to Beau. "I really do. But come on. You're thinking with the wrong head."

Beau couldn't contain a sarcastic laugh. "What a coincidence. Because a few months ago, we were all saying the same thing about *you* when Chef Regale refused to work with the pretty pastry chef you hired." Beau glanced at Allie to drive his point home. "The one sitting in your lap right now."

"That's different," Marc ground out. "Allie was qualified for the job."

"No arguments there," Beau said. "But I recall telling you to keep it in your pants—that it was a bad example to sleep with a staffer. So don't preach to me about thinking with the wrong head. No offense, Allie," he added with an apologetic wave. "You know we all love you."

"None taken," she mumbled, cheeks darkening as she glanced at her lap.

Marc's jaw tightened. Like a snorting bull, he sucked an audible breath through his nose.

"Here we go. Pay up." Ella-Claire held a hand toward Alex, who begrudgingly slapped a five-dollar bill into her palm. "I knew you two couldn't go five minutes without fighting."

"We're not fighting," Beau told her. "We're debating."

The look Marc gave him said he was debating tossing Beau overboard. "If you're so confident in your choice, let's put it to a vote. All in favor of hiring Devyn to manage the education center—and all the infants, toddlers, and preschoolers in it—raise your hands."

Beau glanced around the table. Only one hand went up: Allie's. She shrugged and told her husband, "She's my sister. Dev's always been there when I needed her, and she takes a lot of pride in what she does. If she's committed to this, you can trust that she'll go all in."

Marc blew out a long breath. He took a while to think it over before slashing a hand through the air.

"No. I like Devyn, but I'm not comfortable putting her in charge. Anyway, it would be a slap in the face to everyone who's got seniority."

"How about a compromise, then?" Allie offered. "What if we move Mrs. Grayson to the director position and put Devyn in charge of the eight-to-twelve-year-old group?"

A few seconds ticked by in silence. With a twist of his lips, Marc conceded, "I guess that could work."

Beau thought it over and nodded. "I can agree to that."

"Then it's settled," Marc said, though the darkness in his voice contradicted his words. If he didn't need Beau's money so badly, he would have probably given back the check and resumed his dictatorship over the boat. "Let's get on track. We have a lot to discuss."

From there, the conversation turned to subjects like sanitation and supplies, but the mood never bounced back. Shoulders were stiff, eyes were downcast, and when Marc adjourned the meeting, everyone rattled off a list of to-dos and scattered like buckshot. Even Allie invented an excuse about calling the chef to coordinate meal plans, but Beau knew she used the same dessert menu for the whole season.

Once they were alone, Beau turned to Marc. He had to be sure that fancy white captain's hat wasn't so firmly cemented onto his brother's head that it couldn't be shared. "Are you sure you can handle this?"

"*This* being what, exactly?"

"All of it. Me being here, calling the shots without your blessing."

"You think I can't take a partner at the helm?"

Beau flashed a palm. "Just sayin'."

"Look, you made a decision from an emotional place," Marc said. "It was a mistake, and I don't regret calling you out on it. I'll do it again if I have to, which I'm sure I will."

"That goes both ways, Captain."

"Damn right, it does." Marc sniffed a teasing laugh. "Know what else goes both ways?"

"Enlighten me."

"Not sleeping with the staff." Folding his arms, Marc parroted Beau's words from the cruise when Allie had first come on board. "She's your employee now, and you've got no business chasing her skirt. So keep it in your pants, big brother." Then he clapped Beau on the arm and walked away, calling over his shoulder, "Good luck with that."

Beau grumbled, "Asshole" under his breath and stalked outside to the second-floor deck, where he let the breeze cool his temper by a few degrees.

Beau's motives for hiring Devyn had nothing to do with getting laid. He had seen her in action senior year when she'd volunteered at Cedar Bayou Elementary. Even though she'd grown a thicker skin since then, she was still the same girl who'd baked a giant sheet cake and divided it up to help the students understand fractions when nothing else had worked. If he closed his eyes, he could still see the sparkle of pride in her gaze when she'd told him about that day's lesson. She was so radiant it felt like staring at the sun.

Okay, if he was being honest, he *did* like the idea of being close to her for the next two weeks, but that didn't mean he was thinking with his dick.

When a flashy Mercedes Benz pulled into the parking lot, Beau forgot his troubles, the security specialist in him taking over. The black sedan parked beside his beat-up Chevy and cut the engine, but nobody on staff drove a car like that. The driver had probably taken a wrong turn. Beau strode toward the bow ramp for a closer look, and the passenger door opened, revealing a familiar shapely leg.

It was Devyn's. He'd slung that same leg over his shoulder enough times to know.

But who had given her a ride? Resting both elbows on the deck rail, he leaned down and squinted to bring the driver into focus. One masculine wrist was slung over the steering wheel, but he couldn't see anything more. Then Devyn shifted, leaning against the man in what looked a lot like a cuddle.

A completely irrational surge of jealousy heated Beau from his scalp to his toes. He had no claim on Devyn, but that didn't stop him from grasping the rail with both hands to suppress the urge to charge down the stairs and tear off the driver's-side door. A few deep breaths later, Beau finally regained control of his body.

What the hell was wrong with him? He needed to get his shit together.

His brother was right about one thing—Beau was in command now, and it was time to act like it. He had no business making hotheaded decisions . . . like grabbing his fake girlfriend by the shoulders and kissing her into a frenzy right there in front of Mercedes Man.

No, that was a bad idea. Instead, Beau stayed put and watched the pair from a distance . . . because he had a right to know what was going on with his employee.

He was just being a responsible boss. Nothing wrong with that.

Chapter 3

"One more signature, right here." Warren Larabee pointed to the bottom of the W-9 form, and Devyn leaned in to scrawl her name on the proverbial dotted line. She tried not to press against his shoulder, but in the car's close quarters, it couldn't be helped. He inspected the tax document and tucked it into a manila file folder. "We're all set. Call me when the cruise is over, and we'll work out the details."

"Sounds great," Devyn said, though she certainly didn't *feel* great about this decision. Her stomach had lurched and twisted ever since she'd picked up Warren's business card last night. "Thanks for the ride, by the way."

"No problem." He grinned at her while scratching the stubble along his jawline. "But I have to ask. What changed your mind about the cemetery tour?"

Oh, nothing really. Having my car repo'd. Wearing someone else's dress to my reunion. The overdue rent notice stapled to my door. My ex getting a front row seat for all of it. "Just had a change of heart."

"Huh." Warren didn't seem to buy her excuse, but he wasn't complaining. "Well, whatever the reason, I'm glad to have you on the team. Welcome to Larabee Amusements."

They said good-bye, and Devyn watched him drive away before she faced her new workplace. Then her heavy stomach sank another inch.

To anyone else, the *Belle of the Bayou* would seem like a Mark Twain fantasy come to life. Its wood decks were waxed to a high gloss and lined with oversize rocking chairs. Each outward-facing room was framed by an arch of freshly painted white latticework, which contrasted brilliantly against the massive red paddle wheel anchoring the stern and the dual black smokestacks stretching toward the sky. As historical reproductions went, the *Belle* was at the top of her class.

But Devyn saw this boat for what it really was: a lion's den.

And the biggest beast of them all was standing on the second-level deck glaring at her as if she'd already let him down. She checked her watch and yelled, "Save the lecture, Dumont. I'm ten minutes early."

Wood planks squeaked beneath Beau's considerable weight as he clomped down the stairs to meet her at the head of the ramp. The way he narrowed those hazel green eyes at her made Devyn wonder if she had dressed inappropriately. She didn't see a problem with her khaki skirt and floral T-shirt, but what did she know?

"It's business casual until the cruise next week, right?" she asked.

He ignored the question and jutted his chin toward the parking lot. "Who was that?"

"Who?" She glanced over her shoulder at the vacant asphalt.

"That guy who drove you here."

The mere mention of Warren Larabee had her gaze dropping to the tips of her white canvas sneakers. She wasn't ready to admit to anyone—not even her sister—that she had accepted a job to lead cemetery tours. It was too shameful. So she returned Beau's glare and squared her shoulders. "None of your business, that's who." Then she skirted his massive body and stepped onto the deck. "Why don't you just point me in the right direction so I can start my job?"

He didn't say anything at first. But when he was done staring her down, he abruptly turned and strode inside without a word. She followed, wondering what had crawled up his butt so early this morning.

She instantly regretted thinking about his butt.

Against Devyn's will, her focus locked onto the rock-hard contours of his backside displayed beneath thin, faded jeans that cupped him in all the right places. From there, she watched his long, powerful legs move through the halls in strides so brisk she scurried to keep up. As spectacular as it was, his lower half paled in comparison to the muscled planes of his back and a pair of shoulders so broad they stretched the fabric of his T-shirt to near transparency.

Damn it. Why did he have to look so scrumptious?

Devyn was no angel. She'd partied with her fair

share of men over the years, but it would take three standard hotties to equal one Beau Dumont. He had the most strikingly male physique she'd ever seen. It was what had drawn her eye when they'd first met in high school. She'd been a junior varsity cheerleader, and he'd been the captain of the football team. She remembered standing on the sidelines admiring him during one of the games when she should have been doing toe-touches. He had a body that said *Don't worry, baby. You're safe. Nothing can hurt you while I'm around.*

It was a shame that what was inside didn't match his outside appearance. Because no girl was safe in Beau Dumont's presence.

He led her across a wide lobby to the check-in desk, which was labeled the PURSER'S STATION. A twenty-something brunette with a shoulder-length ponytail stood behind the counter and squinted at her computer. Devyn recognized the girl as Ella-Claire, Marc's half sister. Their paths had crossed a time or two since the wedding, and she seemed nice enough.

"Hey, darlin'," Beau said to Ella. "Can you take care of Miss Mauvais's paperwork?"

Ella flicked a glance at Devyn before offering Beau a warm smile. Seriously warm. As in the sufficient temperature to bake an apple pie. "For you?" she chirped. "Anything."

Oh, barf.

Devyn didn't know why she cared, but the whole exchange left her feeling queasy. Maybe it was all the Bacardi she drank over the weekend. She was pushing thirty now, and she couldn't hold her liquor like she used to.

Ella-Claire handed Devyn a clipboard full of papers. "I'll get you a staff polo. What's your size?"

"Medium," Beau answered for her.

After a knowing smile and a wink—yes, an actual wink—Ella trotted off to the back room to retrieve a shirt. When she returned, she slid it across the counter and started talking with Beau about onshore excursions in Natchez.

While filling out her paperwork, Devyn recalled that Marc and Ella-Claire shared the same mom but had different fathers, while Beau and Marc shared the same dad, but had different mothers. Which meant that Beau wasn't actually related to the pretty young thing. *Wonder if he's nailed her yet,* Devyn thought. With his track record, it seemed likely.

Not that she cared or anything.

Devyn had just finished signing her second W-9 of the day when blond twins, who both resembled a young Matt Damon, strode behind the counter and began rifling through the cabinets. She'd met the pair at her sister's wedding reception, but she couldn't remember their names or tell them apart, so she secretly referred to them as Thing One and Thing Two.

"Hey there, gorgeous," said Thing One, making more eye contact with Devyn's chest than anything else. "Welcome aboard. I'm Nick. If you need anything—and I mean *anything*—I'm your man."

Devyn plastered on a sickly sweet grin. "Hi, Nick. Quit staring at my tits, or you'll be wearing this clipboard like an enema."

Thing Two burst out laughing and slapped his twin brother on the back. "I like her. Good call, Beau."

Beau didn't seem to think Devyn was quite as hilarious, but his lips twitched and his gaze sparkled when it landed on hers. For no reason at all, Devyn's pulse hitched. Probably that second cup of coffee. Yeah, that had to be it.

Beau must have completely gotten over whatever was irritating him, because he grinned as he led her away from the lobby and toward the education center at the heart of the boat.

"You'll bunk with a roommate once the cruise starts," he explained as they wound their way through the narrow halls. "There's not much space, so pack light."

"Can I bunk with Allie?"

"You can try," he said. "But I don't think Marc's bed is big enough for the three of you."

Devyn's cheeks heated. "Sometimes I forget they're married."

"Don't worry," Beau said with a hint of sarcasm. "You'll have plenty of reminders when you're around them twenty-four seven."

She was about to ask if Allie was here today when Beau ushered her inside a room that resembled a daycare center. A few travel cribs lined the far wall with a changing station in the corner. On the opposite side of a movable room partition stood a rectangular class-room table. Squishy foam alphabet tiles carpeted the floor, and a glance at the ceiling revealed paper chains strung from corner to corner.

Why had he brought her in here?

"There's been a small change of plan," Beau said. "We're putting you in charge of the oldest group, the eight-to-twelve-year-olds."

"Oldest group?" she repeated in a daze.

"There aren't many on this trip. You won't have more than ten, and that's assuming their parents drop them off every day. Some folks don't."

Devyn swallowed hard. This wasn't the kind of ed-ucation center she'd had in mind. She'd pictured a mini museum where she would hand out pamphlets and recite historical facts for passengers who gave a shit about things like that.

Clearly, she'd been wrong.

She envisioned the room at full capacity, dozens of shrieking rug rats varying in age from infants to twelve-year-olds, each demanding attention for a very specific set of needs. This was a problem. Devyn didn't even like kids. They were exhausting and selfish and they smelled like peanut butter and warm cheese.

"I'm a babysitter?" she asked. "For two solid weeks?"

The way Beau's mouth dropped open made her think she'd offended him. "There are no babysitters here. We offer more than child care. You'll be teaching the kids about river travel, everything from the history of steamers in the Civil War to the math and science behind steam engines. We've got a collection of lesson plans all ready to go."

Okay, so a *glorified* babysitter. "This isn't what I expected."

"What did you think I was hiring you to do?"

After she explained it to him, Beau shook his head. "We already have an onboard historian—our pawpaw."

"Your grandpa?" They actually let that cantankerous old geezer interact with the public? "The same guy who brews moonshine and sells it in baby food jars at the farmer's market?"

Beau scratched the back of his neck and took a sudden interest in his shoes. "Yeah, that's him."

"Isn't there somewhere else you can use me?"

When Beau glanced up, a hint of mischief twinkled in his eyes. "I can think of a dozen delightful ways to use you, Kitten. But the only staffer I need is right here in the center."

Devyn slumped against the doorjamb and sighed, too deflated to think of a witty comeback. She could barely tolerate two hours in the company of little kids, let alone two weeks. The worst part was that after this assignment lurked an equally soul-sucking job of playing dress-up and leading strangers to her ancestors' graves. There seemed to be no end in sight to her troubles, no second chances.

This was her life now.

"Don't look so excited," Beau said, his tone flat.

"It's just . . ."

"This isn't what you expected," he finished.

"Yeah." She pulled in a fortifying breath. "But don't worry. I'll survive. I can handle almost anything for two weeks."

"Nice attitude." Beau's mood shifted, darkening while he folded both arms across his chest. "Because that's what every kid wants—to feel like a temporary burden for you to survive."

She spun on him. "How dare you try to dump a guilt trip on me! I didn't ask for this. You strong-armed me into coming here, remember?"

"Yeah." He closed the distance between them until they stood an inch apart, with the set of his shoulders every bit as tight as his mouth. Even though she hadn't done anything wrong, his heated stare made Devyn want to hide her face. "I thought this job would be good for you."

He couldn't be serious. "Good for me, how?"

Beau pointed at the miniature chairs surrounding the classroom table. "This was your dream once—and you were good at it. Maybe you've forgotten, but I haven't. I was hoping you could reconnect with that old passion and do something with your life."

She matched his stubborn stance, folding her arms and refusing to look at him. What Beau didn't seem to comprehend was that high school was a long time ago. A lot had changed since then. Including herself.

Beau cupped her chin and turned her to face him. "I know how you bounce from one dead-end job to the next. Allie told me. You're floundering, Dev."

"No, I'm not."

"Yes, you are. And you're better than that."

She pushed away his hand, but she couldn't refute his words. There was truth in his statement—the kind of raw honesty that settled in her lungs and choked her.

"Spend the day here," he said. "Go through the lesson plans. Decide whether this is something you think you could be good at. If it's not, I'll let you off the hook." He lowered his head and used his eyes to deliver an ultimatum. "All or nothing. I won't let you half-ass it. Are we clear?"

Devyn nodded.

"I'll be in the casino installing some new slots," he said. "Come find me when you make up your mind."

"Baking soda?"

Devyn stepped inside the walk-in pantry and scanned the shelves until she found what she was looking for. She pulled back the industrial-sized plastic lid and peered inside. "Half a can."

"I'll add it to the list." Allie scribbled on her notepad.

After an hour of skimming riverboat-themed craft ideas and rolling her eyes at cheesy historical role-playing activities, Devyn had snuck out of the education center to the boat's galley to help her sister inventory ingredients. The task wasn't exactly a thrill ride, but at least she was in good company. Besides, she had spent so much time at the Sweet Spot bakery that she felt at home with flour in her hair and Crisco beneath her fingernails.

"I wish I could work in here with you," Devyn said.

"That makes a hell of a lot more sense than sticking me in the romper room."

Instead of weighing in with her opinion, Allie bent over her notepad and pretended to study the list she'd made—the one with only a handful of items on it.

Something was up.

"What?" Devyn asked. "Spit it out."

Allie bit her lip and glanced up with an apology in her mismatched amber-gray eyes. "I know you're not happy in the education center, and I can empathize. During the last cruise, I had to serve drinks in the casino because Chef Regale wouldn't let me in the galley. It was demeaning. But Beau really went to bat for you this morning to get you that position."

"What?" That made no sense. Beau had practically forced her into taking the job, which implied that he was desperate. Allie made it sound like there were a swarm of applicants.

"At the family meeting," Allie said, "there were a few . . . well . . . *concerns* about letting you work with the kids. But Beau wouldn't back down. It caused a fight, and things are still kind of awkward between the brothers."

Devyn's lips parted. "Nobody wants me here?" She sounded hurt, even to her own ears, though she didn't know why she cared. She didn't even like the Dumonts.

"I want you here," Allie promised. "Beau does, too. But the rest of the family"—she cringed and spoke her next words through her teeth—"they think you're a little scary."

"Me?" Devyn repeated, pointing at herself. "I'm not scary!"

Allie tipped her head and raised a brow. "Did you or did you not threaten to shove a clipboard up Nicky's ass?"

"Psh, that doesn't count," Devyn said with a flick of her wrist. "The skeevy bastard had it coming."

"Maybe, but you could have handled it like a professional." Allie tucked her pencil behind one ear. "And Ella-Claire is afraid you don't like her."

Devyn splayed both hands. "But I didn't do anything!"

"That's exactly the point," Allie said. "You didn't smile or shake her hand or show any interest in her as a person. What was she supposed to think?"

Allie was wrong about one thing. Devyn *had* shown an interest in Ella-Claire, but only as it applied to Beau. She still wanted to know if the two had done the deed. "Okay, so I could have been a little friendlier. But that doesn't mean I'm a terrifying monster who eats children."

"I know that." Allie's face broke into a gentle smile, and she crossed the galley to rest a hand on Devyn's shoulder. "You're my best friend and the finest person I've ever met. Look at how you helped me get the Sweet Spot off the ground. You could have done anything with the money Mom and Dad left us, but you used it to help buy the shop." Her eyes misted over.

Allie was such a softie. If she discovered the sad state of Devyn's bank account, she'd probably take out a second mortgage on the bakery and give back that money. Which was why she couldn't find out.

"Any good sister would have done the same," Devyn mumbled.

"Don't be so sure," Allie said. "You're special, whether or not you believe it. I want everyone else to see the real you, but first you have to let them in. It wouldn't kill you to lighten up, either."

Even if Devyn agreed with her sister's advice, which she didn't, what was the point of forging friendships with a family who had spent the last century using and discarding women? Memère had jinxed their line for a reason—her Dumont lover had ditched her at the altar, and all these years later, the men in that clan still couldn't keep it in their pants. Just look at Beau's dad. That sleaze had enough offspring to populate a small country.

The doubt must have shown on Devyn's face, because Allie said, "They're good people. Even Beau. I know it hurt when he ran out on you—I was there to pick up the pieces—but he's not that same selfish boy anymore. He's trying to make amends. And he has faith in you."

For some odd reason, that burned even worse than hearing that his brothers didn't want her here. Devyn's chest grew heavy when she remembered the disappointment on Beau's face and the way his voice had gone soft when he'd given her the option to quit. She hated that Beau had the power to make her feel ashamed, but he did.

"You should stay and give it a try," Allie said. "What's the worst that can happen?"

"I could get pinkeye. That stuff runs rampant in day cares."

"Never killed anyone."

"What about norovirus? I could die from dehydration."

"The nurse has meds for that."

"The boat could sink."

Allie playfully shoved Devyn's shoulder. "Then we'll go down together. It'll be way more interesting than dying of old age."

A smile played across Devyn's lips. Leave it to Allie to put things in perspective. "Okay, but if we have a *Titanic* moment, you'd better not let me go like Rose did to Jack."

"Never. You're stuck with me." Allie gathered her in a hug.

"Can you handle inventory on your own?" Devyn asked. "I need to find Beau."

"Go ahead." Allie offered a gentle push toward the door to make her point. "But be sweet to him, okay? He really did—"

"Go to bat for me," Devyn finished. "Yeah, yeah. I know."

What she didn't know was why he'd fought so hard. Refusing to give it any further thought, she left the galley and followed the signs to the casino on the second floor. When she reached the double doors, she steeled herself and walked inside.

The noise of Metallica greeted her on the stereo, along with the vibrant greens of felt-covered blackjack tables and the flash of neon beer signs. Even with the overhead lights turned on and the rows of electronic slots lying dormant, Devyn was so visually over-whelmed that it took a moment to spot Beau in the back of the room near the bar. He didn't notice as she approached, so she kept her footsteps quiet and watched him work.

A sheen of sweat had glued Beau's T-shirt to his skin as he hauled an outdated video poker machine from the bar and replaced it with a new one featuring wiz-ards or maybe a vampire theme. It was hard to tell be-cause Devyn was too distracted by the man installing it. His powerful biceps bunched as he repositioned the heavy machinery. He was so completely male that it stopped Devyn in her tracks. He must have sensed her watching, because he turned and widened his eyes in surprise.

"Hey." Beau lifted the front of his shirt and used it to wipe the sweat from his face. "I didn't hear you come in."

God help her. His flat slab of a belly was even harder than she remembered, all rippling muscle with a dust-ing of dark hair that encircled his navel and dipped below the waistband of his jeans. In another lifetime, she'd spent hours lying beside him in the cool shaded grass and let her fingernails trace that happy trail to where it ended. Which had resulted in a whole lot of heavy breathing. Her body remembered all too well.

Even now, her blood warmed with recognition and sent heat pooling south of the border.

Damn her Judas lady bits.

"You done?" he asked, pointing at his exposed stomach. "Or do you want another minute?" When she answered by way of her middle finger, he tugged down his shirt. "So, did you make a decision?"

"Yeah," she said. "I'm sticking around."

"Really?" The way his whole face lit up told her he wasn't expecting that answer. "I'm glad to hear it."

Devyn studied her fingernails and pretended that his reaction didn't cause her heart to swell. "What can I say? I love a challenge."

"Come up with your own lesson plans if you want," he said. "Let Ella-Claire know if you need any supplies, but try to keep it to a small list. We're on a budget."

"Sure." The room began to feel small with the two of them standing there, Beau smiling at her like she'd just told him he won the Powerball. She took a step back, and then another. But she couldn't leave before saying one last thing. "Thanks, by the way."

"For what?"

"Allie told me what you did. I don't know why you want me around so badly, but I'm glad you stood up for me."

A crooked grin tugged Beau's lips as he leaned an elbow on the bar. "Why, Devyn Mauvais. Are you being nice?"

She heaved a sigh. Why did he have to go and ruin

it? "Enjoy it while you can. This is a onetime deal." Then she left the sweaty caveman to his work and returned to the education center.

She'd rock this job, if for no other reason than to spite the Dumonts.

Chapter 4

When the day came for the *Belle* to embark on a two-week tour of the Mississippi, Devyn reported for duty wearing a frilly lace-up corset dress instead of her uniform of a staff polo and khakis. Her costume wasn't the most historically accurate of reproductions—in fact, she looked more like a pirate's wench than a proper lady of the Victorian era—but the kids in the education center wouldn't know that. They'd see her outfit and beg to dress up themselves; then she'd launch into an enthralling history lesson that would captivate them for the rest of the afternoon.

That was the goal, anyway.

But first she needed to get her room assignment and drop off her duffel bag. When she approached the purser's desk, Ella-Claire glanced up from her computer and did a double take.

Devyn smiled, remembering her sister's words about lightening up. "History by immersion," she said. "We're playing dress-up in the center today."

"Aww." Ella tipped her head as if admiring a puppy. "What a fun idea."

Fun wasn't the word Devyn had in mind, but whatever. She dug into her dress pocket and handed over a tiny red satchel tied with yellow string, a peace offering to make up for their shaky first encounter. "I made some gris-gris for you. It's for love and luck."

Ella brought a grateful hand to her breast, her gaze softening. "Allie used to make these for me, but she quit."

"I know," Devyn said.

The fact that Allie had abandoned their heritage was a bone of contention between them. Allie claimed she had never believed in voodoo, that she'd faked the rituals and told her clients what they needed to hear to help them change. She called it self-fulfilling prophesy. Devyn called it faithlessness. Tomato, to-m*ah*-to.

"She said this kind was your favorite."

"Thanks," Ella said. Still beaming, she pocketed her gift. "That was thoughtful of you."

"Anyway, I need my room assignment so I can get settled in." Devyn hoped her roommate didn't snore. She was a light sleeper, and if the Dumonts thought she was scary now, they should see her after a bout of insomnia.

Instead of looking up the information, Ella watched her in silent contemplation. When she spoke, her words were tentative. "There's an open spot in my room. If you want it."

Luckily, Devyn was able to maintain her smile, despite mingled feelings on the offer. Ella-Claire seemed like a sweet girl, but if they had both slept with Beau . . . well, that could make for an awkward two weeks on the water. However, there was no way to decline the invitation without hurting Ella's feelings, so in the end, the decision made itself.

Devyn made a show of widening her eyes in enthusiasm. "Really? That would be awesome! Allie's told me so many wonderful things about you."

"You, too!" Ella said as she flashed a thousand-watt smile that made Devyn instantly regret any negative thoughts she'd had about the girl. Ella was so excited that her ponytail was swinging. "Here," she said, handing over an old-fashioned key on a string. "Staff rooms are down below. We're in lucky number thirteen. I already took the bottom bunk, so I hope you don't mind the top."

Bunk beds? Devyn suppressed a sigh. What was next, days-of-the-week underpants and juice boxes? "That's my favorite," she lied smoothly. "See you around, roomie."

She made her way down to room thirteen and unlocked the door. When she let herself inside, she nearly banged her shins on the bed frame. She had assumed the rooms would be small, but this was more like a closet. Between the bunks and a single dresser pressed against the side wall, there was barely enough room to turn around. And she had to share this space with a roommate?

Good thing she wasn't claustrophobic.

She tossed her duffel onto the top mattress and noticed an adjoining doorway. It seemed they had their own bathroom. That was something to be grateful for . . . or so she thought. A peek inside showed nothing but a miniature sink and a standing shower stall, the whole bathroom no bigger than an airplane lavatory. Where was the toilet?

She texted the question to her sister.

Moments later, Allie replied, *Check behind the shower curtain.*

Devyn pulled aside the plastic panel and gasped out loud. Her fingers flew over the cell phone screen. *Are you f-ing kidding me? A toilet in the shower??? That's so wrong!*

Biting her lip, she glanced at her duffel bag. She hadn't unpacked it yet. If she hurried, she might be able to give her resignation and escape before the boat pulled away from the dock.

I know, right? Allie texted. *Even the suites are like that. You get used to it after a while.*

"Not friggin' likely," Devyn muttered. *We can drink when we're off duty, right? Because I'm going to need a stiff one later.*

Allie replied, *That's what SHE said.* ☺

A much-needed laugh shook Devyn's chest. *You're warped. Wish me luck today.*

You make your own luck.

No arguments there. And since there was no use in delaying the inevitable, Devyn headed to the education center for her first day of "school."

She found the room empty, which didn't surprise her because the passengers were still boarding. The quiet was exactly what she needed to calm her jittery pulse, so she used the lull to her advantage by arranging a variety of hats and old-style vests on the table, along with the scavenger hunt worksheets she'd prepared. She had just finished going over her plans for the day when heavy footsteps drew her attention to the doorway.

Only one person could make such a clatter walking on foam tiles, and when she turned to face him, her already unstable pulse skipped a beat. Beau was in uniform—wearing a gold-embellished white dress shirt and coat over freshly-pressed slacks, a black tie knotted at the base of his broad neck. The effect was strikingly debonair, even with sunglasses pushed atop his head.

Clearly God was trying to test her.

Grinning like the devil himself, Beau appraised her costume, and in a few smooth strides, he closed the distance between them. Devyn knew she should back up, but he held her captive with his mesmerizing green gaze, and her feet refused to budge. He smelled delicious in his unique way. Familiar, like Irish Spring soap and store-brand shampoo. No frills for this man.

"Nice." His words dripped honey while he dragged an index finger slowly down the length of her corset laces, then all the way back up again. "*Very* nice."

Devyn's corset stays must have been too tight, because it took a moment to catch her breath. "You're not too painful to look at either."

"Not too painful?" he repeated with a deep chuckle. "Enough with the wild praise, darlin'. You're making me blush."

Darlin'. Like that meant anything. He said it to all the girls, including Devyn's new roommate. The reminder helped snap her out of whatever lusty haze she'd fallen into. She smacked his hand and skirted the table to gain some distance. "I've got a job to do, so if you don't mind . . ."

"Not at all." In one quick motion, he snagged her fingers and bent to sweep a kiss over her knuckles. His eyes never left hers, and she felt the touch of his lips in more places than just her hand. "I'll be back to check on you later."

Before she could tell him not to bother, he strode from the room.

Devyn blew out a breath and tried to refocus. She tracked down ten pencils and clipboards, just in case all of her students showed up for the scavenger hunt, but an hour passed without the pitter-patter of any feet, little or otherwise. Eventually the room director, who doubled as one of the infant caregivers, joined her.

Mrs. Grayson explained that most passengers would keep their children with them on the first day, to acclimate them to the new environment. "The only people who'll make drop-offs today," she confided behind her hand, "are the ones who don't want their kids here."

"But if the parents want to be alone, why bring the

kids at all?" Devyn had seen the brochures, and more specifically, the fare breakdown. Two weeks aboard the *Belle* cost more than the same number of nights at a top-notch Caribbean resort. And kids weren't free.

Mrs. Grayson turned up her palms. "It happens. More often than not, because of custody arrangements or last-minute changes of plan."

"Ah." Devyn understood. "It's Mom's week to have the kids, and Dad can't keep them."

"Something like that."

As it turned out, the woman nailed it. When the first—and only—children shuffled into the education center that afternoon, they were brothers tagging along on a honeymoon with their mom and brand-new step-dad. Devyn didn't know which was worse, having to bring your kids on your honeymoon, or being the kid. Because, seriously. How awkward.

The first boy, a shaggy-haired nine-year-old in a Super Mario Bros. T-shirt, crept into the room in baby steps while scanning his surroundings. When his gaze landed on the video gaming station in the back corner, he stood a bit straighter and lengthened his stride until he stood before Devyn with a hopeful grin.

But his big brother clearly resented being here. Wearing a Saints ball cap and a frown, the twelve-year-old sauntered forward with both hands shoved in his pockets and gave an eye roll that said, *I'm too old for this shit.*

Devyn felt him loud and clear. *Welcome to my world, kid.* She brightened her smile and invited the boys to join her at the table, where she'd arranged all her materials. "I'm Miss Mauvais, and I'm glad you came. It was getting too quiet in here."

The younger one pointed at the gaming station. "Do you have *Super Smash Brothers Brawl*?"

Devyn blinked at him. Was he speaking English?

Without asking permission, he bolted to the corner and tore open the plastic bin of games, then started digging through dozens of cases. His brother shuffled over in his Converse Chucks and picked through a second bin. Neither had seemed to notice her costume, or maybe they just didn't care. Devyn looked to Mrs. Grayson for guidance, but found none. The woman told Devyn she was taking her lunch break and left her alone with the boys.

She watched them pluck a case from the bin and inspect the gaming disk for scratches. When the older brother moved to turn on the Nintendo, she stopped him.

"Here's the thing . . ." Devyn took the game from them and set it next to the television. "I know it's vacation, but I'm supposed to teach you something." She glanced at the information cards their mother had filled out. "In fact, I have to sign some forms telling your school what you learned on this trip, or your absence won't be excused."

Both boys groaned.

"Hey," she said, resting a hand on her heart. "I don't make the rules."

"But this is supposed to be fun," whined the younger boy. "Mom promised."

"I'll make you a deal," Devyn said. "For every two minutes you spend with me, I'll give you one minute on the Nintendo. That should give you about an hour to play after the main lesson."

The older brother pursed his lips in consideration, obviously doing that math. "Together or separate?"

"Together," she said. "There's only one console, so you'll have to pick two-player games anyway."

He heaved an epic sigh worthy of the most angst-ridden tween. "Fine. Whatever." He gave his brother a knowing look. "It's not like we have a say in *any* of this."

Devyn had a feeling the kid was referring to more than just a history lesson. "I hear your mom got married. That's exciting, huh?"

A glare was his only reply.

Devyn didn't let it get her down. With this age group, sulking was par for the course. "It was nice of her to bring you on the honeymoon. My parents never took me anywhere."

When neither boy responded, she decided to dispense with the pleasantries. "Here." She handed them each a clipboard, then swept a hand over the dress-up clothes on the table. "Pick an outfit and we'll get this party started."

The nine-year-old—whose name was Will, according to his information card—eagerly snatched up a satin top hat and a gentlemanly vest and put them on. But his older brother, Jason, was having none of that nonsense. He folded his arms and cocked his head to the side in the unmistakable gesture for *Oh, hell naw.*

"Or not," she mumbled.

The first item on the scavenger hunt list was to learn the emergency exit that led outside to the lifeboats. Devyn showed the boys how to follow the signs to the main deck, and for the next couple of hours, she led them on an activity-based tour of the most useful parts of the boat: the main dining hall, the purser's desk, the library, the theater, and the recreation room. When she caught Jason checking his watch, she took the brothers to the pilothouse to watch Marc drive the *Belle.* Even Devyn was impressed by the gadgetry on display, but instead of admiring the control panels or asking to blow the steam whistle, the boys checked the time and told her they'd earned an hour on the Nintendo.

Devyn was forced to admit she'd lost the battle. With a heavy heart, she accompanied her students back to the education center, where they spent the rest of the afternoon playing an old video game they admittedly didn't even like. The figurative cherry on her sundae of failure was when Beau dropped in to check on her, exactly as he'd promised.

She hugged a clipboard to her chest as he took the seat across from her at the table. "It's not what you think," she said, nodding toward the noises of *BOING, BOING, BOING, BWOOP!* "They earned that game."

"Relax, hon." Beau rested an arm on the back of a vacant chair beside him, easy like Sunday morning. And it would be easy for him. He'd spent half his childhood on this boat. "You don't know what I'm thinking."

"Spare me. These kids are neck-deep in Mario World, and you think I'm not doing my job."

He laughed under his breath, shaking his head. "Not even close."

"Oh, yeah?" She leaned toward him with a challenge in her voice. "What, then?"

An impish grin played on his lips. "Maybe I saw you a few hours ago when you walked through the lobby," he said, reaching across the table to take her clipboard, his voice lowering to a whisper. "Maybe I noticed how freakin' hot you were in that dress, and I couldn't get you out of my head all day. Maybe I walked in here and imagined undoing all those laces . . . with my teeth." He wagged his brows. "Maybe that's what I was thinking."

Devyn's cheeks grew warm when she imagined him untying her corset laces, but in her fantasy, Beau used his strong, dexterous hands. The tips of his fingers would be rough when they brushed her skin, and her breasts would fit perfectly within his big palms—she remembered that detail quite well.

"Wouldn't surprise me." Devyn let her curls fall forward, hoping to conceal the blush he'd brought to her face. "Your mind's always in the gutter."

"Not always," he objected. "Only when you're around."

She didn't believe that—once a Dumont, always a Dumont.

Deciding to derail that train of thought, she turned her attention to the boys. "Anyway, I had to bribe them to participate in my lesson. From the way they acted, you'd think I was dragging them over fifty yards of broken glass."

"Give yourself some slack," Beau said. "They're kids on vacation. Everyone needs some down time."

Devyn supposed he was right, but she hated that the boys would leave here and dread returning in the morning. "Still. How do I make it fun for them?"

Beau shrugged and stated the obvious. "They're boys." When she gave him a *No shit, Sherlock* glare, he added, "Appeal to what boys like."

"And what's that?"

He cracked his knuckles and thought about it. "When I was that age, I was into country music, video games, football, and girls. Not necessarily in that order."

Devyn grabbed her clipboard away from him. "Real helpful, thanks."

"Oh, and blowing things up. That's some good, clean, redneck fun, right there."

"You're a regular genius," she said with an eye roll. "However can I repay your sage advice?"

When he grinned, she quickly amended, "Don't answer that."

Laughing, Beau stood from the table and ruffled her

hair. "You'll be fine. Just dip a little deeper into your bag of tricks, that's all."

"You make it sound so simple," Devyn said as she straightened her curls and slouched. What she needed was more tricks in her bag.

"They're boys. It doesn't get any simpler than that."

But he was wrong.

Over the next three days, Devyn dug all the way to the bottom of her bag of tricks, to no avail. Her lesson on the math and science of paddle-wheel propulsion was a bust, the kids tuned out her informative lecture on the economy of interstate trade, and one boy actually nodded off while playing the "boat race" board game she'd spent all day building.

She was officially tapped out.

"How about crafts?" suggested Ella-Claire one night from the bottom bunk. "Maybe a scrapbook of their trip? The students can color pictures and keep a journal for a keepsake to take home."

Devyn shifted on her mattress to dodge a rogue spring poking her hip. "These kids are too old for crafts. They're in that weird in-between age when they're too young to sit still for lectures but too mature for crayons and finger paint. I'm competing for their attention with Mario and Luigi, and I'm getting my ass kicked."

"Well, in all fairness, they do have Princess Peach."

"And Yoshi."

"Yeah," Ella said. "The deck is totally stacked against you."

A series of musical knocks rapped at the door, followed by a man's voice. He sounded close, as if he'd pushed his lips against the crack between the door and the wall. "Elles-Bells," he called. "You awake?"

"Elles-Bells?" asked Devyn.

"It's Alex. Mind if I let him in?"

"Go ahead. All my interesting parts are covered."

Ella flipped back her blanket and answered the door . . . wearing nothing but a T-shirt that barely covered her panties, something that didn't escape Devyn's notice. When Ella turned on the light and let Thing Two inside, her wardrobe choice didn't escape his notice either. His eyes flew cartoonishly wide and locked on to Ella's legs.

"You could have told me you weren't decent," he said, still staring.

"Dork." Playfully, Ella shoved him in the shoulder. But unlike the casual touches she gave the other Dumont brothers, this one lingered. She threaded an arm through his and peered up at him with more than just warmth in her gaze—this was full-on heat. Interesting. "You saw a lot more than this when we went tubing on Saturday."

A dopey smile broke out on Thing Two's face. "*And* when we went fishing the weekend before that. God bless that little string bikini of yours." He parked his backside on the edge of the dresser and seemed to notice Devyn for the first time. When he spotted her, his brows jumped like she'd caught him doing something wrong, and he detangled his arm from Ella's. Very interesting. "Oh," he said with a shaky wave. "Hey, Devyn."

She waved back and propped on one elbow to study him. Devyn was no behavioral analyst, but it seemed like Thing Two had a *thing* for Marc's half sister. Devyn pointed back and forth between the pair. "You two are . . ." She trailed off, thick with the implication.

"Friends," Thing Two said quickly, and with a bit more emphasis than necessary.

"Best friends," Ella clarified. "Since we were kids."

"Uh-huh." Best friends with benefits, probably. "How sweet."

While Thing Two and Ella-Claire huddled around his iPhone to watch a funny video he'd found online, Devyn pulled her own cell from beneath her pillow.

Ella-Claire and Alex, she texted her sister, *are they an item?*

A few minutes later, Allie texted back. *Officially? No. Marc would lose his shit. None of the brothers have laid a hand on Ella. Unofficially? Yeah, they're both totally sprung. It's kind of cute.*

Devyn found herself smiling, but not out of joy for the secret lovers currently giggling at the latest SNL digital short. She smiled because of the other thing Allie told her: if none of the Dumont brothers had touched Ella-Claire, it meant Ella and Beau hadn't knocked boots. Devyn shouldn't mind either way, but there was no denying that her chest felt lighter than it had five minutes ago.

Don't be a sap, she criticized inwardly. *This doesn't mean anything.*

To dial down her excitement a few notches, she forced herself to recall the morning after graduation, when she'd awoken naked and alone in a two-person sleeping bag, hungover and snuggling the school mascot she and Beau had "liberated" the night before from its pen. She'd trusted Beau with her heart, and he'd skipped town without so much as a good-bye. A six-word note had arrived in the mail from boot camp a couple of weeks later, but his half illegible *Sorry, Dev, I joined the Marines* was no consolation for what she'd suffered.

He'd hurt her once, and he would do it again if she gave him the chance.

Her sister's words turned over in her head. *He's not that same selfish boy anymore. He's trying to make amends. And he has faith in you.*

Was that true?

Devyn didn't know. But no matter how hard she tried to push Beau Dumont out of her thoughts, she drifted to sleep dreaming about one of her happiest memories—their first date.

Instead of defaulting to dinner and a movie, Beau had borrowed his pawpaw's boat and motored them to his top-secret fishing hole, the one he'd never even shared with his brothers. The fact that he trusted her with something so special made Devyn's heart flutter, and she couldn't stop sneaking sideways glances at his full mouth as they dangled their poles in the water. It was a perfect spring evening, the low sun sharpening the angles of Beau's masculine cheekbones and bringing out the reddish hues in his hair.

He was breathtaking.

"Any nibbles?" he whispered, nodding at her motionless fishing line.

Devyn shook her head. She wanted to talk to him, but the nervous butterflies in her tummy had stolen her voice.

"Soon," he promised, then winked and nearly made her ovaries explode. "This place is magical. The fish can't resist me here."

Devyn couldn't imagine a living creature resisting Beau in *any* location, but instead of saying so, she blushed and gazed out at the water.

He was right. Within minutes, she hooked a five-pound catfish. The gleam of admiration in Beau's eyes made her want to throw it back and catch an even bigger one, but she reeled in the fish and settled against Beau's chest when he moved behind her.

"Nice catch," Beau murmured in her ear as he pulled the hook free. "You're a natural."

Devyn turned to look at him. "I can't take the credit. Like you said, this place is enchanted."

His lips slid into a crooked grin, and just like that, she was done for. He glanced at her mouth for one infinite moment while her heart thumped in anticipation of his next move. Then, right there, with a squirming catfish in hand, Beau kissed her for the first time.

It was remarkably tender—a light brush of lips that lingered, making her feel like the most cherished girl in the bayou. When he pulled back, he smiled down at her and whispered, "Magical."

She agreed. Something was blooming between them . . . something unearthly. And she loved every minute of it.

Chapter 5

"Come on, cowboy," Beau muttered to himself. "Keep your hands where I can see 'em."

Pressing his nose against the one-way glass, Beau squinted across the casino to the high-dollar poker table, where a gambler in his mid-forties and wearing a black Stetson kept dropping one hand into his lap. Anyone with a lick of common sense knew better than to do that, especially the professionals. Beau supposed it was possible the cowboy had a case of jock itch, but he doubted it.

He checked the closed circuit television feed on the monitor affixed to the wall, but the overhead view was no better. For the life of him, he couldn't tell whether the gambler was innocently digging in his pocket for a stick of gum or swapping out cards. If the guy was cheating, he was as subtle about it as a bullhorn.

Beau checked the floor for Nicky, spotting him making the rounds near the craps table. He called his brother's cell and watched him answer it.

"Be cool," Beau said. "But I don't like what I'm see-ing at the high stakes poker table. Check out the guy in the black cowboy hat."

Nick had worked the casino floor since the day he'd turned twenty-one, so he knew to rotate casually and flick a glance in that direction. He pretended to wave his congratulations to a slot winner while reporting to Beau. "Dark wash jeans, black Laredos, nursing a whisky sour, and a little twitchy?"

Damn, that boy was good. "You got it."

"Want me to pay him a visit?"

"Yeah, but be friendly." They needed to proceed with caution. Each passenger had paid a pretty penny for two luxurious, stress-free weeks on board the *Belle*, and Beau's first priority was keeping the customers happy and coming back for more. Word of mouth ad-vertising was king, and nothing would turn off a return traveler faster than an insult . . . like a false accusation of cheating. "Bring the table a round of drinks," he said. "Some complimentary sandwiches, too. That should get you plenty close."

"I'm on it."

While Nick put in his order at the bar, Beau watched the overhead feed. He made a mental note to talk with the blackjack dealer about the tipping procedure. He didn't suspect the woman of anything shady, but once in a while, a gambler would slide over a chip to tip her, and she'd neglect to tap it on the table before dropping it in her shirt pocket. It was standard prac-tice to help Beau identify legitimate money leaving the table, and she should know better. Aside from that, everything looked kosher. There were barely any vacant stools at the gaming tables, and all the slots were occupied.

That was what Beau liked to see.

He noticed Nicky balancing a tray on one arm and making his way to the poker table. With a disarming smile, Nick set a drink in front of each player. If Beau hadn't been looking for it, he never would have noticed his brother's gaze dipping into the cowboy's lap. After handing out a few sandwiches, Nick strode back to the bar and disappeared off camera into the storage area, which meant he would soon be joining Beau in the security room.

The door opened and Nick slid inside with a laugh. "Well, he's cheating, but not on us."

"Translation, please?"

Nicky held up his left hand. "Dude's wearing a wedding band, and he's sexting his mistress. Or maybe the girl's just a booty call. I can't be sure, but he's certainly looking to hook up with someone named Jill."

Beau let out a breath, both relieved the guy wasn't scamming the house and annoyed by the infidelity. Having grown up watching his mama's heart shatter after each of his daddy's indiscretions, he had no tolerance for assholes who fooled around. He hated his dad for keeping Mama on the hook all those years, coming around every so often to spend a night or two, staying just long enough to get her hopes up again. Despite popular opinion, breaking up really wasn't hard to do.

If you didn't want to be with your lover, you should end it before moving on.

Beau glanced out the one-way glass at the cowboy, who'd just glanced into his lap to tap another text. He wanted to give the guy the benefit of the doubt.

"How do you know he's not sexting with his wife?" he asked.

"Easy," Nick said. "Because his last message said *I'll meet you in your suite as soon as my wife falls asleep.*"

Beau shook his head in contempt. "Dickhead."

Nicky shrugged and checked his own messages, seemingly unbothered by the stranger's behavior. Probably because the twins' mama had wised up and kicked Daddy to the curb shortly after she gave birth. Then she'd married a pharmacist and never looked back. Nick and Alex had escaped the fate of most Dumont boys, winding up with a white picket fence. They didn't understand how it was for Marc, Beau, and little Jackson—or Worm, as folks called him. The three of them knew the shame of wanting to protect their mothers and falling short. No doubt the new baby that Daddy had sired would learn soon enough, too.

Poor kid.

Beau realized he was clenching his jaw, so he took a deep breath and shook off thoughts of his father. The old man wasn't worth it.

"Hey," he said to Nicky. "Take over for me, will you? I'm cutting out for a break." It was four thirty, and if he hurried, he could catch the end of Devyn's lesson before the education center closed for the day. Seeing her gorgeous face never failed to cheer him up, and recently she gave him two smiles for every glare—progress.

"You got it, boss."

On his way out, Beau crossed through the casino and discreetly offered a few of the high rollers free tickets to an offshore excursion in Natchez. Then he left behind the plinking noise of slot payouts and stepped into the blissful silence of the hallway. When he reached the education center, he inched open the door and tiptoed inside.

Devyn had tacked a diagrammed steam engine poster to the wall, and she stood beside it, pointing to the high pressure cylinder. "Exhaust steam comes from here . . ." She trailed off and blew a lock of hair from her eye, then sighed when she noticed two boys playing rock-paper-scissors under the table.

"Can we play Nintendo now?" asked the oldest kid in the group, a blond who crossed his arms and slouched in his chair.

The girl next to him asked, "When's my mom coming?"

Beau took a knee on the foam tiles beside the table. When Devyn noticed him, she attempted a grin, but it didn't reach her eyes. She looked like she needed a hug.

"Can we go outside again?" lisped the youngest boy.

"No, I want to finish explaining how the *Belle*'s engine works," Devyn said. "Don't you think it's awesome that something as simple as steam can power this big boat?"

The kids provided their answer in the form of silence.

Devyn hooked a thumb at the poster. "After the steam leaves this chamber . . ." She paused again and locked eyes with him, and then something new sparked behind her gaze. Her lips parted in thought for a few moments before she said, "You know what? Forget this. Who likes to blow stuff up?"

Backs straightened and eyebrows rose. Scattered cries of *Yeah!* and *Me!* and *I do!* filled the room while Beau's stomach dropped an inch. Where was Devyn going with this?

"Blowing up something is called an explosion," she explained. "Does anyone know what the opposite of 'explode' is?"

The slouchy kid said, "Implode."

"Exactly." Devyn bent low to make eye contact with her now-attentive class. "Who wants to see me make a Coke can implode using the power of steam?"

Every hand in the room shot up.

"Okay, then." She pointed to Beau with a grin so infectious it lifted the corners of his own mouth. "Mr. Dumont, would you like to be my assistant?"

"Yes, ma'am." He pushed up from the floor and rubbed his hands together, relieved that she had no plans to ignite the boat. "Just tell me what to do."

"I saw an electric hot plate in the break room," Devyn said. "I'll need that and a pot of cold water. A pair of tongs, too. Oh, and an empty Coke can."

"Hot plate, tongs, cold water, Coke," he repeated. "Be right back."

Ten minutes later, he returned with the supplies and helped Devyn set up her experiment on the table while the kids sat at a safe distance, cross-legged on the floor. She put a small amount of water in the Coke can and set it on the burner to boil, then placed the pot of cold water in the center of the table. When a light mist wafted up from the can, she held a piece of black paper behind it so the kids could see the steam.

"Look," Devyn said, holding her palm over the can. "It's just a tiny bit of steam. Not even enough to burn me."

It was five o'clock, and several parents had filed into the room to pick up their little ones. Beau welcomed them to take a seat beside their kids, and soon Devyn had a captive audience of nearly twenty onlookers.

"Now watch what happens when I turn it upside down in the pot of cold water." Using the tongs, she clasped the bottom of the Coke can. "The temperature difference is going to create a vacuum and make the can . . ." She leaned forward and raised an expectant brow.

"Implode!" shouted the kids.

"That's right." She paused, heightening the anticipation. "Is everyone ready?"

The children nodded.

"Count down with me," Devyn said. "Three . . . two . . . one!"

She turned the can upside down, and the instant it touched the surface of the water, a loud *THWOOP!* thundered in the air, making the kids jump. Just like that, the can was decimated, completely crushed as if she'd taken a sledgehammer to it. Devyn held her tongs forward to show everyone.

Wild applause broke out from the audience. From the look of admiration in the kids' eyes, you'd think Devyn had summoned fire from her hands. She flourished the crushed can and took a bow.

"Thank you," she said with a playful wink. "I'm here all week. Don't forget to tip your server."

The oldest kid perked up and begged, "Do it again!"

"Tomorrow," Devyn promised. "I'll plan some other steam projects, too. So be here bright and early."

The children nodded eagerly and bounced on their toes, still chattering about the experiment as their parents led them into the hallway. Once the center had vacated, Beau told the director, "I'd like a word with Miss Mauvais. You can go on to supper, and I'll make sure to lock up when we leave." After Mrs. Grayson made her exit, Beau shut the door behind her and turned to Devyn.

"That was amazing," he said. "You knocked it out of the ball park."

She waved him off with a grin.

"How did you come up with the idea?"

A glow radiated from Dev's face, the unmistakable pride of a job well done. "I saw someone run the same experiment my freshman year in college, but I'd forgotten all about it. Then you came in, and I remembered what you said about blowing things up." She used a hand to mimic an explosion. "Boom. It triggered a memory."

"And you made fun of my *sage advice*," he teased. "Guess I'm useful for something, after all."

"Very useful." The joy shining behind her gaze made Beau's chest tight. He couldn't recall any reward greater than seeing her this happy. "Thank you, Beau."

Beau. She'd said his name.

Such a simple thing, and yet the gentle sound of it on her tongue lit him up like the Vegas strip. A surge of emotions swelled inside his lungs, and he acted without thinking. He eliminated the distance between them and took Devyn's face between his hands. Then he fulfilled his greatest fantasy from the last ten years—he kissed her.

Her lips were every bit as soft as he remembered, the honeyed taste of her mouth so achingly familiar that it gave him chills, even after all this time. If he thought the *Belle* felt like home, it was nothing compared to kissing Devyn.

Now he was home.

Despite the drive to take more, he didn't rush. Instead, he moved with deliberate care to give her a chance to respond, and when she opened to him, he explored her thoroughly with slow, sensual licks that had her groaning into his mouth.

Locking both arms around his neck, Dev stood on tiptoe and angled her head to deepen the kiss. The tip of her soft tongue stroked his while every inch of her body crushed against him. Beau's tenuous grasp on control snapped in half. He fisted her shirt and hugged her closer while he plundered her mouth with a decade's worth of bottled-up passion.

Suddenly, he couldn't get enough. It was as if a vacuum had opened up inside him, just like the flattened Coke can, and nothing but Devyn could fill the void. Every drop of blood in his body turned hot and rushed between his legs, every part of him begging to be inside her. He made love to her mouth, stopping only long enough to steal a ragged breath.

Before he knew what he'd done, he'd pushed her against the wall and lifted her by her ass so she could wrap her legs around him. She wasted no time in hooking her ankles behind his back and straining against the ridge of his erection. A shock of pleasure tore through his groin and ricocheted down the length of his thighs. He swallowed a curse and rocked into her.

At the contact, Devyn made the same adorable mewling sound that had earned her nickname back in high school. It was the hottest fucking noise on the planet, and Beau damn near blew in his pants.

"Kitten," he whispered against her mouth. "I missed you."

She pulled back, panting. Her eyes were thick with lust, her lips slick and swollen. She opened her mouth to speak but shut it again and darted a glance at the wide display windows lining the front wall. Then she nodded toward the other side of the room.

"Supply closet," she said. "Hurry."

Devyn's wish was his command.

Careful not to trip over discarded toys and games, he carried her to the closet and threw open the door. A glance inside made him wonder if they would both fit.

Shelves cluttered with Play-Doh, paints, and craft supplies lined the closet walls on three sides with a vacuum cleaner taking up half the floor space. There wouldn't be room to turn around, but he didn't much care. He ducked his head and wedged their bodies inside, then shut the door, enveloping them in darkness.

Devyn didn't miss a beat. With her legs still wrapped around his waist, she unbuttoned his dress coat and rubbed her hands up and down his chest, sucking in a breath as if she'd just seen the Grand Canyon for the first time. He wanted to touch her too, ached to feel the weight of her breast in his palm. Beau supported her with one arm and tried slipping his free hand up the front of her shirt, but he banged his elbow on the shelf and knocked an object to the floor with a *thunk*. For an instant, he worried there might be paint seeping onto the carpet, but then Devyn started grinding again, and she wiped his mind clean of everything but the sweet pressure building behind his fly.

"Damn, baby." He nuzzled the side of her neck and gently nipped her delicate flesh. "You feel so good."

"Mmm," she agreed, digging her heels into his backside for more leverage.

Beau's eyes had adjusted to the darkness, and he pulled back to gaze at her. He repeated, "I missed you. Tell me you missed me, too."

Dev's teeth flashed as she grinned at him. "You talk too much." She leaned closer and licked his top lip. "I think you've forgotten what your tongue is for."

Beau chuckled. Maybe she wasn't ready to forgive

him, but it was hard to be disappointed while she was riding his jock. Beau used a thumb to tease her nipple to a tight point, wishing like hell she'd worn that flimsy lace-up dress instead of a shirt and pants. And wishing twice as hard that he'd brought a condom. If he had, he'd be inside her right now.

"There's not enough room in here, Kitten," he murmured. "But if you come back to my suite, I'll peel off your clothes and make you eat those words." Then he traced the shell of her ear with his tongue to show that he still knew how to use it. "And you'll know what you've been missing."

She groaned, writhing in his arms. "It's unearthly," she whispered. "Just like the first time."

"What?" he asked.

"Nothing. Enough with the chitchat. Shut up and finish what you started."

Devyn would get no arguments from him. He kissed her, pressing her against the shelving while he thrust between her thighs in an imitation of what he wanted to do with her in bed.

Each stroke made him harder than the last, and soon the tight space was filled with the sounds of labored breathing and groans of pleasure. It occurred to him that he'd left the center door unlocked, and anyone who walked in would overhear. But Beau couldn't bring himself to care. All that mattered was release from the pressure building low in his gut.

When Devyn began panting and arching wildly against him, he quickened the tempo until she made the whimpering noise that'd always told him she was on the brink. Kisses turned clumsy as they moved together in a frenzied rhythm, the friction of their bodies making Beau throb until he couldn't hold out any longer. He remembered how Devyn liked it, so he squeezed her ass hard while rotating his hips in circles, and she came undone.

Digging her nails into his shoulders, she tipped back her head and muffled a cry while riding out her orgasm. Her ecstasy spurred his own, and seconds later, Beau bucked against her with a low groan. Violent spasms of pleasure erupted between his thighs, and he saw stars as he spilled in hot release. He rested his head against the base of Devyn's neck, his heart thundering so loud it rang in his ears. The quakes kept racking him long after his climax ended, and he rocked into her until every drop was wrung from his core.

He regained use of his brain by gradual degrees, and when his world righted itself, he was grinning like a dope and so satisfied he could have floated away on a breeze.

"Holy shit," he breathed. "We've still got it."

"I know, right?"

He kissed her forehead and gave quiet laugh. "Only you."

"*Only me* what?" she asked defensively.

"Could make me come so hard . . . or in my pants." It was going to be an uncomfortable walk back to his cabin. "It's like senior year all over again. Remember that time we snuck into the janitor's closet during study hall? I had to go to football practice with cold, wet boxers. Couldn't run worth a damn, and the coach chewed my ass."

Devyn didn't seem to enjoy hearing that. Instead of laughing with him, she detangled her legs and planted both feet on the floor, then pressed a palm to his chest in a silent message to give her some space. "I need to clean up out there."

Her abrupt reaction stunned him into a beat of silence. "You okay?"

"Fine," she insisted. "But it's cramped in here. I can't breathe."

As soon as he opened the door and took a step back, she slipped around him and began picking up toys from the floor with the single-minded determination of a lady on a mission. She didn't even pause to let her eyes adjust to the light. In seconds, she'd collected an armful and deposited the toys in the nearest bin. Beau moved forward to help her, but she extended a palm like a traffic cop.

"I've got this," she said. "You probably have a lot to do, so you can go."

Was that a dismissal? It sure sounded like one.

"Hey." He tried to catch her gaze, but she wouldn't look at him. "What's wrong?"

She folded a board game in half and shoved it inside a box. "Nothing."

"Did I hurt you?"

"Of course not."

"You came before I did, right?"

"Yes. It was great, thanks."

It was great, thanks? What was this, a business transaction?

Beau retraced his steps, trying to figure out where he'd gone wrong. Everything was fine until he'd mentioned senior year. He figured their past wasn't quite water under the bridge, but bringing up one of their best times together shouldn't have caused her to shut down.

He snagged her by the elbow. "Talk to me. Are you all right?"

When she spun on him, there was defiance in her eyes. "I'm always all right." She pointed a little red fire truck at him and repeated, "Always. I've been fine for the last ten years, and there's nothing wrong with me now."

"Why are you mad at me?" he asked. "You told me to finish what I started, and I did."

"I'm not mad at you." She threw the truck into the bin with enough force to send another toy bouncing out to the floor.

"Funny," he said. "When I woke up this morning, I didn't have 'dumbass' tattooed on my forehead." He pointed at his temple. "Is it on there now?"

She glared at him.

"I'm not an idiot, Dev. Tell me what I did wrong."

Devyn spent the next couple of minutes in silence, scurrying about the room and tidying up while Beau stood there with his arms folded, refusing to budge until she answered him. After she was finished, she stowed the electric burner inside the closet they'd recently vacated and closed the doors with a gentle *click*. She kept her back to him when she finally spoke.

"You didn't do anything wrong." Her voice was soft but wounded, like she was fighting off tears. But when he moved to join her, she extended an arm to keep him at a distance. "It's been a long day. Just go, all right?"

No. Nothing about this felt all right. "You're making me worried."

"Look, we had a good time." Her voice wasn't soft now, the frost on her tongue virtually cooling the room by a few degrees. "The fact that I don't want to cuddle afterward doesn't mean there's anything wrong with me. I'm not a clinger. I never was."

Beau wasn't stupid, and he knew what she was doing—pushing him to leave. He didn't want to walk away, but clearly she had no intention of lowering her defenses. If he stayed, it would only antagonize her. "Fine, I'll go. But I'm gonna check on you later."

She sniffed a dry laugh. "I'm not going to jump overboard because of you, Dumont. No need to flatter yourself."

A spark of anger flared in his chest. After what he'd done on graduation night, he expected to work hard to earn back Devyn's trust. But that didn't mean he would be her personal whipping boy. He walked behind her, stopping when he noticed her shoulders stiffen. He bent to her ear and said, "Since I came back to town, I've done nothing but help you, and you've thrown it in my face every time. I don't know what crawled up your ass, but come find me when you're ready to apologize. I'll be waiting."

Then he buttoned his coat, reclaimed his Man Card, and stalked back to his room to change clothes. It was a cold, sticky walk up the stairwell, which perfectly matched his mood.

So much for feeling satisfied.

Chapter 6

"This is your third batch." Allie pulled a wire basket from the deep fryer and shook bits of breaded okra onto a clean plate, then dusted them with garlic salt and parmesan cheese, just like Mama used to do. She slid the plate across the gleaming stainless steel island. "After this, the kitchen is closed, so you'd better go on and tell me what's bothering you."

Devyn pulled another beer from the industrial-sized fridge and popped the top. She took a long gulp, but all the beer and comfort food in the world wouldn't push down the self-loathing lodged in her throat. "I'm weak." She took another swig and added, "And pathetic."

"Oh, come on. Weak?" Allie pushed a stool to the opposite side of the island and took a seat. "This coming from the girl who tracked down my fifth-grade bully and gave him an atomic wedgie on the playground?"

Devyn smiled at the memory. The kid had outweighed her by fifteen pounds, but she'd had the height advantage, which had come in handy for tugging the waistband of his tighty-whities over his head. "Hey, nobody messes with my sister."

"Or *my* sister," Allie said. "So tell me what's wrong."

A frown replaced Devyn's smile, and she shoved a bite of okra into her mouth.

Allie pointed back and forth from the beer to the fried okra. "This has man trouble written all over it."

"Beau," she mumbled around her food. "Who else?"

"What did he do?"

"Strangely enough, it's not what he did," Devyn said. "It's what I did."

"Okay, so what did you do?"

Devyn used a fork to stab at the innocent chunks of okra. "After graduation, when he made all those promises and then skipped out on me, I swore I'd never take him back."

She had spent more time than she wanted to admit fantasizing about how he'd drop to his knees and beg for a second chance. In her daydreams, she had scoffed and told Beau to go to hell, then climbed inside her silver Maserati and sped away with her hot Italian boyfriend. So much for that. "He's back in town less than a month. A few crooked smiles and a handful of pretty words, and I'm dry humping him in the day-care closet."

Allie's eyes flew wide. "You did what in the where?"

"You heard me."

Devyn recalled the night of her high school reunion,

when Beau had told everyone their song was "Bump n' Grind." How appropriate. "Tell me that's not the weakest, most pathetic thing ever."

Allie's lips twitched in a poorly concealed grin as she reached for the okra. Clearly she wasn't taking this seriously. "You got some over-the-clothes action from a big, hunky guy. I'd say that's the opposite of pathetic."

"Not just any big, hunky guy, and you know it," Devyn said, raising the beer to her lips, but then she slammed the bottle back onto the steely counter. "When he kissed me, I forgot about everything I felt ten years ago—the fear when I couldn't find him, the embarrassment of being the last to know he joined the marines, the heartbreak when I realized he was gone forever. All of it just vanished."

Until afterward, when he'd mentioned the time they had fooled around in the janitor's closet. Then all those old emotions had come rushing back in a tidal wave that'd nearly had her in tears.

"Cut yourself some slack," Allie said. "You two loved each other once. Those were powerful feelings, and it sounds like neither of you really moved on."

"Maybe." But still, Devyn hated herself for how Beau had snapped his fingers and she'd come—no pun intended—faster than a bullet train. "It gets worse. He didn't like the way I acted when we, you know, were done, so he laid a guilt trip on me." She shook her head in disbelief. "After dumping me like a load of garbage, he weaseled his way between my legs again and somehow *I'm* the bad guy."

"Why are you the bad guy?"

Devyn hunched over her plate and mumbled, "I was kind of mean to him."

"Kind of?"

"Okay, totally mean. But I didn't know what to do," Devyn said, helplessly turning up her palms. "I was freaking out, and I needed to be alone. He wouldn't take a hint. He wanted to stand around and talk about the 'good old days'"—she made air quotes—"which weren't all that good, trust me."

"So you bit his head off," Allie said with a nod. "I know how you operate."

"Hey," Devyn said. That stung. "Whose side are you on anyway?"

Allie didn't hesitate to say, "Yours. Always yours. Never doubt that." She folded both arms and rested them on the island. "But you have a habit of striking out when you feel cornered or threatened. What I don't think you understand is that Beau's not a threat to you."

"How do you know?" Devyn asked, because deep down, she felt threatened and her instincts had never led her astray. "Nothing's changed." When Allie took a breath to argue, Devyn cut her off. "All right, so maybe Beau's changed. Maybe he's a new man with good intentions. But the curse is still the same. It's only a matter of time before he screws me over again, because that's what Dumont men do."

Allie rolled her eyes. "Not this nonsense."

"Yes, this *nonsense*." After everything that had happened, Devyn couldn't believe her sister still denied the curse. "The Dumont men are hexed. Don't try to blame parental example and self-fulfilling prophesy, because the women get married and ride off into the sunset—just not the guys."

"There's a perfectly good explaina—"

"Not to mention," Devyn interrupted, "the freaky stuff that happened to Marc when you two got serious." At the wedding reception, Marc had confided that each time he'd tried asking Allie to move in with him, he was unable to speak the words. He had said it was like having an invisible pillow stuffed over his face. "And when he wanted to marry you, every imaginable force of nature stood in his way."

"A coincidence," Allie said. "Nothing more."

"Oh, yeah? What about Memère's ring?" It was no coincidence that Marc had stumbled upon the engagement ring his great-great-grandfather had given their great-great-grandmother before the old fool had ditched her at the altar and suffered a curse for it.

"He was in the right place at the right time."

"Fine," Devyn said, because she'd saved her best argument for last. "Then explain the birthmark."

Exactly as expected, Allie didn't have anything to say to that.

Each Dumont man was born with a wine-colored splotch on the skin above his heart. Marc's birthmark had mysteriously disappeared on his wedding night while his brothers had retained theirs. It was how Devyn knew he'd broken the curse only for himself, not the entire family.

Allie scowled, obviously trying to come up with some psychobabble scientific explanation for what she stubbornly refused to acknowledge. "I haven't figured that out yet. But I'm sure there's a logical reason for it."

"There *is* a logical reason," Devyn said. "Memère's hex."

"Fine." The flatness of Allie's tone warned she was switching tactics. "For argument's sake, let's say there actually is a hex on the Dumonts."

That wasn't hard to do. "Okay."

"Marc and I proved that it can be broken."

"It wasn't easy, though."

"No, it wasn't," Allie agreed. "But nothing worthwhile ever is." She paused to munch on a bite of fried okra, then reached across to steal a sip of beer. "Remember how hard you tried to break the curse for me and Marc?"

Devyn nodded.

"Why not do the same for yourself?"

Because there were plenty of fish in the sea—fish without baggage. "What makes you think I want to?"

Allie glanced at the two empty plates of comfort food, cocking a brow as if no further explanation was necessary.

"Okay, so Beau and I have chemistry," Devyn admitted. "Truckloads of it. But that's not enough to make a relationship last. And besides, I couldn't break the curse for Marc. He had to do it himself."

"*Purest faith shall set you free,*" Allie said, reciting the last line from Memère's spell. Her gaze turned soft, and for a moment, she sounded like a believer. "All the two of you need is faith."

Whatever. All Devyn needed was to get off this boat and back to her regular life—the one that didn't include Beau Dumont. Which reminded her . . . "Hey, I've been meaning to tell you something."

"Is it how wonderful I am?"

"Well, that's a given," Devyn said smiling, but she kept her gaze fixed on an empty beer bottle. "About a week ago, a guy offered me a job and I took it."

"That's great!"

"Yeah," Devyn said, resolving to be positive. "It's a unique opportunity, and the owner's excited to have me on the team."

"What kind of job is it?"

Devyn cleared her throat and studied her fingernails. "I'm going to lead haunted graveyard tours in Cedar Bayou," she said; then she chanced a peek at her sister.

For a pregnant beat, Allie froze and her lips parted. She quickly recovered with a congratulatory smile, but her original reaction spoke volumes. "How perfect is that? Nobody knows more about Memère's history than you do."

"Mmm-hmm." Suddenly Devyn didn't want to talk about her new job anymore. Even her sister, who had little esteem for their voodoo heritage, recognized the shame of exploiting it. "Just wanted to let you know."

"I'm happy if you're happy," Allie said, reaching across the island to offer a gentle nudge. "But you're not exactly turning cartwheels."

Devyn shrugged and picked up one last bite of okra. "It's money."

She popped the morsel in her mouth, but her appetite had died, so she tossed it back onto the plate. "Thanks for the snacks. I'm heading to bed."

"Hope you feel better in the morning," Allie said. "If not, come back and I'll make Mama's warm bread pudding with an extra dash of lemon. That always cheers me up."

Devyn hugged her sister and turned to go, but her footsteps were heavier than before. She was pretty sure not even bread pudding could fix what ailed her.

Devyn didn't sleep well that night, or the night afterward. She tossed and turned on her narrow bunk. Just when the lazy haze of slumber would begin to wash over her, she'd see the hurt in Beau's eyes and jerk awake while his words echoed in her head.

Come find me when you're ready to apologize. I'll be waiting.

"Fat chance." Devyn punched her pillow to fluff it, then faced the ceiling. She hadn't done anything wrong. She hadn't asked him to kiss her, and she hadn't asked for this job. He'd muscled his way into her life without permission. He was the one who owed her an apology— ten years' worth of *I'm sorry*—not the other way around.

So why was guilt chewing a hole in her stomach?

"Damn you, Beau Dumont," she whispered in the darkness. "Damn you for making me feel like this. And damn myself for giving you the power to do it."

Ella-Claire stirred from the bottom bunk, mumbling in her sleep and smacking her lips, so Devyn kept quiet and tried to lie still. Sleep finally took her as the blackness of night gave way to the purple bruise of morning, and the alarm sounded way too soon for her weary body.

She washed in a daze, too exhausted to cast her usual scowl at the shower-toilet, and she made for the coffee station in the dining hall before her hair was even dry.

While stirring her creamer, she couldn't help discreetly scanning the passengers and crew for the object of her angst. It wasn't hard to spot him. Beau stood a full head and shoulders above everyone else, his white uniform a stark contrast against a sea of polo shirts and button-downs as he entered the room. He smiled and nodded *good morning* to everyone in his path, but he didn't spare a glance in Devyn's direction when he topped off his travel thermos with black coffee.

He stood close enough to fill her space with the mingled scents of roasted Colombian beans and aftershave. It was a pleasing homey smell, evoking memories of Sunday mornings with her family. Devyn leaned behind him to toss her sugar packet in the trash. Ready to bury the hatchet, she brought a cardboard cup to her lips and faced Beau to give him a chance to acknowledge her.

But he didn't.

Instead, he screwed on his thermos lid and turned to

leave. He waved at everyone but her and strolled out the door without looking back. The bite of rejection made Devyn's shoulders round forward. He was really going to do this—freeze her out until she apologized. For the thousandth time, she wondered why Beau's approval mattered so much to her. Clearly she needed professional help.

Fine, she thought. *Let him stew a while. I'm not apologizing.*

She lasted all of eight hours.

When five o'clock rolled around and the education center emptied, Devyn was ready to jump out of her skin. Each minute had ticked by in torturously slow degrees until it felt like time was going in reverse. All day, her focus had been shot. It had taken three tries to get her candle-powered mini steamboat to work, because Beau had dominated her brain and clumsied her fingers.

She refused to examine the reasons why, but she couldn't stand knowing he was upset with her. It didn't mean she wanted a repeat performance of their closet adventure, and it didn't mean she wanted to be friends. She would make her apology quick and sterile, and then things could go back to normal.

As normal as they ever were.

After cleaning up and preparing her materials for the next day, Devyn walked to the casino, figuring she'd find Beau there. She stopped in front of the dou-

ble doors to take a fortifying breath and wipe her
clammy palms on her pants. She could do this—be the
bigger person. Five minutes of eating crow would re-
store her sanity.

It was a worthy trade.

Shaking back her hair, she strode inside. An over-
load of sensations smacked her in the face as she
scanned the crowded room for Beau's stubborn auburn
head. Between the flashing lights, the clamoring machines, and the boisterous cheering from the craps table, she had to make three passes before realizing he
wasn't there.

A hand tapped her on the shoulder, and she spun
around to find Thing One smiling at her. She knew it
was him because he still hadn't learned to keep his
gaze away from her boobs.

"Looking for the boss man?" he asked.

Devyn nodded. "Where is he?"

"In the security room," he said, pointing to a swinging door behind the bar. "Go through the storage area;
then it's the first door on the right."

She followed his directions and strode toward the
bar. Her knees trembled and her heart pounded the
closer she got to the storage area, but she pushed open
the door without hesitation.

Ripping off the Band-Aid, and all that.

To her surprise, Beau was already waiting for her.
The door to the security room was open, and he leaned
against the jamb with both arms folded across his chest,

his face a blank mask. He'd removed his jacket and rolled up his sleeves, revealing muscled forearms that heightened her anxiety level. It wasn't easy to meet his chilly gaze, but she forced herself to look him in the eyes.

"How did you know I was here?" she asked.

Beau nodded behind him. "One-way glass. I saw you coming."

"Oh." She cleared her throat and blotted her palms again. "Is this a bad time? Because I can come back later."

To his credit, Beau didn't stare her down or make her grovel. He kept his expression impassive, but moved out of the way and swept a hand to invite her inside.

The security headquarters was about the same size as her bedroom, but at least ten degrees warmer thanks to a table full of computer equipment and a flat-screen monitor hanging on the wall. That explained why Beau had removed his jacket.

While he shut the door and dragged over a folding chair, Devyn glanced out the one-way glass and wondered what had gone through his mind when he'd watched her cross the casino floor. She had expected him to gloat or at least offer one of his signature smirks, but he was being unusually mature. She wasn't sure if that would make her apology easier or not.

"Have a seat," he said, lowering to his swiveling office chair.

Devyn preferred to stand, so she walked behind the

chair and gripped its metal back for support. Beau didn't seem to mind, probably because they were eye level now. Since delaying the inevitable wouldn't make this any easier, she jumped right in.

"You know why I'm here," she said, staring out the glass without seeing anything. "I was upset, and I shouldn't have taken it out on you. I'm sorry. You didn't deserve that."

He didn't say anything at first, just shifted on his seat. When he spoke, there was no trace of resentment in his tone. "Thank you. I know that wasn't easy."

"I can admit when I'm wrong."

"But still."

"Yeah," she conceded. "Nothing between us is ever easy."

He blew out a breath and seemed to relax a bit. "Can I ask what I did to make you mad? Because I keep replaying it in my mind, trying to figure out where I went wrong. It's been driving me crazy. Whatever I did, I promise I wasn't trying to upset you."

Devyn's heart warmed with the knowledge that their spat had affected both of them. She met his gaze, humbled by the concern she saw there. It gave her the courage to tell him the truth. "It's my issue. I don't like thinking about our past. Reminiscing about old times might make you laugh, but for me, memory lane is paved with land mines and broken glass."

"Was it really that bad?" He blinked at her. "I know I messed up, but—"

"You hurt me, Beau." Devyn couldn't believe she'd just said that out loud. She had spent so much time pretending otherwise, but it felt good to admit the truth, like dropping a barbell she'd carried for too long. "And everything is tainted because of that. Even the good times."

He stood from his chair and reached for her, but seemed to think better of it. "I'm really sorry, Dev. I wish I could make you understand how much I regret leaving." While keeping his distance, he paused until he caught her eye. "I panicked and I ran. We can blame the curse or my own immaturity, but either way it was wrong. I've spent the last decade kicking my own ass for ruining what we had, and I never got you out of my head." He tapped his temple and repeated, "Never. I don't think I ever will."

Devyn squeezed the metal chair while her eyes prickled. She didn't want to hear how much he'd missed her. All she had come here to do was apologize and leave. If Beau kept going on like this, she would have to shut him down by admitting something she'd kept buried from everyone, even her sister. Devyn had refused to think about it for the last decade. In fact, she'd done such a good job at blocking the memory that it didn't seem real anymore.

"Let me try to make amends," he went on. "Can't we start over? We'll go as slow as you want. I'll take you out to dinner and I promise I won't lay a hand on—"

"You don't get it." Devyn's voice cracked, and she paused to blink back tears. "There's more."

Beau shook his head in confusion.

She filled her lungs and announced, "You got me pregnant."

"What?" He braced one hand on the wall while his jaw went slack. Stammering, he tried several times to get the words out. "When? Why didn't you say anything?"

"I didn't know at first. I took a test the same day your letter came in the mail." She lifted a shoulder. "Then I got my period a few days later, and then there was no reason to tell you. What was the point? You were long gone, and we were over."

Silently, he lowered to his chair.

"But those three days before the miscarriage? They were awful." Devyn drew a shuddering breath. "Not because I was young and alone. I knew my family would help with the baby and the military would garnish your wages. I'd have enough support to get by. That wasn't what scared me."

Beau just stared at her, so she blotted her eyes and went on. "What scared me the most was knowing what happens to the kids in your family. And to their mothers. You left me behind to travel the world, and I was just another Dumont castoff, tied to you forever by a baby you would've ignored except on holidays, assuming you happened to be in town."

Beau's voice was barely audible when he asked, "Did you really think that?"

"Yes. I got a glimpse of what could have been," Devyn said. "This might sound hateful, and I don't mean any disrespect, but I almost ended up like your mama. I don't want that for myself. No man is worth it."

Not even the only man she'd ever loved.

Devyn took a deep breath and continued. "That's why we can't start over. That's why I don't want to reminisce about sneaking off to the janitor's closet. If I could erase all that from my memory, I would."

Judging by the lack of color in his cheeks, Beau hadn't quite absorbed the news yet. Devyn understood. At eighteen, it had taken her two full hours to acknowledge the second blue line on her pregnancy test. She had kept staring at it like the results might change if she blinked enough times.

"Look, I didn't come here to lay anything heavy on you," she said. "I just want you to know where we stand—and why I can't go back." Then she corrected, "Why *we* can't go back. I don't want that kind of life."

Beau dragged a hand over his face and stared into empty space for so long that he seemed to have forgotten she was there. She took that as her cue to leave.

"I'm sorry for snapping at you the other day. That's all I came here to tell you."

When he didn't answer, she folded her chair and leaned it against the wall, then quietly let herself out.

Devyn had thought that apologizing to Beau would make her feel better, but when she stepped into the casino, each electric chirp pierced her skull like a jackhammer. It was as if she had shed her skin, and now her nerves were exposed. Needing to escape, she jogged across the floor and didn't stop until she'd reached the ship's galley.

With moisture welling in her eyes, she asked her sister, "Is that offer of bread pudding still on the table?"

Allie dropped her cup of flour and rushed to offer a hug. "Oh, honey. You bet it is. And ice cream, too."

Chapter 7

During recon training, the marines had tested the limits of Beau's body and mind to the breaking point through a series of drills most men couldn't survive. He'd suffered in silence for three months of the most grueling physical exertion imaginable, like *The Longest Day*, an eighteen-hour test of endurance where he had puked and dry heaved so much it was a wonder his stomach hadn't ruptured. But that was child's play compared to the nighttime exercises. Exhausted from a full day of swimming, running, and towing boats with his bare hands, he had been ordered to hold his position in pitch darkness while his instructors attacked him with blank artillery and tear gas.

It was goddamned terrifying.

With no gas mask, he'd used his sweat-soaked T-shirt to cover his mouth and nose, fighting the urge to retreat to the next sand dune for a breath of clean air. His eyes and throat had burned hotter than hellfire, panic had surged through his veins, and it was the most unnatural thing in the world to lie there and breathe that poison.

He kind of felt that way now—suffocated and confused.

Conflicting emotions of anger, loss, and shame pressed against his lungs to smother him as real as the tear gas that had brought him to his knees. The longer he sat in the security room, the harder his pulse rushed. His muscles tensed, and his blood boiled. He wanted to fight someone, but he didn't know why.

Who was he even mad at?

Not Devyn. She hadn't done anything wrong. And yet the mental echo of her words made him want to punch a hole in the wall.

I almost ended up like your mama.

He sucked a breath through his nose and shot to his feet, then paced a circuit around the room in an effort to burn off some rage. What in the ever-loving hell was wrong with him?

Two quick knocks sounded from the door, and Nicky poked his head inside. His blond brows shot up, telling Beau how crazy he must look. "You okay?" Nick asked. "Devyn ran out of here like the room was on fire."

Beau couldn't worry about her right now. He needed to get out of here and blow off some steam.

"Take over for a while, will you? I'm going to the gym."

"Sure." Nick seemed concerned, but he clearly knew better than to pry. "Take the rest of the night off if you want. I'll pull Alex from the purser's desk. We can hold down the fort."

On his way out the door, Beau clapped his brother on the arm and said, "Thanks." Then he charged upstairs to his suite while avoiding eye contact with everyone he passed.

After changing clothes, he jogged to the gym, pleased to find it empty. He glanced at the clock and realized it was dinnertime, which meant he would have the place to himself for a solid hour or two. Beau scanned the workout equipment to find the right outlet. Soon he spotted it—a red punching bag hanging from the ceiling in the corner of the room. His lips curved and his fists clenched in anticipation.

Perfect.

Two hours later, Beau's knuckles were raw and he could barely lift his arms, but he felt nearly human again. He swiped the back of his hand across his forehead and geared up for one last swing, a grand finale with all his weight behind it. When his right hook connected with the bag, a loud smack echoed through the gym, and one of the bag's reinforcement straps tore, causing it to hang from the ceiling at a skewed angle.

Beau swore under his breath. He should have quit while he was ahead.

"See?" said a male voice from behind him. "This is why we can't have nice things."

Marc strode into view with his jacket slung over one arm and his captain's hat in hand. He must have come off duty in the pilothouse, because he'd loosened his tie and undone the first few buttons of his dress shirt.

Beau didn't need to ask how his brother had ended up here.

"Nicky ratted me out."

"More or less," Marc said. He took a seat on one of those silly Nautilus machines that women used to work their inner thighs—the kind that spread their legs wide open. "He asked me to check on you. Said he hasn't seen you this pissed since the day I broke your nose."

Beau chuckled dryly, remembering the first and last time he had ever dissed Marc's mother. Deep in his teenage heart, he'd known better, but he'd cracked a joke about the woman to score a laugh with his friends. "I deserved that."

"Yes, you did," Marc agreed. "But let's not change the subject. Nick also said you had a fight with Devyn."

"That's not true."

"You sure?" Marc said, standing as he grabbed a clean towel from a nearby table. He handed it to Beau while wrinkling his nose in distaste. "You need a shower."

"The answer is yes," Beau said. He used the towel to wipe down his sweaty face. "To both of those statements. Dev and I aren't fighting." And he sure as hell needed a shower. He smelled like roadkill.

"Okay." The way Marc drew out the word sounded like he didn't buy it. "Then why the bloody knuckles? What did that innocent punching bag ever do to you?"

Beau glanced down and noticed a smudge of blood

across the back of his right hand. Again, he wished he had quit before that final throw that broke the bag. He grabbed a clean towel and wrapped it around his knuckles while stalling for an excuse. Beau honestly didn't know what to say, because he didn't understand what had come over him.

"Spit it out," Marc said.

Beau sat on the matted floor and flicked a glance at his brother. The two of them had never been close—in fact, they'd spent most of their teenage years at each other's throats—but they had a lot in common, like a deadbeat dad. It prompted him to ask, "Did you ever worry that you'd turn out like the old man?"

From the way Marc's chin dropped, he wasn't anticipating that question. He glanced down at his captain's hat, perhaps recalling all the years their father had worn it. "Maybe a little. I never wanted to repeat his mistakes. That's why I always kept it wrapped when I took a woman home."

Beau sensed that his brother had left something unsaid. "But . . . ?"

"But Allie pointed out something when we were dating," he said, leaning forward to rest both elbows on his knees. "She said I was exactly like Daddy, just without all the kids." He sniffed a humorless laugh. "I didn't like hearing that, but she was right. I fooled around with half the parish and never stayed with one woman long enough to make it count. The only difference between me and Daddy was I had nothing to show for it."

"So in all those years," Beau said, "you never slipped one past the goalie?"

"Not that I know of."

"What if you had?"

"Gotten some girl pregnant?"

"Yeah." Beau pretended to inspect the bruised knuckles on his left hand. "What would you have done?"

Marc shrugged. "The right thing, I guess. I would've manned up and taken care of the kid."

"Would you have married the mother?"

A look of incredulity crossed Marc's face, along with a nervous grin. "Let's not get carried away. That's a really bad reason to get married. I would have made sure she was taken care of." Then he clarified, "Financially, I mean. I wouldn't have used her as a permanent booty call the way Daddy did with our mamas."

Beau was glad to hear that. "I would have married her."

Marc cocked his head. "Married who?"

Uh-oh. He hadn't meant to say that out loud. "No one in particular," he lied. "If I'd gotten a girl in trouble, I would have tried to make an honest go of it. That's all I was sayin'."

Marc scrutinized him for a long moment. "Is there anything you want to tell me?"

Beau pushed up from the floor. "Nope."

"So you're all right?"

"Yep," he said, hooking a thumb at the battered punching bag. "You can take that out of my wages, Captain. I'm off to the shower."

Marc waved a hand in front of his nose. "It's about damn time."

A grin lifted the corners of Beau's mouth. Though he'd never admit it, he was glad Nicky had sent Marc down here. This chat had helped him understand what had been eating him, and more important, what he needed to do about it.

On his way back to his suite, he sent Devyn a text. *I need to talk to you. My room in twenty minutes. Won't take long, promise.*

Devyn's cell chimed from her back pocket to announce an incoming text. With a bowl of bread pudding in one hand, she used the other to retrieve her phone and swipe the glass. Her heart jumped when she read the message, and she hid the screen so Allie couldn't see.

"What does Beau want?" Allie asked from the other side of the island. "That was him, right?"

Damn it. "How did you know?"

Allie toasted her with a glass of milk. "It's the *Oh, shit!* face. You only make it when he's around." She took a bite of her own bread pudding. "So what did he want?"

"To talk."

"That's probably a good idea."

"To talk in his *suite*."

A devilish smile spread over Allie's face. "A very good idea."

"No, it's a very bad idea."

Devyn hadn't told her sister about the miscarriage.

For all Allie knew, Beau wanted to talk about the weather. But that wasn't what he had in mind, and Devyn had no interest in dredging up those memories. She had finally calmed down after three desserts. Besides, the last place she needed to meet Beau was in his bedroom. They'd be horizontal before the door clicked shut. "You know what happens when we're alone."

Allie rolled her eyes. "It's not like your pants will come flying off the second you cross the threshold."

"Psh." Close enough.

"Tell you what," Allie said. "Go talk to him. If you're not back here in half an hour, I'll come up there and knock on his door. And I won't stop until one of you answers."

"You would do that? Run booty interference?"

"Just one of the many services I offer."

Devyn began to take her sister's suggestion seriously. After the bomb she had dropped on Beau, it was only natural that he'd have questions. And aside from bedrooms—and closets—there weren't many private places to talk aboard the boat. "Okay," she decided. "But you might have to use some muscle to get me out of there."

"Seriously?"

"Yes, seriously," she said. Her sister didn't understand the power of Beau's sexual magnetism. "Promise that you'll make me leave, no matter what."

"Fine," Allie said flatly. "I promise."

"Just give me a few minutes to get up there."

Devyn made a pit stop in her room to splash cool water on her face. It didn't do much to alleviate the puffiness beneath her reddened eyes, but the refreshing chill gave her a much needed energy boost.

Soon she was standing in front of Beau's door, every bit as nervous as when she had come to apologize earlier that evening. Beau certainly did have a way of making her heart race. She'd probably burned off a serving of bread pudding just standing here working up the courage to knock.

She held her breath and rapped her knuckles on the door. Moments later, the door swung open and that breath whooshed out in a rush as Devyn fought to keep the shock from parting her lips.

Beau stood there . . . wearing nothing but a towel.

Oh, God. She was screwed.

"I said twenty minutes," he told her, gripping the white terrycloth at his waist. "I'm not dressed yet."

Yes, she could see that. In fact, she could see a lot of things, like the contours of his muscled shoulders and broad chest, his hair-encircled nipples tightened to hard buds. Her own traitorous nipples puckered to match. Her gaze was held hostage by the overwhelming masculinity of him, from the thick column of his neck down to his lean, powerful legs. He must have just stepped out of the shower, because water droplets rested along the ridge of his pectorals, and the scent of soap carried into the hall. Even with a burgundy stain over his heart and battle scars marring his flesh, he was a glorious sight to behold.

Devyn swallowed hard. "My bad," was all she could say.

"Come on in."

He turned and strode into the room, and she followed, reluctantly shutting the door behind her. Maybe she should have told Allie to come in fifteen minutes. A lot could happen in half an hour.

Don't be stupid, Devyn chided herself. *You can handle this.*

But then Beau dropped his towel, revealing the hard curves of his naked ass, and a wave of desire slammed into her with so much force she stumbled back a step. "Holy Mother of God," she cried, still unable to look away. "You could have warned me!" Her fingers twitched to grab those muscled cheeks and hold on tight.

"What's the big deal?" Beau continued digging through his dresser drawer until he found a pair of athletic shorts and pulled them on. "It's nothing you haven't seen before."

"Common courtesy," she said. "I don't run around naked in front of *you.*"

He glanced over his bare shoulder with the crooked grin that had always been her kryptonite. "Feel free. It wouldn't bother me in the least."

Devyn took a moment to close her eyes and refocus. When she opened them, she did her best to train her gaze on his face. "You wanted to talk."

"Yes." His playful smile disappeared and he took a seat on the edge of the bed. He gestured for her to join him. "Thanks for coming. I wasn't sure if you would."

Devyn didn't want to sit beside him, so she scanned the room for a less dangerous position. His suite was about three times the size of hers, but it was still small enough to put her within an arm's reach no matter where she sat. She chose a cushioned chair in the corner. A couple of feet of distance was better than nothing.

Devyn folded her arms. "I know it was a shock, telling you about the pregnancy like that. I figured you'd need some time to process. I mean, there was never an actual baby. But still."

"But still," he agreed. "There was. For a few weeks, at least."

Devyn had never allowed herself to think of the baby that way. It was less painful to say her period had shown up late than to admit she and Beau had conceived a child and then lost it. "So, are you okay?"

"I am now. But I was mixed up at first. Took a while to figure out why."

"It's probably scary," she said. "Knowing how close you came to being a dad."

"No, that's not it." Beau shifted on the mattress, leaning forward to lock their gazes. "But before we go any further, I want to say I'm sorry you had to face that alone. I should have been there when you took the test. Hell, I should have bought it from the store and held your hand while we waited for the lines to show up. If I could change that, I would."

She nodded to accept his apology. "It was a long time ago."

"I'm sorry all the same," he said. "And what shook

me today wasn't the fact that we almost had a baby. It was that you thought I'd handle the situation like my old man. I'm not him. I would have stepped up, Dev."

Devyn didn't doubt that he believed it, but she wasn't so sure Beau would've done right by her. "It's easy to sit here ten years later and say what you would have done."

"No." He shook his head, his expression deadly serious. "I hated what my dad did to my mama. I watched him break her. I still can't stand to be in the same room with him. I hate that I have his eyes, his smile, or any part of his DNA." In challenge, he pointed a finger at her. "Did I ever mess around behind your back while we were dating?"

Devyn shrank back. "I don't think so."

"The answer is *no*. I don't cheat, and that's because I'm nothing like him." Beau's cheeks had reddened, and he stopped to suck in a few breaths. "If you'd written to me and said you were pregnant, I would have sent for you. It would've been *me* who broke the curse for the first time, not Marc. I would've married you, hexes be damned, and I would have loved that baby. Because I loved you."

He waited until she looked up at him before speaking again. "I need you to know that."

Devyn wrung her hands and willed away the telltale prickle behind her eyes. She was done crying over this man. "You and me, married fresh out of high school?" She scoffed. "We wouldn't have lasted six months."

"Maybe," he said. "Maybe not. But I would've bent over backward to try and make it work. Don't doubt that."

Why was he bringing this up? Did he enjoy twisting her heart, making her reopen wounds that had nearly healed?

"Well, it doesn't matter anyway. What's done is done, and the pregnancy was over as soon as it began."

"It *does* matter," he said. Pushing off the bed, Beau knelt at her feet and braced both hands on the armrests of her chair, essentially trapping her in place. "You said we can't start over because you don't want my mother's life. This is me telling you that won't happen."

Now she saw where he was going with this. For a split second, Devyn understood how Beau had felt all those years ago when he'd panicked and skipped town. Her heart rushed and she would have fled if she weren't blocked by two hundred pounds of solid man. He was too close, the heat from his exposed skin settling over her, weakening her resolve.

"If you don't want to give me a second chance, then fine," he said, taking one of her hands between both of his, so strong and warm. "I'll respect that. But make your choice for the right reasons, not because you're afraid I'll turn into my father. I'm not him, and I never will be."

Devyn needed space, but she couldn't bring herself to push him away—not even when he tipped their foreheads together and slid his rough palms up the length of her arms.

"Do you hear me, Dev?" he murmured while trailing his fingertips along her jawline. "Say you believe me."

Against her will, Devyn's hands gravitated to the inside bend of Beau's elbows, then traced the rock-hard curves of muscle all the way to his shoulders. His skin was hot and smooth beneath her fingers, an oh so familiar sensation she'd missed for far too long. Her knees parted an inch, and then another, allowing him to nudge his massive body in between. She didn't want to run anymore. Instead, she locked both legs around Beau's hips to hold him there.

"Please." He cradled her face while his lips brushed hers in a whisper kiss. "Tell me."

Letting her eyelids flutter shut, Devyn nodded within the confines of his powerful hands. "I believe you."

Using the tip of his tongue, he traced her bottom lip and she instantly opened for him. But he teased her with his mouth, nipping at her without getting too close, forcing her to lean forward and chase his tongue. "Do you want this?" he asked with another brush of lips. "I need to hear that you want me."

"Yes," Devyn said. She could do this—indulge in some steamy action with her ex—as long as she kept her feelings out of the equation. So she threw her arms around Beau's neck and thrust her tongue into his mouth in a kiss that turned from hot to scintillating in an instant. Groaning, he pulled her into a crushing embrace and captured her mouth like a soldier headed for war. Her lips throbbed, but she wanted it harder. Desperation overtook her, and she clawed at his shoulders as if to pull herself inside him.

Beau tugged her hips out of the chair, and before she knew what had happened, Devyn was flat on her back while a wall of delicious muscle pressed her into the carpet. He parted her thighs and settled between them, then slid the full length of his erection against her from base to tip and back again. Pure pleasure had her bowing back with a gasp, but she wanted more than dry friction this time.

She wanted everything.

"Inside me," she ordered, reaching between them to unbutton her pants. "Right now."

Beau didn't argue. He pushed aside her hand and took over. In seconds, he had her zipper down, and he roughly shoved her pants to her ankles, where they remained trapped against her shoes. Her panties soon followed. She started to kick them off, but Beau touched her for the first time in earnest, and she was helpless to do anything but moan with the pleasure.

"Mercy," he whispered, spreading moisture over her folds in an erotic massage. "You're already wet for me." He made a male noise of appreciation and repeated, "So wet."

She opened wider for him and shamelessly begged with her hips. When he skimmed a thumb over her sensitive bud, she made an embarrassing mewing noise and rocked against his hand. Propping on one elbow, he studied her while barely dipping a finger inside, playing at her entrance until she grew aching and swollen with need. In turn, she reached into his shorts and curled a hand around the steely length of him, and then stroked his shaft, teasing him with a feather touch that drew beads of arousal to the tip.

Their breathing came in ragged gasps for the next few minutes as they locked eyes and drove each other toward the brink. When a sheen of sweat had broken out across Beau's forehead, he asked, "Are you on the Pill?"

"I have an IUD."

"Do you want me to get a condom?"

"No." Devyn couldn't wait that long. Tugging him closer, she used his satin head to stroke the juncture of her thighs until Beau groaned and nudged inside an inch. That first luscious invasion felt so good that Devyn's toes curled in her shoes.

"More," she pleaded. "Hurry."

But Beau took his time, using his plump tip to stretch her so slowly she had to bite her lip to contain a scream. "God, baby." His eyes clenched tightly as he struggled for control. "You feel so good it's unreal."

Panting, she rolled her hips to take him an inch deeper when someone pounded on the bedroom door and yelled her name. "No!" Devyn cried, suddenly remembering the instructions she'd given her sister. "No, no, no!"

Confused, Beau glanced at the door. "Ignore it. Whoever it is, they can come back later."

Another series of knocks sounded, followed by Allie's voice. "Answer the door, Devyn. I'm not going away until you do."

"It's okay," Devyn shouted to her sister. "Forget what I said before. I'm fine."

"No dice," Allie said, pounding her fist harder. "I'm not leaving without you. Don't make me call Marc to bring the master key, because I will!"

Devyn looked at the virile body braced above her, especially the long, thick erection poised between her thighs, and she gave a pitiful whimper. She told Beau, "We have to stop for a minute."

After taking in the situation, he gaped with disbelief. "You told her to come here and cockblock me?"

"Kind of." Devyn scooted away from him and tugged up her pants. "Just wait, and I'll get rid of her."

Beau pulled up his shorts and pushed to his knees with a grunt of frustration. "You never cease to amaze me, Dev."

"Hold that thought." Without bothering to zip her khakis, she rushed to the door and opened it a crack. Allie peered back at her, gripping her hips like a maiden aunt, guardian of virtue. "Go away," Devyn hissed. "I don't need you."

Before she could shut the door, Allie wedged her shoe inside. "A deal is a deal. You're coming with me."

"No, I mean it—"

Allie flashed a palm. "If you change your mind, Beau will still be here in the morning." Delivering a pointed look, she added, "*After* you've had a chance to clear the hormones out of your system."

"Please let me stay? I promise I'll never ask you for anything, ever again."

"Begging won't work."

"Pleeeeeeease?"

"Come quietly, or I'll drag you out by force."

"Pretty please with a cherry on top?"

"Not even with whipped cream and sprinkles."

Devyn let her head thunk against the wall. "You're not going to leave, are you?"

"Nope, so you might as well tell him good-bye."

Why did Allie have to be such a good sister?

"Fine," Devyn sighed. "Give me a second."

"I'll give you ten."

Of course, Beau had overheard the entire conversation. He was standing out of view against the side wall, watching her like he didn't know whether to ruffle her curls or wring her neck. "You've got to go," he said flatly.

"Yeah, sorry."

He blew out a dry laugh that assured he wasn't angry, only frustrated. He moved in and pressed a chaste kiss to her cheek. "It's okay. I told you we could take it slow, and I meant that. I've got all the time in the world."

When Devyn slipped into the hall and shut the door

behind her, Allie made a show of inspecting her wrinkled pants and untucked shirt.

"Tsk, tsk." Smiling, Allie gave a disapproving shake of her head. "You're so easy."

Devyn slung an arm around her sister's neck as they strode toward the stairwell. "You have no idea."

Chapter 8

Everything changed after that night.

Logically, Devyn knew she should stay away from Beau. She fully acknowledged that she was playing with fire, and since he'd burned her once, he would probably do it again. But try telling that to her raging libido.

Beau had given her a taste of perfection, and now a hunger had opened up so deep inside her that it eclipsed everything else. He'd even dominated her sleep, appearing in dreams to stroke her with his masterful fingers and impale her with his iron shaft. She had awoken from each fantasy gasping, suspended a hairsbreadth from climax and unable to do a damn thing about it because Ella-Claire was a light sleeper.

If there was a female equivalent for blue balls, Devyn had it.

As the days passed, she found herself rationalizing a relationship with Beau—nothing serious, of course. No flowery poems or *I love you*s or promises of forever. She would keep it casual and guard her heart. She'd even reflected that a fling would be good for her health. Didn't scientists claim that orgasms released endorphins and decreased stress? Who couldn't use a few more endorphins? Maybe if she took things nice and slow—seriously slow, as in molasses speed—there was no harm in letting Beau try to earn back her trust.

Right?

But it seemed like she was trying too hard to convince herself, which usually meant something was wrong. For that reason, she avoided him and threw all her energy into her job at the education center. Or she tried to, at least. There was no escaping Beau in such close quarters. Their paths crossed several times a day, like at the coffee station each morning.

Right now, he stood so near that the sleeve of his starched white jacket brushed her bare elbow. Devyn focused on peeling back the foil lid to her creamer, but the intoxicating scent of Beau's aftershave had her fingers slipping. As he took his first sip of coffee, she slid a covert glance at him to watch the muscles work in his throat. Her heart rushed at the sight, sending heated blood to some pretty interesting places. No man had a right to look so sexy this early in the morning.

"Want some help with that?" he asked.

Devyn nearly dropped her creamer. "No, thanks. I've got it."

Beau's lips quirked in a grin when he caught her staring at his neck. He lowered his voice to a deep rumble that flowed over her like warm honey. "How'd you sleep last night?"

"Fine," she lied. "You?"

"Like a baby." Leaning another inch into her space, he murmured in her ear, "I've got that great big suite all to myself. Gives me plenty of room to spread out naked on my king-sized bed."

Devyn's eyes closed while her skin pricked into goose bumps.

"Wouldn't mind sharing it, though," he added. "If you asked me real nice. But I can't guarantee you'll get much sleep. In fact, I promise you won't."

The creamer slipped from her hands and plunked to the table. Without missing a beat, Beau picked it up and handed it to her, then told her to have a great day and strode from the room.

Damn it. He was enjoying this, the arrogant bastard . . . the delicious, hard-bodied, toe-curling arrogant bastard.

Devyn shook her head to clear it. Forget the creamer, she would drink her coffee black today. She grabbed an apple turnover and headed for the education center, but she realized halfway down the hall that she'd forgotten a handout on her dresser. When she returned to her room and opened the door, she drew back in shock, sending coffee sloshing over the rim of her cardboard cup.

Ella-Claire sat on the dresser while Thing Two braced his hands on either side of her hips and leaned in for a kiss. At the interruption, they flinched and turned toward Devyn with noticeably different reactions—guilt from him, sexual frustration from Ella-Claire. By now,

Devyn could recognize the symptoms of a woman un-fulfilled.

"Uh," Thing Two stammered, giving a fake business-like nod at Ella. "I think we got that lash out of your eye."

"Oh, come off it," Devyn said. She shut the door and pointed in a silent request to her handout, which was stuck under Ella's butt. "She didn't have anything in her eye. You were macking on your half brother's half sister." God, that sounded even more absurd when she said it out loud. "Your secret's safe with me. But don't insult my intelligence by pretending nothing's going on. Just sack up and own it."

It seemed her advice was wasted on Thing Two. He mumbled an excuse about running payroll and promptly bolted from the room.

Ella handed over the sheet of paper while deflating like an old balloon.

"Sorry about that," Devyn said. "If I'd known you wanted to be alone, I would have come back later. Next time, hang something on the door like a hat or a hair elastic so I'll get the message."

"It doesn't matter." Ella-Claire sank back against the dresser. "Even if he *had* finally kissed me, I doubt he would ever do it again."

"Wait a minute." Devyn had assumed the two were already getting it on. They shot off so many sparks she expected someone to lose an eye. "You haven't kissed yet?"

Ella shook her head, sending her ponytail into motion. "Nothing more than a peck on the cheek. I was telling the truth when I said Alex and I are best friends."

Wow, Devyn's smutty radar was off. "But you want more?"

The girl shrugged and picked at her manicure. "Yes. Maybe. I always had feelings for Alex, but I kept him in the friend zone. He was a player, just like his brothers," she said, glancing at Devyn. "You know, a typical Dumont guy."

"Yeah," Devyn deadpanned. "I know."

"But in the last few months, he's changed. Matured. He takes on extra duties around here instead of hitting the bars, and he hasn't been with anyone since the time he and Nicky accidentally slept with the jazz singer."

Devyn shook her head in disbelief. Only a Dumont man could end up in the middle of an unintentional three-way.

"It's a long story," Ella said. "Anyway, I've started to think there could be hope for him, that maybe he'd end up more like Marc and less like their dad."

"But you're worried about the curse," Devyn said, completely understanding. It was a valid concern.

Ella flapped a hand. "I don't believe in all that."

You should. "Then what's the problem?"

"It's Marc," Ella said with a frustrated sigh. "He can barely stand for any of his brothers to look at me. If he found out that Alex almost kissed me, he'd throw him overboard. I'm not even kidding."

"I get that." Devyn had felt protective of her own sister when Allie had gotten involved with a Dumont.

"But you're an adult, and sooner or later he needs to respect your wishes."

"That's what I keep telling Alex, but he idolizes Marc," Ella said, staring at the door as if replaying how quickly Thing Two had fled the scene. "I don't think he's scared of what Marc might do to him. I think he's afraid of disappointing his big brother." She drew a stuttered breath. "But what about me? Why don't I matter? Why is it okay to disappoint his best friend?"

Devyn felt a prickle of sympathy for the girl. If Thing Two wasn't ready to pursue a relationship with Ella, it would seem he hadn't matured all that much. Devyn crossed the small room and unzipped her duffel bag, then found a sachet of gris-gris. She had mixed a batch last night to untangle her own muddled emotions.

Handing the pouch to Ella-Claire, she said, "Here, this is for clarity of heart, so keep it in your pocket. It will help lead you in the right direction, but you'll have to do some of the work yourself."

Ella nodded for her to go on.

"It's time to have a 'Come to Jesus' talk with Thing Two." At the girl's puzzled expression, Devyn corrected, "I mean with Alex. Be clear about what you want, and tell him to make a choice—no more straddling the line. Either he's in, or he's out. But don't let him string you along." She gave Ella's arm an encouraging squeeze. "You're a smart, beautiful young woman, and if he's not willing to fight for you, then he's not worthy."

Ella smiled and a tear spilled down her cheek. There

was gratitude in her gaze, but fear too, like she already knew what Alex's response would be and she didn't want it confirmed.

"Be strong," Devyn told her. "Don't settle for less than what you deserve."

When Ella promised to take the advice to heart, Devyn left for the education center, where her counseling skills came in handy for the second time that day.

Jason, the older sibling of the honeymoon crashers, sat on the floor in the corner of the room, slouched against the wall with the bill of his Saints ball cap pulled down over his eyes. On a typical day, he dragged into the room with a heavy sigh and an eye roll, but a reluctant smile would follow once Devyn set up a science experiment. This morning something was clearly wrong. He had never looked so dejected.

Nearby, his younger brother immersed himself in *Super Mario World*, fingers flying over the control buttons, his tongue pressed against the corner of his mouth while his gaze stayed fixed on the television screen. Nothing out of the ordinary with that one.

None of her other students had arrived, so she sat beside Jason in the corner and tipped up his hat. "Hey, there," she said. "You okay?"

His eyes met hers for an instant before he jerked down the bill. "I don't feel good. I just want to be left alone."

She touched his cheek with the back of her hand, noting that he didn't feel warm. "Do I need to send you to the infirmary?" Her instincts said no, but it was worth asking.

Jason brought both knees to his chest and shook his head.

"Should I page your mom?"

The boy made a noise of contempt. "She probably wouldn't come. She's too busy with Dave." He said *Dave* like it was the foulest of swears, which explained a lot.

"Ah." Blended family angst. That was a hard transition to make, and Devyn didn't envy any of them. "Sounds like you're not a fan of your new step-dad. He seems like a nice guy to me."

Another grunt.

"I don't know Dave that well," Devyn said, "but I've noticed something important about him that makes me think he's a good man."

Slowly, Jason lifted the bill of his cap and peered at her. "Like what?"

"The way he looks at your mom." Devyn gave a serious nod. "When they come to drop you off and pick you up, he acts like she's the only woman on the boat." She thumbed toward the infants on the other side of the partition. "When Cameron's mom showed up yesterday in a bikini top, every guy in the room stared at her. But your step-dad didn't even notice. He was too busy holding your mom's hand and kissing the top of her head."

Jason made a *yuck* face. "He always does that."

"Seems like he really loves her." When the boy shrugged with indifference, Devyn asked, "Isn't that what you want? Someone who thinks your mom is the most important person in the world?"

Jason dodged the question. "*He's* not the most important person to her. That's me and my brother."

"Of course." Now Devyn understood the root of the problem. Jason felt displaced. "And that will never change. A mother's love for her children is like nothing else on earth. But you know what?"

"What?"

"Someday you and your brother are going to grow up and leave home." She knew the boy wouldn't believe her if she said so, but there would soon come a time when his mother was no longer the center of his world. "Eventually, you'll start your own family. And think how lonely your mom would be if she didn't have your step-dad to keep her company."

That seemed to get through to him. Jason pursed his lips and stared at the foam-tiled floor for a few moments. "I'll always take care of her, no matter what."

"I know you will," Devyn said. "But you'll have a job and a wife and kids. That will take up a lot of your time." When he didn't respond, she gently tweaked his ball cap. "Don't you want your mom to have a best friend who loves her? Someone to make her happy when you're not there?"

"I guess."

"Then maybe give Dave a break. Maybe give your mom one, too. Starting a brand-new family is kind of hard, and they're going to need your help—especially as the big brother. William looks to you as an example. If you treat your step-dad like a friend, he'll do the same." She nudged him with her elbow. "What do you think?"

Jason peeked up with understanding in his eyes. "Yeah, I guess I can do that."

"Good," she told him. "That's the best wedding present you could give your mom." Devyn threw a glance at Will. "Now let's peel your brother off the Nintendo and set up an experiment."

Jason grinned up at her. "First, can we implode another Coke can?"

"You bet." Then she added the usual disclaimer, "As long as you explain the science behind it."

"I can do that in my sleep," he boasted. Then he said something that melted Devyn's heart. "'Cause you're a real good teacher."

"Thanks for taking such good care of the boys," Jason's mother said at pick-up. "It's like I get my own class every night because they can't stop talking about what they learned. I wish they were this excited about school back home."

"It's my pleasure." And Devyn meant every word. She'd grown to enjoy her time in the center—the light of discovery in the children's eyes, and the increasing admiration behind their smiles. A couple of the students had even pilfered flowers from the lobby vases to give her each morning, which touched her more deeply than she wanted to admit. "See you tomorrow."

As she waved good-bye and began tidying the room, a fierce warmth glowed beneath Devyn's breastbone. It had been such a long time since she'd felt the sensation that it took her a few moments to identify what it was—pride.

She smiled to herself and studied the hand-drawn maps the children had made that afternoon, each stop along the Mississippi labeled according to nineteenth-century trade. Will's depiction of a beaver pelt looked more like a Brillo Pad, but at least he'd understood the significance of fur as currency.

She was good at this. Really good. And more than that, she liked it.

The cell phone vibrated in Devyn's pocket, interrupting her reverie. She didn't recognize the incoming number and hesitated before answering.

"Hello?"

"Hi," said a man's voice. "It's Warren Larabee."

Instantly, the glow inside Devyn's chest morphed into a chill of dread. She'd been so distracted lately that she had forgotten about the job that awaited her back home.

"Miss Mauvais?" he asked when she didn't respond. "Is this a bad time?"

"Not at all," she said with a manufactured smile. "I just finished my shift, so your timing is perfect."

"Good. I wanted to run something past you real quick." Warren launched into a spiel about the grave-yard tour and how excited the team was to script a reenactment of Memère's botched wedding day. "Juliette was jilted at the altar by a local, right?" Warren asked. "Edward Dumont? He's buried at the same cemetery."

"Yes," Devyn said. "Then she cursed his line so the men in that family would never find lasting love."

"Uh-huh. The team wants to know if you have anything of hers that we can use for authenticity." He paused for a beat as if talking with his hands. "Her wedding dress or her veil, maybe. A bridal portrait would be nice. You'd be surprised how much an artifact can add to the spooky mood during a haunted tour."

Devyn swallowed a lump of shame. Just thinking about putting her great-great-grandmother's personal articles on display to "add to the spooky mood" made her want to take a shower. She couldn't believe she was even having this conversation.

"Miss Mauvais? Are you still there?"

"Yeah, sorry. I was just thinking," she said. "Let me check with my sister and get back to you. She has most of our family heirlooms in storage at her place." The second part was true, but Devyn had no intention of giving Larabee Amusements anything that belonged to Memère. "I'll call you as soon as I know."

They disconnected and Devyn exhaled a heavy breath.

"Who was that?"

She whirled around to find Beau watching her through the open door. Right away, he pushed both palms forward and disclaimed, "I wasn't eavesdropping."

Sure, he wasn't. "Then why do you care who I was talking to?"

"Because I heard you mention my family's curse." He stepped inside and shut the door behind him. "That's not typical small talk, even for you."

"In other words, you were eavesdropping."

"Don't split hairs," he said. "Who was on the phone?"

"No one you know."

Beau grumbled under his breath. "It was Mercedes Man, wasn't it?"

"Who?"

"You know," he said, waving a hand. "The guy who drove you here on the first day."

In the span of two seconds, Beau's features hardened while a set of creases played across his forehead. If Devyn didn't know better, she'd think he was jealous. "His name is Warren, and if you must know, yes, that was him on the phone."

Twin brows formed a slash above Beau's green eyes. "Who's this guy to you?"

Devyn bit back a smile. "Oh, my God. You *are* jealous."

"Don't be ridiculous. It was just a question."

She drew a breath to tell him it was none of his concern, but that didn't seem entirely true anymore. Devyn didn't know how to label her relationship with Beau—they weren't quite friends, and they weren't quite lovers—but something had grown between them. To the point that she wanted to admit the truth because his unease fed her own.

"I'm not involved with Warren," she said. "He's my boss."

Beau didn't seem to like that any better. "I'm your boss."

She laughed at his reaction. "That's a stretch, and this is only temporary."

"Since when do you work for this guy?"

"Technically, I haven't started yet."

"What's the job?"

Devyn's lips parted in silence. The answer was easy enough, but she couldn't manage to shake it off her tongue. Some secret part of her feared Beau's judgment, and there was no doubt he would disapprove. He would tell her this was another dead-end job and that she was floundering. She didn't want to hear it—the truth hurt.

"That bad, huh?" he asked, arms folded.

She deflected with a casual shrug. "Well, I'm not shooting a porno."

"Good to know. Sex tapes are bad news." He grinned. "Unless you want to make one with me, because we'd keep it to ourselves. Then I'm cool with it."

"Naturally." She found herself smiling. "I'll bet you'd even supply the camera."

"The tripod, too. Just say the word." Beau crossed the padded floor until he'd invaded her personal space, but she didn't back away. She didn't want to. He tucked a stray curl behind her ear. "Talk to me, Kitten. I can tell you're not happy about this job."

She blinked up at Beau. He was so strong and steady and in control. For the first time in her life, she wished she could be more like him. "Nobody's happy with their jobs. That's why we call it a *job*."

"You're stalling."

"Okay, fine," she said. "I hate it. You happy now?"

"Thrilled," he said sarcastically. "Why do you keep dodging the question?"

"Because the last thing I need is another lecture from you about my future."

She expected him to get defensive, but instead Beau nodded solemnly and said, "No lectures. I'll just listen."

"You mean that?"

"I promise."

Devyn narrowed one eye at him, and when he didn't falter, she took a deep breath and told him everything. She included each mortifying detail, from selling her "little trinkets" in a shop near the graveyard to Warren's recent request for her great-great-grandmother's personal effects. She unloaded all of her frustrations, and when she was finished, she felt a little bit lighter.

Beau didn't say anything at first. Then he smoothed a gentle hand over her hair. "I can understand why you're upset. You've always taken a lot of pride in your family's legacy."

She waited for him to go on, but he didn't. She made an *And?* motion with one hand.

"That's it," he said. "I'm sorry you're in this position."

"Really?" she asked. She couldn't believe that he had no advice and no condescension for her. "That's all you're going to say?"

"Yep."

Beau was actually being supportive and listening.

She hadn't seen that coming. "Thanks for lending an ear."

"Any time," he said, picking up a hand puppet from the floor and tossing it into the nearest toy bin. "Hey, I was about to grab some dinner and take it back to the security room. Want to join me? I've got the night shift, and it gets awfully quiet in there by myself." He played it cool and tucked both hands in his pockets, but the expectant way he looked at her betrayed how badly he craved her company.

About as badly as she craved his.

Devyn chewed her bottom lip. She knew full well what would happen if she put herself behind a closed door with Beau. History would repeat itself. Maybe that's why she couldn't tell him no. "Sounds great," she said. "I'm starved."

Chapter 9

Beau was no idiot.

He knew when to keep his trap shut, and this was one of those times. As he followed Devyn along the staff room buffet line, he filled his plate with an assortment of savory sides and resisted the urge to tell her that leading ghost tours was the worst fucking idea he'd ever heard. A blind man could see that traipsing around in a graveyard was a waste of Devyn's God-given talent. What she really needed was a satisfying career where she could grow, not another short-term job.

But getting Devyn to admit that would take finesse.

So he bit his tongue and feigned interest in a vat of smothered chicken breasts, at least grateful that Mercedes Man wasn't a boyfriend. Then Devyn dropped her napkin and bent to pick it up, and all thoughts of cemetery tours vanished. Beau stood there absently holding the bread tongs as he admired the long, tanned legs on display beneath her khaki skirt, not to mention the slope of her gorgeous ass.

Damn, he'd love to sink his teeth into those firm cheeks.

She stood and pointed to the bread basket. "Those buns look delicious."

"Oh, honey," Beau said, plunking one onto her plate. "They're downright mouthwatering."

Balancing her plate on one arm, she glanced at the desserts, then across the room at the drink station. "How are we going to carry all this to the casino?"

Beau scanned the room until he found a serving tray. "I'll take our dinners upstairs. See if you can snag another tray from the galley for the rest."

"What do you want to drink?" she asked.

"Iced tea."

"And for dessert?"

Your sweet buns. "Pecan pie, I guess."

While Beau arranged their supper on the tray and covered them with stainless steel domes, Marc ambled up with a glass of Coke in hand. Marc was still on duty in a freshly pressed captain's uniform, his hair smoothed into a low ponytail that made Beau want to offer him a Midol and a subscription to *Cosmo.*

"Hungry much?" asked Marc, pointing at the plates. "It's a miracle we turn a profit with you on board."

"Half of that is mine," Devyn said. "Though you have a point. I've never seen anyone pack it away like your brother."

"Hey, I've been meaning to tell you," Marc said to Devyn. "Everyone's raving about your lessons in the education center. Keep up the good work."

Devyn stood an inch straighter and grinned. "Thanks."

Changing the subject, Marc leveled a challenging gaze at Beau. "So where are you two gonna eat?"

Beau bristled at the question. It was none of his brother's business where he ate, or with whom. "Does it matter?"

"Not really," Marc said with a shrug. "Just wondering if I should send Allie to your suite in twenty minutes so she can turn the hose on you two." He kept his tone casual, but arched one brow in a message that he knew what was brewing between Beau and his ex.

Devyn grumbled and tossed a handful of napkins onto the tray. "Allie has a big mouth."

"She's my wife," Marc said. "We tell each other everything."

"Everything?" Beau asked. "Even how I caught Nora trying to sneak into your room a few weeks ago?"

Devyn spun on Marc. "Who the hell is Nora?"

"And old girlfriend of Marc's," Beau told her. "Red hair, legs up to here."

"She was *not* my girlfriend!" When Marc's shout drew a few curious gazes, he lowered his voice to a hiss. "She was a booty call, and barely that. There was no reason to tell Allie. It would only upset her, and now that Nora knows I'm married, she'll back off."

"Slippery slope, Captain," Beau said.

"Mind your own damn business."

Beau smiled. "Gladly. If you'll do the same."

Clearly Beau had made his point. Marc fired a glare at him and stalked away.

"Well, that was awkward," Devyn said, tucking a couple of forks between their plates. "I'm going to run to the galley for another tray. And to remind my sister that loose lips sink ships."

"Sounds good." Beau bent to whisper in Devyn's ear. "But don't tell her about the redhead. Marc's a cantankerous bastard, but he's only got eyes for Allie, and I don't want to make trouble. He really did read Nora the riot act when she snuck on board. She won't come back."

Devyn smiled up at him with an admiring gleam in her gaze, like she was proud of him. Either that or he had something between his teeth and she thought it was funny.

Beau scrubbed a finger over his front enamel. "What?"

"You're a halfway decent brother, you know that?"

A soft laugh shook his chest. "I know a few folks who would tell you otherwise."

"Whatever." She gave his shoulder a nudge. "Go ahead to the casino. I'll meet you there in a few."

"Remember," he said. "Iced tea and—"

"Pecan pie," she called over her shoulder. "No worries, Dumont. I know what you like."

"No doubt about that," he mumbled to himself while watching her skirt-clad rear end sashay out of sight. He blew out a breath and cradled their dinner tray in one arm, then made his way to the casino's security room.

When he opened the door, Nicky was kicked back in the swiveling office chair studying the live feed on the flat-screen. "Hey," he said, keeping his gaze fixed on footage of the roulette table.

"How goes it?"

Nicky offered a noncommittal grunt. "I've been eagle-eyeing this guy, and I can't find anything wrong."

Beau set his dinner tray on a tiny folding table near the computers, careful to keep a safe distance from the expensive equipment. "Patience, little brother." Part of Beau's job as casino manager was keeping track of each table's income. Mathematical probability ensured a predictable payout for each one, and if there was a significant change in earnings, he needed to figure out why. The roulette wheel had generated a lot less loot in the past few days, and Beau suspected one of the staffers was skimming off the top. "Everything's recorded. Sooner or later, he'll slip up."

Nicky stood from the chair and stretched, rubbing his lower back. He glanced at the two covered plates and used his eyes to issue a silent question.

"Dev's keeping me company," Beau said. And before his brother could warn him, he added, "Marc already knows, so if he seems pissier than usual tonight, that's why. Probably best not to poke the bear."

Nick took a moment to study him before saying, "You're really into Devyn, huh?"

Beau saw no reason to deny it. "Always have been."

"Oh," Nick said, cringing a little. "I thought she was an old fling, nothing more."

Beau narrowed one eye at Nicky. The last time he'd

seen this much guilt cross his brother's face, Nick had used the pantry to hook up with a server and spilled the last bottle of pure Mexican vanilla in the process. "What did you do?"

"Nothing," Nick said a bit too quickly. "Didn't lay a hand on her." He backed toward the door. "I'll make sure nobody bothers you two tonight." And in a flash, he was gone.

Didn't lay a hand on her. That meant Nicky had swung and struck out. Beau decided that Devyn was right—he *was* a good brother. Because he'd decided to let Nicky keep his balls.

Beau shrugged out of his dress jacket, already over-heated in the cramped space. He stood before the one-way glass and watched the casino floor come alive with guests trickling in from the dining hall. Nobody out-side the family knew it, but Beau had tweaked the eve-ning entertainment schedule so passengers had forty minutes of downtime before the theater shows began. About half the guests used the lull to return to their cabins or grab an after-dinner drink. The other half had migrated into the casino. That one small adjustment had increased their income by enough to replace all the outdoor furniture next season.

Not too shabby, if he did say so himself.

He spotted Devyn on the floor and his stomach jumped, exactly like it used to do each time he'd caught a glimpse of her in high school. He shook his head in disbelief. Between the marines and his private contract work, ten lifetimes worth of adrenaline had traveled through his veins, but nothing stirred him the way Devyn did.

She worked her way through the crowd with a smile, allowing guests the right of way and occasionally glancing at the mirror behind the bar as if she sensed him watching. Though she couldn't see him, Beau found himself smiling at her. His dinner invitation had been a total Hail Mary. He couldn't believe she'd actually said yes, not after the distance she'd put between them since their botched lovemaking. His grin widened in anticipation the closer she strode toward the bar, but his mouth turned down when a familiar man snagged her by the elbow.

It was that douche bag cowboy, the one cheating on his wife. And judging by the slippery smirk on the asshole's face, one mistress wasn't enough to satisfy him. The guy crowded Devyn's space as they spoke; then he bent to her ear before tweaking her chin and striding toward the craps table.

Beau was thankful to be stuck behind an inch of solid glass, otherwise he would've shown Casanova Cowboy the exit—right over the second-story deck rail.

After taking a calming breath, he held the door open for Devyn, who beamed while unloading their drinks and desserts onto the folding table.

"Did you see that guy?" she asked. "He just hit on me, wearing a wedding ring and everything."

"And you're smiling because . . . ?"

Dev stood an inch straighter, raising her chin with

pride. "Because I handled it like a professional. Instead of threatening to shove my tray up his ass, I said *not interested.*"

Beau couldn't help laughing. She looked like she'd just won a blue ribbon at the state fair. "That's my girl."

"I can't wait to tell Allie," Dev said as she pulled up a chair and sat at the table. "At least this time it'll benefit me when she blabs to Marc."

"Do I detect a hint of resentment?" Beau asked, unfolding another chair. He sat down across from her. Their knees bumped and he adjusted his legs to give her more room. "Not that I'm judging. You two have always been close, and now she's got a new favorite."

Devyn gasped in mock outrage and began cutting into her chicken. "That's not it." Then she paused and waved her knife in the air while she said, "Okay, maybe a little. I always thought it would be *sisters before misters* if one of us got married."

Beau chuckled under his breath and scooped up a bite of mashed potatoes. "I guess Marc gives her something that you don't."

"Ew," she said, lightly kicking him in the ankle. "Can we not discuss what your brother *gives* my sister? At least not while I'm eating."

"Says the woman who sent that sister to cockblock me."

"That was nothing—just a little interference," Devyn said around a bite of green beans. "We didn't swap stories afterward."

Beau leaned forward enough to brush the outside of

her thigh with his. He held her gaze, lowering his voice to a murmur. "So you didn't tell her I had you on the floor with your pants around your ankles?" When Devyn's cheeks blushed, he added, "Or that I was half-way inside you when she tried to bust down the door?"

Dev swallowed hard and shook her head.

"Good. Some things should be kept private." He threw her a teasing wink. "Like how blazing hot you felt when I slid my—"

"This chicken's fantastic," she said, her voice trembling. "Don't you think?"

He kept their gazes locked for another heartbeat before trying a bite. The breast was seared to perfection, but it needed a kick. "I'd have added a pinch of cayenne to the marinade."

"I forgot that you used to run the galley," she said. "Do you miss it?"

Beau didn't have to ponder the question. "No. If you think it's hot in here, imagine running around in that kitchen with a full staff at your elbow."

He didn't mind cooking—in fact, dicing veggies while nursing a cold beer took the edge off a rough day—but not feeding hundreds of guests and a crew. That was some serious pressure.

"Allie says you're better than most gourmets."

He lifted one shoulder and said, "I'm a man of many talents."

Instead of commenting, Devyn shoved a forkful of mashed potatoes into her mouth.

"I've never cooked for you, have I?" he asked. When she shook her head, he suggested, "How about tomorrow, when we stop in Natchez? The galley will shut down after the guests leave for their excursions, so I can probably sneak in there to make us lunch."

She bit her bottom lip and apologized with her eyes. "It's tempting, but if I don't get off this boat for a few hours, I'm going to need a padded cell and a Xanax script."

Beau understood. Two weeks on the water would seem like an eternity to a landlubber. "New plan. I'll cook lunch for us and pack it in a basket. Then we can find a place to eat on nice, solid ground."

She pretended to study her plate, but a gradual smile spread across her lips, and when she flicked a glance at him, her azure eyes were brighter than the Mississippi moon. Beau's heart sprouted wings. He wished he could bottle the way he felt when she looked at him like that—his insides all light and floaty with pleasure. He'd never need another beer as long as he lived.

"That sounds perfect," she said. "Thanks."

"Still hate mushrooms?"

"Are they still a fungus?"

Yes, then. "That's a shame. I make a mean portobello sandwich."

She pointed her fork at him. "People who enjoy the taste of fungus can't be trusted." After another bite, she used a napkin to dab at her mouth and studied him for a long moment. When the watchful silence continued, Beau figured a change in subject was coming. Turned out he was right.

"I never asked what you've been up to these last ten years," she said. "I've seen the scars. Want to tell me about it?"

Beau tipped back his iced tea, taking a few more chugs than necessary as he processed the unwelcome shift in topic. He wasn't angry with Devyn for asking—if anything, her curiosity gave him hope—but that was a decade in his life he didn't like to revisit. He couldn't very well tell her the truth in all its miserable glory. Like the time he lost half his unit when they walked into an ambush and couldn't make contact for reinforcements. Or the day he'd refused to reenlist and the recruiter had accused him of selling out his brothers to make a few bucks doing contract work. Beau could still taste the metallic tang of rage on his tongue.

"You don't have to," she said.

"There's not much to tell." Absently, he picked apart his dinner roll and pressed the bits into his mashed potatoes. When he realized what he was doing, he brushed off his hands and gave Devyn his full attention. "I enlisted for the wrong reasons. It was a knee-jerk reaction because I was hotheaded and afraid. The discipline helped me grow up, I can't deny that, but eventually I figured out that I couldn't make a career out of running."

He liked to think those years weren't wasted, that he'd needed time and distance to appreciate his hot

mess of a family. If he'd stayed in town after graduation, he and Marc might have clawed at each other's
throats until there was no relationship left to salvage.

"Anyway," he said, "I'm glad to be home. This is
where I belong."

"What about working on the *Belle*?" Devyn asked.
"Does it bother you that Marc's captain while you're
managing the casino?"

"Not one bit."

"But he didn't have to invest any money. Your daddy
just gave him the boat."

"For good reason," Beau said. "If it hadn't been for
Marc, the *Belle* wouldn't be operating. Alex and Nicky
helped out, but they're too young for the responsibility.
Marc was the best choice. He was here; I wasn't."

"So you really enjoy this?" She hitched a thumb toward the one-way glass. "You don't want to be captain?"

"Nah, that was Marc's dream, not mine." Beau was
simply happy to be home. It didn't matter whether he
was working in the casino or the galley or the pilothouse—the *Belle* kept his family together in one place,
and that was all that mattered. "I'm a jack-of-all-trades.
I'll go wherever I'm needed."

"Wow." With one cheek stuffed full, Devyn shook
her head as if amazed. "You really have grown up."

"Don't sound so surprised," he said with a chuckle.
"What about you? Allie told me you've had some interesting jobs over the years. Were you really a virtual
dominatrix?" He wasn't sure if he wanted to know

what that entailed. What did she do, text guys a picture of her boot and then tell them to lick the screen? Order them to smack their own asses?

She held up an index finger. "We're not talking about that one."

"How can we *not*?"

"Easy," she said. "You're going to tell me about your job instead." In one long guzzle, she finished her wine, then stood from the table and approached the one-way glass. "What are you looking for when you spy on all these unsuspecting slot pullers?"

He joined her at the window, taking a seat on the tall swiveling office chair. "It's not the slots I'm worried about. Those pretty much take care of themselves," he said as he pointed at the live feed displayed on the flat-screen. "In the slot rows, I only check for theft. You know, folks stealing each other's coin buckets. And I look for unseemly activity."

A few years ago, Marc had busted a couple of honey-mooners near the far wall slots with their hands in each other's pants. Not the kind of family-friendly enter-tainment the staff had in mind.

"Unseemly?" Dev asked, tossing her curls over one shoulder and grinning at him. "Are you talking about exhibitionists? Right here on the sweet little *Belle*?"

"It happens."

"People are crazy. I'll never understand what's so exciting about public sex."

Beau grunted in agreement. "Hiding in the aisles,

barely moving, not making a sound. That's no way to fuck." When she elbowed him in the ribs, he corrected, "I mean, make love."

She stood on tiptoe and peered at the gamblers as if picturing a secret tryst. "I don't see anywhere remotely private enough to pull it off."

Beau left his chair and settled behind her, near enough to catch the floral scent of her shampoo. He rested one hand on her waist and used the other to point out the window. "Right back there," he said into her ear, "near the corner. Someone standing behind that machine is out of sight."

Devyn relaxed into him, bringing the firm cushion of her ass against his fly, and Beau nearly swallowed his tongue. "Except for the ceiling cameras," she pointed out.

All the blood in his body funneled toward his crotch. Devyn's nearness—the warm press of her body and her intoxicating scent—scrambled his thoughts until his words stumbled out in a disjointed murmur against her earlobe. "People . . . tend to forget"—he cleared his throat—"the cameras."

She must have sensed the shift in him, because she stilled for a moment before releasing a shaky breath. "Do they?"

"Oh, yeah," he moaned. He wanted to bury his nose in her curls, so he did. She surprised him by tilting her head aside to bare her neck. Taking full advantage, he nuzzled the patch of skin below her ear and took her waist between both hands. She smelled of sweetness and sex, which wasn't helping the problem growing inside his pants. "It's easy to get caught up in the moment."

She arched her lower back just enough to brush his erection with her bottom. "Distracted by the rush."

"Uh-huh," he said while squinting his eyes shut. As if that would stop the desire from engorging him. He shouldn't have lit this match. The last thing he needed was another night spent with a cramp in his gut. "Listen," he said, groaning when she ground against him again. "I said we could go as slow as you wanted. . . ."

She took his hands and guided them to her breasts.

God bless, she wasn't making this easy. He couldn't stop his palms from molding to her softness. The heavy weight of her breasts was so deliciously familiar, filling his hands to perfection. He skimmed both thumbs over her nipples, pleased to find them already erect. She wanted him, and he loved that.

"And I meant it," he said. "We don't have to rush."

"Mmm," she hummed, bowing back for a heavier touch. "Slow is good."

Then she blew everything to hell by reaching behind her to stroke his erection. She cupped him hard and slid her palm gradually down to his base before sliding it back to the tip, where she circled the underside of his sensitive head with one fingernail. "I like it slow."

He groaned and thrust into her grasp, hoping like crazy she wasn't toying with him. He was hard enough to pound nails. "Baby, you're killing me."

Still stroking him, she used her free hand to cover

his, encouraging him to massage her nipples. When he rolled them between his fingers, she whimpered, tipped back her head to rest on his chest, and said, "What a wonderful way to die."

The last thing Beau wanted to do was stop, but that was exactly what had to happen unless she intended to take him all the way.

"Where's this going, Dev?"

She peered over her shoulder with a hunger in her gaze that matched his own. Her cheeks had grown flushed; her lips parted as she locked eyes with him and asked, "Are there cameras in this room?"

Beau shook his head. "Not a single one."

She blinked up at him, so beautiful it almost hurt to look at her. In that moment, he would have shaved twenty years off his life to have Devyn for one night—to peel off her clothes and consume every inch of her. To make up for the ten years he'd wasted living outside of her bed. Beau held his breath and waited for an answer.

"Good," she said. "Then hurry up and kiss me."

Chapter 10

Devyn didn't need to tell him twice.

Before she had a chance to blink, Beau took her cheek in one hand. She turned her face and arched her neck, rising to meet him while he lowered his mouth to hers. At the contact, she released a whimper that revealed how desperately she wanted him, but she didn't care. She was beyond pride. Her body had taken the wheel, and it was veering full throttle toward the massive, hard man behind her.

One touch had her skin burning with fever, and when the tip of his tongue flicked against her upper lip, chills rushed over Devyn's body. All her cares fell away until there was only Beau—his mouth firm and commanding as he explored her with a seeking tongue. A wave of desire settled between her thighs until she was so hot she could have combusted.

No one kissed like Beau Dumont. No one on earth.

When she broke free for air, he lifted her curls and slid his open mouth down the side of her throat, nibbling a trail to the weak spot at the top of her shoulder. There, he sucked her mercilessly while drawing her close with one powerful arm. Devyn pressed a hand against the window and bit her lip to contain a moan. She wanted to face him, to nestle their bodies together as tightly as she could, but then she glanced through the glass and locked eyes with a stranger on the other side.

A smoldering thrill shot up the length of Devyn's thighs.

In the instant before she remembered the stranger couldn't see them, she feared the man had caught her in the act. She envisioned what he would have seen— Beau kneading one of her breasts and biting her neck while she reached behind to palm his erection. For the briefest of moments, she had thought someone was watching her.

And surprisingly, she'd liked it.

The hint of danger heightened her sensations, each touch twice as erotic as before, and she finally understood the appeal of public sex. It was dangerous and forbidden. Which was hot as hell.

Still gazing out the window, she guided Beau's hand over her hips and whispered, "Touch me."

He made a noise of raw male hunger and tugged the hem of her skirt to her waist, then used a thumbnail to trace swirls around the source of her need, teasing her through the thin fabric of her panties. "Both hands on the glass," he ordered. "I'm not getting off in my pants this time, Kitten."

She did as she was told.

"I'm going to finish inside you," he promised. "But first," he said as his thumb pressed her swollen bud and made her gasp, "you'll come for me." He held the pressure and moved in a circle, rubbing tension into her core. "Again and again, until you can't stand up. By the time I'm ready to make love to you, there won't be a bone left in your body . . . except mine."

Devyn moaned and widened her stance. She was halfway there.

He tucked his hand inside her panties and took her breath away with the delicate play of his fingers. They taunted and probed, sliding between her wet folds with a lethal precision that had her panting Beau's name. He knew what he was doing, knew her body like a favorite song, and he strummed her chords until every muscle in her legs tensed in anticipation of release. Her hands squeaked against the window, a chorus of desperate noises rising from her throat. When she shifted her gaze to meet the eyes of a woman checking her reflection in the mirror, a flare of heat blossomed within her and Devyn went flying over the edge.

She came down slowly to find that Beau had followed the direction of her gaze into the casino. There was a devilish smile in his voice when he pressed his lips to her ear and whispered, "It feels like they're watching us, doesn't it?"

Devyn nodded, unable to form a coherent sentence.

"Did you like that?"

She swallowed and nodded again.

"Then let's try something." After removing her panties, he sat her on the edge of a tall rolling chair and swiveled it to face the window. Then he sank to his knees in front of the chair and propped her left heel on his shoulder. "I want you to pretend we're back there in the slots, hiding in the corner while I remind you what my tongue is for."

She wanted to tell him to wait a few minutes, that she was too sensitive after her climax, but then he licked her soft and slow, and she was powerless to do anything but lie back and surrender to his mouth.

Pure pleasure washed over her as he sucked and nibbled, pausing only long enough to utter a curse and tell her how good she tasted. He dragged the tip of his tongue back and forth over her throbbing flesh while she held tightly to the chair and moaned with inexplicable bliss. When she spread wider for him, he used two fingers to dip inside and stretch her by gradual degrees until he pushed all the way in and pulled back out again. Devyn remembered his instructions, but she couldn't pretend she was anywhere but right here, riding his long fingers while he sucked her to orgasm.

She came hard and fast, crying out into the room without a care for who might overhear. She was too far gone. Her inner walls convulsed around his pistoning fingers until the tremors ceased and she slumped back in the chair, utterly boneless.

Exactly as he'd promised.

Beau nipped at her inner thigh before rising from the floor and giving her a look that would melt steel. He licked off each of his fingers and spoke in a lust-roughened voice. "You're so fucking sweet, Dev. You always were."

The heat behind his gaze sent a new shiver of desire down her spine. She glanced at the enormous bulge straining the front of his pants and reached for the zipper. "Now it's my turn to taste you."

"Unh-uh." Wickedly, he grinned and shook his head. "You'll have to take a rain check. I want inside you. Right now."

She tried to stand, but her knees wobbled and gave out, sending her plunking back to the chair.

This seemed to please him. Beau smiled while unbuttoning his pants. "Didn't I say you wouldn't be able to stand up? I'm a man of my word."

Swamped by satisfaction, Devyn couldn't fire a witty comeback. Instead, she mirrored his smile and watched as he lowered his zipper to free his erection. His skin was stretched tight over a delightfully long, wide shaft. He was the living embodiment of masculinity, so big and strong and hard. Despite the two orgasms he'd given her, heat pooled low in Devyn's belly, making her go tingly in all the right places. Her body wanted him—*needed* him—and she was more than ready to take him in.

She spread her thighs for him, and he stepped in between, then gathered her in his arms. "Wrap your legs around my waist," he said. "I'm going to fuck you against the window, with all those people on the other side."

A charge of anticipation unfurled between her legs. The whole experience was so wrong, but in the best way. She couldn't recall the last time sex had made her feel so alive. She clung to Beau's shoulders and locked both ankles at the base of his spine while he grabbed her by the hips and pressed her bare bottom to the glass. The cold shock made her breath catch, but she quickly recovered when he nudged his rounded head inside her.

"Oh, God," she groaned while her eyelids slammed shut. The pleasure. There was no describing it. He'd given her only an inch, and she was already on the verge of coming. "More," she pleaded.

He pulled out to the tip and slid in halfway, until her body protested at the pressure of his girth. Beau hissed through his teeth and held there, trembling with need while she stretched to accommodate him. Then he pulled back and sank in a fraction more, working inside her gradually until he rocked his hips one last time and buried himself to the base.

Devyn held her breath and willed her inner muscles to relax. God, she was so full—so unbelievably full. She hadn't had a man this big in years, not since the last time she and Beau had made love, and the delirious invasion came with a stitch of pain.

"Are you okay?" he asked against her lips.

She nodded. "Just give me a second."

He kissed her in a gentle sweep of lips that told her to take all the time she needed. When her passage had adjusted, she squeezed her inner muscles and ground against him. "Go slow," she whispered.

And he did. He cradled her hips between his powerful hands and moved in and out in a lazy, fluid motion that had her neck arching against the window. He watched her carefully, gauging her reaction. "Is this all right?"

"Yes." *Oh, yes.* Feeling him so deep and hard inside her was the truest form of ecstasy she'd ever known. With his iron shaft gliding so smoothly between her legs, Devyn was much better than all right.

Until he gave her that intense look—the one that said this wasn't just sex.

"Dev . . ." he whispered, then pulled in a shaky breath. Unable to say anything more, he burned her up with his gaze and tipped their foreheads together. In response, her heart swelled and cracked as if to allow him inside, baring herself in a way she hadn't done since graduation night.

Right before he'd abandoned her.

She couldn't keep this up. He was taking too much. But when she let her lids flutter closed to escape the connection, Beau halted his movements.

"Look at me," he whispered. "No hiding. I want all of you." She rolled her hips, but he pressed her hard against the window to keep her immobile. "Want me to stop?"

"No," she cried, hating herself for her weakness even as she strained forward for more friction. She opened her eyes. "Don't you dare."

"That's a good girl."

Beau rewarded her with a rotation of his hips, smiling

when her eyes rolled back in rapture. He quickened the tempo of his thrusts, and she matched each one. Keeping their gazes locked, she dug her fingertips into his shoulders and held tight as the tension built low in her core. She raced toward climax to alleviate the sweet agony, telling herself this didn't mean anything, that she could give Beau her body and keep her soul hidden.

Even though it felt like a lie.

Beau gasped, his rigid control beginning to crack. She could tell he was near the brink, and she was nearly there herself. "Come for me," he murmured, squeezing her ass with those strong fingers. "I want to feel it, Dev."

Then he angled his hips and plunged hard, hitting exactly the right spot. She cried out and begged him to do it again. So he did, over and over, filling the small room with the squeak of her bare skin against the glass and the ragged pull of breath into their lungs. Each slow, slamming thrust increased the pressure until it finally broke into a molten release that sent sparks bursting down her legs. She buried her face in his shoulder and sobbed an incoherent strand of curses as she clenched around his pumping shaft.

"God damn," Beau growled with his forehead pressed to the window. "You feel so fucking good, I can't—" He cut off, and with one final slam of his hips, he stiffened and spilled into her with a low groan. For several heartbeats, he continued swearing under his breath until he placed a kiss below Devyn's ear. "Unreal," he whispered. "That was unreal."

"Mmm," she agreed. It always had been—sex with Beau was never the problem. What came afterward was a different story. "It really *is* a Magic Stick."

He laughed and pulled back to look at her, so happy that it put a hitch in Devyn's pulse. "Abracadabra, honey."

"And you're so modest, too," she teased. "The whole package."

"Let's make some more magic." He kissed her, soft and sweet. "Stay with me tonight. I've got that great big bed—plenty of room to strip you down and tend to anything I missed." In demonstration, he took her breast in hand and swept a thumb over her nipple. "I still haven't kissed you here."

The sweep of his thumb was going to turn her on again if he didn't stop. Devyn had no regrets for what she and Beau had done, but she needed some distance. Her body might be able to handle another round with him, but she couldn't say the same about her heart. If she spent the night in his bed, he would have her wide open and desperate, and he'd make her look into his eyes until he branded her. She wasn't ready for that, wasn't sure if she ever would be. Shaking her head, she unwrapped her legs from around his hips, sucking in a sharp breath of pain when he withdrew.

Maybe her body couldn't handle another round, after all.

"Sore?" he asked, handing over her panties.

It took a couple of tries to get her wobbly legs inside her bikini briefs. "Yeah. It's been a while for me."

He zipped up and smoothed his shirt, trying unsuccessfully to hide a prideful grin. "Stay the night anyway. I won't lay a hand on you."

She arched a disbelieving brow.

"Okay," he conceded, "I might. But I'll be gentle, and you know I'll make it good."

Yes, she knew. But that wasn't the issue. "Not tonight."

"Hey." He stopped what he was doing and took her face between his hands. "Are we all right?"

"Just all right?" she asked. "Didn't we agree that we're magical?"

"You know what I mean."

"We're okay, Dumont." To reassure him, she stood on tiptoe and kissed his nose. "And we're still on for tomorrow. Come get me when lunch is ready."

"At least let me walk you to your room."

She palmed his chest. "No way, not while you're wearing that dopey grin. The whole staff will know what we've been up to."

That dopey grin widened. "You're glowing too, by the way."

Devyn didn't doubt it. And truth be told, that scared her.

So she told him good-bye and returned to her room on shaky knees, for once relieved at the sight of her lumpy, narrow bunk. There, she was safe.

The next morning, the staff formed a line near the bow ramp to wave to the passengers as they left for their daylong excursions in Natchez. In between shaking hands and wishing guests a great day, Beau kept catching Devyn's eye, flashing a secret smile that affected her more than she wanted to admit. The heat in his stunning green eyes made her heartbeat catch, and when she returned to her room to change, she found herself taking extra care with her makeup and deliberating over what to wear.

She finally decided on jeans and a simple, snug-fitting blouse in Beau's favorite color—blue—and let her curls hang loose around her shoulders. She even skipped the antifrizz serum because it felt sticky, and Beau loved playing with her hair. Every choice she made was out of consideration for him.

That's how she knew she was in trouble.

At around noon, he knocked on the door, looking good enough to eat in paper-thin denim and a short sleeve T-shirt that hugged the contours of his muscled chest. He must have come straight from the galley, because he carried the scent of baked bread on his clothes. When a wide smile lifted the corners of his lips, he made her mouth water in more ways than one.

"You look beautiful," he said.

"You're kind of easy on the eyes yourself."

He laughed and lifted a wicker picnic basket for show. "As much as I'd love to stand here and soak up your ridiculous compliments, our lunch is getting cold." Extending an elbow, he asked, "Ready?"

She grabbed her handbag, and they linked their arms to set off toward the dock. At the head of the ramp, they crossed paths with Thing One and Thing Two, but for once, Devyn couldn't tell the twins apart because each man kept his gaze respectfully above the neck. This was unusual, not that she was complaining. Since they were still in uniform, she glanced at their name tags to differentiate between them.

"Hot date?" Nick asked with a crooked grin.

The question didn't faze Beau. "Jealous?"

"Hell, yeah. I'm stuck here running payroll for this guy," he hitched a thumb at his twin, "while he gallivants around Natchez with Ella-Claire."

Alex smiled. "He lost a bet, fair and square."

"I don't know about *fair*," Nick mumbled.

Ignoring his twin brother's complaint, Alex turned to Devyn. "Is Ella still getting ready? She needs to shake her tail feather, or we're going to miss our tour."

Devyn tipped her head in confusion. Ella had been up and out before breakfast. She hadn't even joined the staff that morning to bid farewell to the guests. "She left hours ago. I assumed she was with you."

"No." His blond brows pinched together. "I haven't seen her since yesterday." When he pulled out his cell phone and texted Ella, she didn't reply. A wrinkle of disappointment creased his forehead, and for the briefest of moments, Devyn felt sorry for him. Until she remembered her conversation with Ella-Claire—and the hurt in the young woman's eyes.

It seemed that Ella had drawn a line in the sand. Good for her.

Devyn put the matter behind her as she and Beau

strode down the ramp and onto the dock parking lot. The unyielding pavement felt so good beneath her feet that she stamped her heels a few times against the asphalt, enjoying the energy that resonated up her shins.

Beau cast an amused glance at her. "Better?"

"Much." She pulled in a deep breath of Mississippi air and turned her face to the sun, its rays heating her skin despite autumn's arrival. It was the perfect day for shore leave—clear and ever so breezy with the faint scent of mown grass drifting on the wind.

She turned to Beau and found him watching her with a grin. He shook his head in a slight gesture of disbelief. "I could look at you all day and never get my fill."

Her face heated, so Devyn did what she knew best—she deflected. "Where are we eating?"

"Over there a ways," he said, jutting his chin toward a grassy easement about fifty yards upriver. "It's not a proper park, but there are a few picnic tables overlooking the river. Should be more private than anything we'll find in town."

He surprised her by taking her hand as they walked onward. His fingers felt so perfect when they were laced between hers that Devyn couldn't bring herself to pull away. She enjoyed feeling anchored to him like this, so she swung their joined hands between them and savored the caress of the sun on her shoulders until they reached the first wooden picnic table and settled on opposite sides.

"What did you pack in here?" she asked, lifting the lid to peek inside.

Beau lightly smacked her hand. "Sit down and re-lax," he said, pulling a bottle from the basket and twist-ing off the top. "Here, have a beer."

"Nice." She tipped it back for a deep pull. She didn't know how he managed it, but the beer was ice-cold. "Doesn't matter what else is in there, this lunch is al-ready a winner."

He unpacked the contents: two paper-wrapped pack-ages, a pair of dill pickle spears, half a cheesecake, and a sack of breaded bits she couldn't identify. Then he pointed to the first bundles. "Gourmet grilled cheese sandwiches. Smoked provolone and cured bacon on ar-tisan bread with sun-dried tomato pesto."

"Oh, my God," she moaned. That sounded like heaven. "I just had an orgasm in my mouth."

Beau waggled his brows. "Only one? You know that's not enough for me," he said as he shook the bag, rustling the bread crumbs inside. "Allie told me you love fried okra, so I put a spin on your mama's recipe. Gave it a little kick."

"You do love spice."

"Who doesn't like it hot?" he asked with a wink while opening the bag. "Try one."

She didn't need further persuading. The mixture smelled amazing, like peppers and salted garlic. When she popped a bite in her mouth, the flavors burst across her tongue, and she made a noise of pleasure. "You've got skills, Dumont," she mumbled around the okra. "Mad skills."

"Wait till you try the grilled cheese," he said as he

unwrapped both their sandwiches and grabbed a beer for himself. "You'll fall down at my feet in worship."

Devyn chuckled while she sank her teeth into the crispy bread, but by the time she finished her first bite, she wasn't laughing anymore. The smoky cheese and bacon provided the perfect contrast to the sweet tang of sun-dried tomatoes. Her taste buds were weeping with joy as she devoured the sandwich with no lady-like grace whatsoever. She wished she had an extra stomach so she could keep eating—it was that good.

"Wow," she said, wiping her mouth. "Ex-marine, security specialist, casino pit boss, gourmet chef. Is there anything you can't do?"

"Apparently, I can't get you to spend the night with me," he complained, tipping his beer bottle toward her. "How about it, Kitten? I'm awful lonely in that suite by myself."

Before she could tell him no, the rumble of a nearby vehicle drew her attention to the street. Then, as if it were a scene from her own personal nightmare, a Larabee Amusements tour bus motored past them and turned toward the heart of town. Here she was, having the best culinary experience of her life with a hard-bodied stud begging her to share his bed, and the moment was ruined by the reminder of what awaited her at home.

"There's no escaping it," she said to herself.

Beau watched the bus until it drove out of sight. His voice was full of caution when he said, "You have options, you know."

Devyn propped her chin in one hand, irritated with herself for letting something as trivial as a passing tour bus ruin her lunch. "Not as many as you think."

"Come on, Dev," Beau said. "I've seen you in the education center. You were born to teach. It's not too late to go back to school."

She laughed at the absurdity of it. "How am I supposed to support myself through four years of college *and* pay for tuition and books?" she asked. That ship had sailed long ago. "Most states require teachers to get a masters degree on top of that. I can feel my blood pressure rising just thinking about it."

"So you bite the bullet for a few years," Beau said. From the flippancy in his tone, you'd think they were discussing a cardio workout. "The reward will be worth it."

"And the tuition?" she asked.

"Student loans and grants."

"Sure," she deadpanned. He made it sound so simple. "And who's going to pay my rent while I'm in class all day?"

"It won't be easy—"

"So far, that's the first logical thing to come out of your mouth."

"But there are ways to make it work," he said, ignoring her. "Split rent with a roommate, get a job that fits your hours, look for programs that let you take classes online. If you want it bad enough, you'll figure out a solution."

"Maybe I don't want it that badly." She enjoyed

teaching, but not enough to spend another four years living like a pauper. For once, Devyn wanted to go to dinner without checking the credit balance on her MasterCard. She wanted to feel like an adult, not a college kid. "I appreciate your concern, but just drop it, okay?"

Beau clenched his jaw, but he didn't push. He drew a deep breath through his nose and blew it out. "I care about you. Sue me."

Devin smiled and threw a bread crumb at him. "Thank you. Now, new subject."

"Okay, how about this," he said as he upped the ante by flicking a chunk of okra at her. "Let's talk about the curse."

That caught her off guard. She wasn't sure if she liked this topic any better.

"Specifically," he added, "how we're going to break it."

"*We?*" she asked. No, she definitely didn't like where this was going.

"Yeah, I want you to help me."

Devyn bought herself a few seconds by finishing her beer, but by the time she'd swallowed the last drop, she was no closer to forming a response than before. Months ago, she had tried helping Marc and Allie break the curse . . . and failed. In the end, the only thing that had worked was Marc's determination to marry Allie at any cost. Devyn didn't want to think about marriage—especially not to the man who'd crushed her heart.

When she didn't answer, Beau nudged her across the table. "Hey, take a breath."

She hadn't realized she was holding it.

"I'm not asking for a Vegas wedding," he said. "Just a little help from a friend."

Devyn chanced a glance at him. He'd begun shredding the paper wrapping from his sandwich, a telltale sign that this wasn't an easy request for him to make.

"Growing up," he went on, "I didn't exactly have the *Leave it to Beaver* experience. But I want that someday—a wife and a family, all my kids under one roof. I want to eat pancakes on the weekends and coach little league. I want the picket fence."

The idea of Beau married to another woman, smoothing his hands possessively over her pregnant belly, made Devyn's chest ache. But she refused to dwell on why she felt that way. "I don't know how much good I can do. The Dumonts have the power to undo the hex, not me."

"Purest faith shall set you free," he quoted from Memère's curse. "But what does it mean? What does it look like? I don't understand, and that's where you come in."

Devyn pursed her lips and stared at her beer bottle as if Sam Adams might come to life and tell her what to do. Logically, she knew there was no harm in doing a little digging, but that didn't stop her stomach from pulling into a knot.

"Did I mention," Beau said, pointing at their dessert, "that I brought cheesecake?"

Devyn smiled and shook off whatever shadow had passed over her. Beau was right—he wasn't asking for much. Besides, after all the things he'd done for her, she owed him a favor. "Oh, well that changes everything."

"So you'll do it?"

"You *did* give me an orgasm in my mouth . . ."

"Among other places."

"True," she agreed. "All right, Dumont. I'll help you break the hex."

"Thanks, Dev." His grateful smile made her go all gooey inside. "This means a lot."

"No problem," she said, reminding herself that this wasn't a big deal. "That's what friends are for."

Chapter 11

Beau sipped his iced tea and studied the flat-screen television, analyzing the footage he'd missed a few days ago when he was otherwise occupied with Devyn. The roulette table was still underperforming, and his instincts told him one of the employees was skimming chips. The problem was that in order to pull off the scheme for any significant amount of money, the perp needed a partner—someone working in the cash-out station who would look the other way and trade those chips for greenbacks. It was bad enough to have one thief on the payroll, but a conspiratorial partnership was a whole other level of betrayal. Thinking about it made Beau's fists tighten, and he squinted at the recorded feed in determination to nail the bastards.

But then he spotted Devyn's image, and his focus blew to hell.

She had been walking toward the exit, her hair still mussed from his fingers, and she threw a glance over her shoulder toward the one-way glass where moments before, he'd held her there and made them both dizzy with pleasure. He paused the footage to freeze her in place, then zoomed in to read her expression. Her lips were parted, her eyes glassy beneath a furrowed brow. It didn't take a brain surgeon to identify the emotion etched onto her features.

She was afraid.

That didn't surprise him. He'd sensed her reluctance to let go when she refused to look him in the eyes during lovemaking. Since that night, they'd had sex three more times, but it wasn't the same as it had been in the security room—just a few stolen moments in supply closets and dark corners, with Devyn continuing to refuse to stay the night with him. She was holding back; that was clear. But still, it stung to see the evidence of her anxiety in high definition.

Beau supposed he couldn't blame her. She'd loved him once, and he had made her suffer for it. Trust was earned. Regaining hers would take time.

Luckily, he had plenty of that.

His cell phone buzzed to announce a new text, and he smiled. Devyn must be on her lunch break. He checked the screen and saw that he was right.

Meet me in my room, she told him, *and I'll give you something a lot more filling than a grilled cheese sandwich.*

If Beau had his choice, he'd meet her in his suite and spend all day worshipping her body. But since she wasn't ready for that, he'd take whatever he could get.

I'm on my way, he promised. *Don't start without me.*

*   *   *

Twenty minutes later, Devyn was on all fours, coming harder than a runaway train while he thrust into her from behind. It didn't escape Beau's notice that she was refusing to have face-to-face sex with him, but with her inner muscles clenching around him like a liquid fist, he couldn't bring himself to give a shit. He slammed into her one last time and growled, erupting in a climax he felt all the way to the soles of his feet.

Once he caught his breath, Beau skimmed a loving hand over the bare ass cheeks peeking out from beneath Devyn's skirt. He pulled out slowly and tucked himself back into his pants.

"Much better than a grilled cheese," he agreed. "But I'll be hungry again in a few hours."

Laughing, she retrieved her panties from beneath the bed. "More like a few minutes."

"You know me well." And because of that, she probably knew what was coming next. "Stay with me tonight."

"I can't." She didn't meet his gaze when she pulled on her underwear and lowered her skirt. "I have a roommate, remember? Ella-Claire will notice if I'm missing."

"She's a big girl. I'm pretty sure she had 'the talk' with her mama."

"You're my boss," Devyn reminded him. "We're not supposed to be sleeping together."

Beau didn't bother arguing that he'd already outed himself as her boyfriend at the class reunion, or that Marc knew they were involved and had begrudgingly accepted it. Because that wasn't the real reason she avoided sharing his bed. Instead, he threw her a teasing grin and pleaded, "Come on. All this sneaking around is making me feel cheap."

She folded her arms and returned his smile. "Want me to buy you dinner next time? I can probably scrounge up some flowers, too."

"You're breakin' my heart, darlin'."

"Mmm," she said, crawling toward him. She laced her fingers behind his neck and kissed him until he couldn't tell which way was up. "And yet," she whispered against his lips, "you keep coming back for more."

Beau couldn't deny it, but that didn't mean she had him by the short and curlies. He took back a handful of the power by nibbling his way down the side of her neck while massaging her breast. He grazed the top of her shoulder with his teeth, using one finger to circle her nipple until Devyn whimpered and strained against him. Until she spread her legs and rocked against his thigh. Until he knew he could have her again.

Then he stood up and told her good-bye.

Later that night, she made him pay.

"Dev," he groaned from inside the linen closet, where he stood against a shelf of bath towels while she knelt at his feet, teasingly flicking her tongue over the tip of his erection. She'd been torturing him with whisper licks for what felt like an hour, and now he was so painfully hard that she may have broken his dick.

"Damn it," he swore. "You'll be the death of me."

The thin strip of light leaking inside from the hallway wasn't enough to illuminate the closet, but he could hear the smile in her voice. "I don't want to kill you, Dumont." She wrapped a loose hand around his shaft, barely skimming him as she pumped up and down. "In fact, I'm kind of attached to some of your finer parts."

"Then prove it," he hissed, gripping the shelf behind him.

"Tsk, tsk, tsk." With her fingernails, she brushed the sensitive patch of skin behind his balls, making his jock twitch. "I didn't hear the magic word."

"Please," he said in a rush. This was a matter of life and death. Now was *not* the time for saving face. "Please, Dev."

She pretended to consider his request, then quickly sucked a bead of moisture from his engorged tip before she pulled back, letting the cool air replace her blazing mouth. Beau clenched his teeth, regretting with every fiber of his soul that he'd teased her earlier that day.

Payback was a bitch.

And apparently, Devyn knew it. She rose to her feet and faced him, taking his throbbing length in her hand. "You're so hard," she mused. "Is there someplace you'd like to put this?"

Beau snapped.

Grabbing her around the waist, he sank to the floor and took her with him until she straddled his lap. He shoved up her skirt, hooked a thumb around the crotch of her panties, and positioned himself at the base of her slick entrance. Then, curling an arm behind Devyn's body, he tugged her down while he thrust upward, filling her with a liquid ease that ripped a moan from both their throats.

"Yeah," he murmured. "Right there."

She rode him slowly at first, building to a desperate tempo that was sure to leave rug burns on her knees. So he rolled her to the floor and slung her legs over his shoulders. The new position must have hit her hot spot, because she mewled and cried and cursed as he rocked in and out of her. Between her primal noises of pleasure and the slap of their colliding hips, it was a wonder half the boat couldn't hear them.

Not that he particularly gave a damn at the moment.

"Now it's your turn to beg," he said, pausing to grind a deep rotation against her. "Let's hear the magic word, Kitten."

Her voice was a low whine. "I hate you."

He chuckled to himself. "I don't think so. I think you're loving one of my *finer parts* right now."

"Please," she whispered. Her breaths came in shallow gasps. "Please don't stop."

He didn't make her ask again, mostly because he couldn't hold out for much longer. Drawing on his last shreds of energy, Beau drove into her hard and fast. They came together in a rush of sensation so powerful that he may have left his own body. It was hard to tell, because he was still dizzy with the intoxicating feel of her sex when they untangled their limbs a few moments later.

"Wow," she breathed, adjusting her clothes. "Just wow."

"Seconded." He felt in the darkness for her hand, then gave it an affectionate squeeze. But when he tried to wrap his arm around her, Devyn planted a hasty kiss at his temple.

"I'll text you tomorrow at lunch," she said, moving to her feet before he'd even zipped his pants. She opened the closet door, blinding him with a flash of light from the hallway before she shut it again.

And then she was gone.

What the hell?

Beau sat there, utterly dumbstruck as he tried to process the hasty escape. He was only joking when he'd said their hookups made him cheap, but damned if he didn't feel a little used right now. Was it his imagination, or had they taken a step backward? Each time with Devyn seemed brasher than the last, a series of hit-and-runs with her doing all the running. She was pulling away emotionally and using him to get off.

That's when it struck him—they weren't making love anymore. They were fucking. And not affectionate fucking, either. This was down and dirty, biting and clawing, teasing and swearing, animal sex. The no-strings-attached kind. And as hot as it was, Beau had come too far with Devyn to let their relationship mutate into some one-dimensional friends with benefits arrangement.

He wanted more.

Which meant no more booty calls.

"Shit." His Magic Stick wasn't going to like that, but it would have to take one for the team. "Be strong, big guy," he muttered to his crotch. "Keep your eye on the prize."

"You've got to be strong." Devyn gripped Ella-Claire's upper arms. "Don't cave now, not when he's finally getting a glimpse of what life is like without you."

Ella jutted out her bottom lip. "But I miss him."

"That's good," Devyn said with an encouraging nod. "I'm sure he misses you too. Think about how miserable you are." When Ella's mouth pulled into a frown, Devyn added, "Now imagine Alex feeling the same way."

"How is this supposed to make me feel better?"

"Well, it doesn't," Devyn admitted. "But it's important that Alex realizes two things."

Ella made a *go ahead* motion with her hand.

"First, he has to know you're serious—that you're not making empty threats when you tell him to fish or cut bait," Devyn advised. The same rule applied in the education center. If her students acted the fool and she threatened a consequence, she always had to follow through on it. "If you keep taking him back, he'll learn that you don't mean what you say."

"And second?"

"He's taking you for granted." Devyn paused to let the words sink in. "Some people have to lose what they love in order to appreciate it. Alex might be one of those people. If so, this distance is just what the doctor ordered."

Ella blinked her big blue eyes and puffed a sigh.

"What did Alex say when you told him you wanted more?" Devyn asked.

The girl's shoulders sagged. "He was totally logical about the whole thing. He said he's attracted to me too, but if we cross the line, it could ruin our friendship and mess up the whole family dynamic."

Devyn didn't say so, but she thought Alex had made a valid argument.

"He asked me to imagine what would happen if we dated and then broke up," Ella continued. "How tense and awkward it would be, especially because we all work together. And how things would never be the same between him and Marc."

"Alex would be risking a lot," Devyn pointed out. "More than you, because Marc holds him to a different standard. And you two are barely out of college. The odds that you'll take your friendship to the next level and stay together forever are pretty slim."

Ella folded her arms and made a noise of offense. "A minute ago, you were telling me to stay strong and make him suffer. Now you're agreeing with him. Whose side are you on?"

"Yours, believe it or not." As much as Devyn wanted to see Ella-Claire with the guy of her dreams, she needed to understand all the possible consequences instead of letting her heart call the shots. "By default, a relationship with Alex won't be easy. Have you considered that?"

Ella answered with a question of her own. "Do you

know how hard it is to stand back and watch him with other girls? To be his friend and pretend I don't care when someone slips a phone number in his pocket? Or to laugh it off when I hear one of his brothers tease him about his dates?"

Devyn thought back to her picnic with Beau, when she'd pictured him with a wife and a family that didn't include her. "I can imagine."

"I can't keep going on like this," Ella said. "It hurts too much. Either we take it to the next level, or we go our separate ways so I can move on. Our family dynamic is screwed no matter what, because something has to change. That's what you and Alex don't understand."

"Aw, honey." Devyn squeezed Ella's shoulder, her heart aching for the girl. "I get it. And my original advice still stands. If you want to give Alex an ultimatum, then hold your ground. I hope you get what you want."

A tear spilled from her lashes and trailed down her cheek. "Why does this have to be so hard?"

"Because," Devyn said, "we don't appreciate what comes for free."

The next day, Devyn inhaled her turkey on rye and jogged to her room while trying not to choke on a bite of lettuce. Her lunch break was only forty-five minutes long, and she had already wasted a few of those precious minutes on actual lunch.

Which wasn't what she hungered for.

After letting herself inside, she wrapped a hair elastic around the doorknob in a silent message for her roommate, then undressed down to her matching bra and panty set—black lace, sure to put some extra giddy-up in Beau's pulse. She took a seat on the dresser and sent him a quick text.

I'm in my room, and all my clothes are on the floor, she typed. *The door's unlocked for you. . . .*

His response was almost instantaneous. *I'll be there in five.*

Devyn checked her watch and smiled when Beau made it there in three minutes, not five. Just as she expected, his eyes bulged at the sight of her, but then he shut the door behind him, and something in his expression shifted. Cooled. He raised his gaze to hers and stood near the wall instead of planting himself between her parted thighs.

She hadn't seen that coming.

The longer he stood there silently staring her down, the more exposed Devyn felt. What was taking him so long? Were they going to do this, or not?

"We need to talk," Beau said, tucking both hands in his pockets. "Maybe you should put on your clothes."

Devyn's lungs emptied as her skin flushed with the unchecked embarrassment of rejection. Here she was, on display for him in a few strategically placed scraps of lace, and he suggested she get dressed? Her ears had heard him, but her mind was a little slow on the uptake. Beau had been all over her like a duck on a june bug since he'd come back to town, and now he didn't want her anymore?

"Aw, now." He gave a sympathetic tilt of his head. "Don't look at me like that."

Devyn gasped before she could stop herself. How was she looking at him? Because the only thing more pathetic than rejection was showing how much it hurt. She scrambled off the dresser and lunged for her pants, which lay on the floor with one leg turned inside out. She'd wanted Beau so badly that she hadn't taken the time to undress like a normal person. No, she'd torn the clothes off her body like they were made of acid. Devyn cursed herself as she punched an arm through her khakis in a desperate attempt to right them.

"Stop." Beau snatched away the pants and tossed them over his shoulder. He was in full uniform, and when his gold-embellished coat brushed her bare stomach, she felt naked in an exaggerated way, like she was standing in Times Square in nothing but her birthday suit. "Look at me, Dev."

When she shoved against him with both hands, he wrestled her until she was facing the mirror, then wrapped his powerful arms around hers and held her immobile. Her breathing was heavy as she glared at his reflection, but she didn't bother to struggle. Beau was a tank—six and a half feet of solid muscle. Any attempt to wriggle free would be a waste of energy.

"Let go," she ordered. "You're the one who told me to get dressed."

"Not like this. Hear me out first."

"Okay, talk."

But of course he didn't do that. He stood there and

watched her, easy as you please, until she calmed down enough to unclench her shoulders. Only then did he begin.

"It's not that I don't want you," he said. "Because I do."

She scoffed at him. "Like I care."

"*I* care."

As if to demonstrate, he gathered her hair aside and placed a kiss on her shoulder, holding her gaze as he did. Then he smoothed a rough palm over the outside swell of her hip and continued past her waist, all the way up to her rib cage. Gently, he massaged one breast through her bra before pulling down the stretchy lace to expose her nipple. It pebbled against her will, proving how *very much* she cared.

With a low grumble of appreciation, he circled the puckered tip with his thumb. "I want you more than I want air." And he showed her by pressing the evidence against her backside. "But I'm not a teenager anymore, Dev. I want more than a few minutes with you inside a dark closet. I want everything."

When he licked his fingers and used them to tug at her nipple, Devyn sealed her lips to trap a moan. But that didn't stop wet heat from pooling in her belly, radiating downward until the flesh between her thighs ached.

"I want to spread you out on my bed," he went on, "and strip you naked. Then I'm going to kiss you here." Lightly, he pinched her nipple. "And here," he said, winding a southbound finger over her belly button.

"And especially here." His hand dipped into her panties, where he stroked her halfway to oblivion.

As much as Devyn tried to hide it, desire played across her face, lowering her lids and bringing a blush to her cheeks. Beau's breaths quickened against her neck as he watched the reflection of his fingers playing between her legs. He felt so good—*too* good—and she hated that only Beau had the power to make her lose herself.

"After that," he said, "I'm going to make love to you, and I'll take my sweet time. Then we'll fall asleep while I'm still inside you—and the next time you wake up, you'll already be moaning my name."

At that moment, with Beau rubbing hot tension into her core, she would have agreed to anything if it would make him keep going. And he must have known it, because he pulled his fingers free and took a moment to suck them clean.

"But until then," he told her, "I won't settle for quick and dirty sex." He held her gaze in the mirror as he bent his mouth to her ear. "Just knock on my door when you're ready for the real deal. I'll make you glad you came."

Several minutes later, long after Beau had left her alone and unsatisfied, Devyn stared at her reflection and tried to pinpoint what was bothering her . . . aside from the ache of desire between her legs. There was something else needling at her consciousness, but it was just beyond her grasp.

Realization hit a while later, when she was in the

education center waiting for the kids to return from lunch. Beau had cut her off and issued an ultimatum— exactly like she'd told Ella-Claire to do. Which implied Devyn had done something wrong. She was the fickle partner.

But she hadn't seen herself that way.

She didn't fear commitment or monogamy. Devyn could totally see herself settling down someday and having children. In holding back from Beau, she was only protecting herself from a proven flight risk.

There was nothing wrong with that.

And much like the trouble brewing between Alex and Ella-Claire, there were two sides to the story, two valid reasons for each partner wanting a different outcome. In demanding that she spend the night with him, Beau didn't realize how much he was asking of her. Or maybe he understood and simply didn't care. Either way, she wouldn't be knocking on his bedroom door any time soon.

"Or at all," she clarified to herself. "Like, ever."

Because much like Pandora's box, once she opened that door, there would be no closing it.

Chapter 12

In the two days that followed, Devyn spent her evenings in the galley under the pretense of helping her sister with the baking. In truth, she needed to stay busy. Idle hands were the devil's playground, and if left to their own devices, Devyn's hands would soon find their way into Beau's pants like magnets to steel.

Steel.

That described him all too well, and suddenly she blushed at the recollection of how magnificent he had felt inside her, so hard and deep. She shut down that train of thought and put more weight behind her rolling pin, flattening the pastry dough for tomorrow's breakfast turnovers.

"Hey," she said to her sister. "Can I ask you something?"

"No." Allie shook her head and eyed her sarcastically over a bowl of blackberries. "You're not allowed to talk while providing free labor. Shut up and get back to work."

Devyn snagged a berry from the bowl and tossed it into her mouth, earning her a reproachful look. "Let's imagine that the unthinkable happened, and you lost the bakery and all your income. No insurance money, no emergency fund. You've got nothing to cushion the fall except a paycheck or two."

Allie frowned. "Okay."

"Now imagine that the restaurant of your dreams offered to make you head pastry chef, but they won't give you the job until you graduate from culinary school. And they won't help pay for the tuition or any of your living expenses—it's all on you. Would you do it?"

"Go back to school?"

Devyn nodded. "Knowing that you wouldn't have two nickels to rub together for the next four years, and you'd be up to your neck in student loan debt by the time you graduated."

Allie blew out a low whistle and thought about it for a while before saying, "I don't think so. I'd probably spend more time on the *Belle*. Our dining hall manager is retiring soon, so maybe I'd take over that position."

Devyn didn't know why, but her sister's answer disappointed her. "You wouldn't miss the bakery?"

"Sure I would," Allie said, adding a scoop of sugar to her berries. "But I can still do that here."

"What if you couldn't?" Devyn asked. "If being a pastry chef on the *Belle* wasn't an option, would you go to culinary school then?"

With her lips pursed, Allie considered the question

before shaking her head. "Probably not. I like baking, but I don't have to do it for a living. I could cook at home for my family and not feel like I'm missing out. Besides, I like working here on the boat with Marc. It keeps us close." She giggled to herself. "And he loves nooners. I wouldn't get any of those if I went away to school."

Devyn was beginning to see that comparing her situation to Allie's was an *apples vs. oranges* kind of thing. Allie was a Dumont now, which meant she had a guaranteed job aboard the *Belle*. She was invested here, so supporting the family business was satisfying enough—in more ways than one.

But Devyn wasn't a part of anything larger than herself, which was both liberating and scary in equal measure. She had the freedom to go wherever the wind took her, but no safety net if the wind quit blowing and dropped her out of the sky.

"Why do you ask?" Allie said. "Do you want to go to culinary school?"

"No. Just thinking, that's all."

"About wh—" Allie's eyes went round with realization. "Oh, my god. You're thinking about getting your teaching degree! Devyn, that's great! Do it!"

Devyn held up a floury hand. "Take a chill pill. I'm not *seriously* thinking about it, just giving it a teensy-weensy bit of consideration."

It was only because Beau had planted the bug in her ear. Now that he'd cut her off from the good stuff, she had more free time to kick around those types of thoughts.

"I'm not actually going to do it."

"Why not?"

Devyn scoffed. She couldn't believe her sister had to ask. "For the same reason you wouldn't do it if you lost the bakery. I'm already broke as a joke. With a tuition bill and no way to work full-time, I'll be flat-out destitute—for at least four years. And then there'll be student loan debt after that."

"But they have programs for that," Allie said. "One of my wedding cake clients last year was a teacher. We got to talking, and she told me the government paid off half her student loans because she taught science in a qualifying school."

"A qualifying school?" Devyn asked with an arched brow. "In other words, the kind no one else wants to work at?"

"Oh, please." Allie flapped a hand. "You could handle the toughest students. Besides, those are the kids who need you most. You could make a difference in their lives. Isn't that what you always wanted growing up?"

Yes, it was. And the unique challenge of teaching at-risk students appealed to Devyn more than she let on. That kind of work would never be dull, and the rewards would extend way beyond a paycheck. She felt a brief glimmer of hope—a faint stirring of warmth within her breast—that her dream had come back to life.

But then reality set in.

Four long years of classes, homework, exams, and internships. That subtle stirring of warmth grew cold. In order to become a teacher, she'd first have to be a student. The whole thing was too overwhelming to consider.

"I'm not going back to school," she said in a tone that closed the topic for debate. "It's too late for that."

"Okay . . ." Allie dragged out the word, clearly not letting Devyn off the hook so easily. "But what about the haunted cemetery tours? It's none of my business how much Warren Larabee offered to pay you, but is this a career? Or is it just a job? Because if it's only another temporary job, you're going to find yourself facing this same problem next year. And the year after that. At some point, you have to settle into an occupation for the long haul. Which means you might as well finish your degree now."

"You don't have a degree," Devyn pointed out.

"I don't need one," Allie said. "But if I *did*, I'd suck it up and go back to school."

Devyn pretended to focus on cutting the dough into strips while reflecting on Warren's salary offer. The amount had seemed generous at the time—considering she'd just come home to an overdue rent notice stapled to the front door—but was it enough to support her in the long term? She imagined herself in forty years, hunched over and leading the haunted tour with a walker. Not a pretty sight. Maybe she should negotiate for a bigger piece of the pie.

She was brainstorming ways to ask for a raise when Nick poked his head inside the galley. She knew it was him because a few days ago, she'd noticed that his left eyebrow arched a bit higher than the right, giving the illusion that he always had something naughty on his mind. Which, knowing him, was probably the case.

"Hey, Dev," Nick said. "The boss man wants to see you."

"Great." Devyn blew out a breath, not bothering to ask which of her bosses had summoned her. She knew. "What does he want?"

"Dunno."

"Where is he?"

"Where else? In the security room."

Devyn brushed the flour from her hands and untied her apron. "All right. I'll head up there in a minute."

"He's in a shit mood," Nick warned. "Just sayin'."

A flicker of concern passed through her. It took a lot to get Beau riled up. Devyn wondered what had happened to ruin his mood, and she found herself quickening the pace to wash her hands so she could get to him faster. Maybe she should take some iced tea and his favorite dessert, too.

"Do we have any pecan pie left from supper?" she asked Allie.

Her sister grinned knowingly. "In the fridge."

Beau liked his pie warm, so Devyn heated up a slice and topped it with a scoop of vanilla bean ice cream, then filled a travel cup with iced tea and set off for the casino. As usual, he saw her coming through the one-way glass and already had the security room door open for her when she arrived.

Beau might have been in a dark mood before, but when he spotted the rich ice cream melting over warm pecan pie, his eyes brightened. "Is that for me?"

Devyn held it out to him, along with the cup. "This, too. I heard you're having a rough night."

When he took the offerings, he watched her for several charged moments with so much gratitude that Devyn tingled all over. She knew she shouldn't be sending mixed messages, but she couldn't bring herself to not care for him. Making Beau smile like this—especially after a hard day—brought her a deep sense of satisfaction, similar to the way she felt after a grand slam lesson in the education center.

"Thanks." He took his pie to the swiveling chair parked in front of the observation window and sat on half of the seat, then motioned for her to share the spot beside him. "This'll take the edge off."

There wasn't much space next to his big body, but Devyn settled in best as she could and peered through the glass. The casino was at half capacity, probably because the theater shows were in progress, so she could see all the way to the craps table at the rear of the room. While Beau ate his pie, she studied the passengers, some laughing at their losses while others sat at the gaming tables with the laser focus of seasoned gamblers. Muffled noises of electronic chirps and cheers filtered into the room to punctuate the occasional scrape of Beau's fork against the plate. It was kind of nice sitting there beside him, enjoying his body heat and a few minutes of quiet company.

Once he'd finished his pie, Devyn asked, "Feel better?"

"Much," he said as he wrapped a casual arm around her and pulled her in for a hug. "That was real sweet of you."

"What happened today? Want to talk about it?"

He huffed a sigh and pointed out the window. "See the employee manning the roulette wheel?"

Devyn brought the man into focus—tall and lanky, mid-thirties, brown hair. He wore a red staff polo shirt and a natural smile that said he genuinely enjoyed his job. "What about him?"

"I'm pretty sure he's skimming chips. I've been watching him for days, and I can't figure out how he's doing it," Beau said, setting down his cup with enough force to shake the computer table. "It's driving me crazy."

That came as a surprise to her. Devyn didn't know the guy, but he had one of those honest faces, the kind she tended to trust automatically. "How do you know it's him?"

"Because his table has been underperforming." Beau explained how part of his job involved tracking each table and gaming machine to make sure they generated the predicted income. "There's only one reason for a steady drop like that."

"But how do you know he's the one stealing?" she asked.

"He's the only one who mans that table."

"What about during his lunch break?"

"We shut it down for the hour," Beau said. "The casino doesn't see much action during lunch, so it doesn't pay to get another employee to cover it."

Devyn leaned forward to study the man more closely. Compared to the other dealers, all business with their tight mouths and their chilly gazes, he seemed so friendly. He even bent down to pick up a woman's handbag for her when she dropped it—a sweet gesture, but a bit naïve as it left the table unsupervised for a split second. That made Devyn wonder if someone else had noticed the man's helpful nature . . . and taken advantage of it.

"What if it's a passenger?" Devyn asked. "Or more than one passenger working together?" She could envision it: one partner distracting the dealer while the other covertly palmed a handful of chips from the table. If they did it right, they could bend over the chips to hide the act from the ceiling cameras.

Beau grunted in doubt. "I don't know. These folks aren't breezing in here from off the street. They've paid a shitload of money for their tickets. I can count the number of times on one hand that we've busted a guest for stealing."

Devyn shrugged. "Rich people steal sometimes. For the thrill of it."

"Yeah, but still."

"Couldn't hurt to check out the footage again," she said. "Look at it from a different perspective. You might notice something you missed before."

"I guess," he said, peering down at her, so close to her that their lips nearly touched. His gaze dropped to her mouth, but he made no move to kiss her. Devyn didn't know whether to feel relieved or annoyed. She liked kissing him. "Want to help?" he asked.

When she didn't answer right away—because she was too busy brooding over why he wouldn't kiss her—he saved the moment by adding, "I miss having you around."

"Yeah?" she asked, a smile flittering across her lips.

"That's the real reason I sent Nicky to get you," Beau said as he coiled a lock of her hair around his finger and flashed a crooked grin that made her stomach flip. "Just because we're not sleeping together doesn't mean we can't hang out." He made his eyebrows bob. "Though I'm happy to correct that first part whenever you want."

Devyn laughed and reclaimed her hair, glad to hear that he wanted her, though she shouldn't have cared either way. "I'll help look at the security tapes, Dumont. But you're sleeping alone tonight."

He set up the recorded feed on the big screen monitor, and for the next hour, Devyn watched the footage while Beau surveyed the casino through the window. She looked for anything out of the ordinary—guests repeatedly knocking items to the floor or monopolizing the roulette dealer's attention—but so far it all seemed aboveboard.

When her eyes couldn't take the strain any longer, she promised to return tomorrow. Beau gave her a gentlemanly kiss on the hand before they parted, but there was nothing tame about the hunger in his gaze when his lips brushed her knuckles. If his intent was to keep her awake half the night, he accomplished his goal. It was stubborn determination, and maybe a little bit of pride, that kept Devyn in her bunk.

The next night didn't yield any breakthroughs either, but she enjoyed spending the evening curled up beside Beau on their shared chair, his powerful arm wrapped around her so sure and steady. To pass the time while they studied the footage, they talked about where they'd traveled since high school and their favorite places to visit. It turned out they were both partial to beaches. Beau told her about Hisaronu Bay in Turkey, two stretches of sandy beach with aquamarine waters and a nearly constant breeze perfect for windsurfing.

"I want to take you there someday," he said, as if making plans together for the future was a foregone conclusion.

Devyn wasn't sure how she felt about that, so she kept the conversation moving. "My favorite is Caneel Bay in Saint John. I took a private charter there from Saint Thomas and spent the day snorkeling." She didn't mention that she'd taken the trip with an ex. "It's warm and gorgeous, and getting to the Virgin Islands is easy because you don't need a passport."

From there, they compared their favorite movies and discovered they were both fans of slapstick comedies, specifically Monty Python films and spoofs like Austin Powers.

"Monty Python's *Holy Grail* is the funniest thing

ever committed to film," Beau declared. "Especially the scene where King Arthur asks the French guard to join his quest to find the grail—"

"And the guard says, *We already have one*," Devyn interrupted with a giggle-snort. "Best line ever!"

"I was just going to say the same thing," Beau said, smiling down at her in wonder. "I can't believe you like that movie. How did I never know that about you?"

Devyn propped her chin on his chest and returned his smile. "Well, we didn't do a whole lot of talking when we dated."

"True," he said with a chuckle. "And I guess we fell into the same pattern here on the boat."

"You know what they say about old habits . . ."

"Mmm," he agreed. He kissed her forehead and returned his attention to the recorded feed on the monitor. "I'm glad we're finally getting to know each other. I like you, Devyn Mauvais."

She grinned and settled into his embrace, utterly content for the first time in recent memory. "You're not so bad either, Dumont."

The following night, they were sharing stories of their most embarrassing moments when Devyn noticed something strange on the monitor. She sat up and leaned closer to the screen, then asked Beau to pause the footage.

"Look right there," she said, pointing to a familiar cowboy hat. It was the married asshole who had hit on her last week. The man leaned a hip against the roulette table to place a bet, which wasn't what bothered her. "Now check this out." She indicated a busty young blonde standing across from the cowboy, placing a wager of her own.

"What about them?" Beau asked.

"They're not a couple, or at least they don't act like it." She'd noticed while observing the casino floor that the cowboy was a loner. Aside from an occasional tip of his hat, he didn't engage in conversation with the other gamblers. "I've never seen them talk."

"Okay . . ."

"But they keep coming to the roulette table and standing right across from each other." That struck Devyn as odd. "Why would two strangers feel the urge to play roulette at exactly the same time—and assume the same positions at the table?"

Beau wrinkled his forehead and played the overhead feed in slow motion. For the next several minutes, they scrutinized every frame containing the couple, but didn't turn up any evidence of theft. The cowboy lost two bets and ambled off to the nearest blackjack table while the blonde strode to the bar for a glass of wine.

Devyn didn't have a lick of proof, but her instincts blared a red alert. "Something's up with those two," she muttered to herself. "I can feel it."

"Maybe she's Jill," Beau said.

"Who's Jill?"

"His mistress." Beau explained how he and Nicky had checked out the guy for suspicious behavior at the poker table, and glimpsed a text message to his lover.

"He's not a total idiot, but apparently not enough to canoodle in public with the other woman."

Devyn wasn't convinced. "Do you have a smaller camera? Something I can wear, or plant near the roulette wheel?"

Beau shook his head.

She slid him a disbelieving glare. "What kind of ex-military security buff doesn't have a spy cam?"

He shrugged. "The kind running security on a historic riverboat."

"Well, the ceiling cameras aren't cutting it." She needed a way to get a low, hands-level view of the dealer's chips, since that's where any theft was likely coming from. "How late does the cowboy usually hang around?"

"Till closing," Beau said. "He's a big player."

In more ways than one, the cheating jerk. Devyn had an idea to get a closer look. It wasn't the most brilliant plan she'd ever concocted, but it was worth a shot. "I'm guessing employees aren't allowed to gamble here or fraternize with guests, right?"

"Not if they want to keep their jobs."

"I'm going back to my room to change," she said. "Tell Nicky that I'm going to hang out on the floor for a while, and not to bother me."

Beau eyed her while folding both arms over his massive chest. "Why? What have you got up your sleeve?"

"Nothing," Devyn said with a wink. "*Yet.*"

Twenty minutes later, she was back in the casino wearing a push-up bra and her lowest cut blouse, the one that showed enough boob to stop traffic. It also had long sleeves that flared at the wrist . . . perfect for concealing a handheld camera, or in her case, a cell phone with video capacity.

She scanned the room for a black cowboy hat and found it bent over the roulette wheel. Perfect timing. Devyn made her way to the opposite side of the table, not surprised to find the blonde there. The woman pulled a ten-dollar chip from her sequined clutch and bet on red. Devyn settled beside the blonde and pretended to study the wheel, then bent just enough at the waist to bring her cleavage into prime view for anyone facing her.

It didn't take long for the cowboy to notice. Devyn didn't make direct eye contact, but through her periphery, she could see him ogling. So she stood there and let him get his fill. The blonde made a sound of annoyance, barely audible, but loud enough to tell Devyn the woman didn't like competing for the cowboy's attention.

So the two *were* involved. At least that suspicion was confirmed.

"Last call for bets," the dealer announced. After a few players tossed down their chips, he waved a hand over the table. "No more wagers."

All eyes were on the tiny white roulette ball—even the dealer's—when he put it in motion. Discreetly, Devyn tapped her cell phone screen, setting it to record while she angled the camera lens toward the dealer's chips and pretended to watch the circling ball. It bounced a few times and landed on black, causing half the table to groan and the other half to cheer. But Devyn didn't stick around to watch the payout. She had what she'd come for.

She strode away toward the bar and rejoined Beau in the security room.

Beau stared at her half-exposed chest while greeting her at the door. "Interesting wardrobe choice. Not that I'm complaining, mind you."

Devyn glanced down at the girls, grinning at her partners in crime. "They got the job done. Anyone facing me was too distracted to notice this." She held up her cell phone. "Now let's see if I caught anything good."

Huddling around her small screen, they watched the recording with bated breath. The footage was a bit shaky, and she'd captured only half the dealer's chip rack in the video frame, but it was the right half. The shadow of a sequined clutch passed over the stacks, and then a set of slim, fair fingers quickly slipped beneath it to capture a single one-hundred-dollar chip. The theft wasn't grand enough to alert the dealer, but quite the haul when spread out over the course of an evening. Or a week. The pair had probably scammed thousands by now.

"Well, son of a bitch," Beau muttered. "You were right."

Devyn cupped an ear. "Come again? I didn't hear you."

Laughing, he took her face between his hands and

gently tipped back her head. He held her gaze for a few heartbeats, giving her a chance to pull away. When she didn't, he murmured, "You were right," and then kissed her, soft and slow.

Beau didn't crowd her, and he didn't rush. He tasted her with shallow licks that served to multiply her hunger instead of sate it. Devyn hadn't truly realized until then how much she'd missed this—his warmth, his strength, the feeling of safety within his arms. The kiss turned her knees soft, and when he pulled back, it was way too soon.

He skimmed a thumb over her bottom lip and whispered, "I'd better go find Marc."

Dizzied by the rush of sensation, it took Devyn a moment to understand. "Oh, right. So you can call the police."

"Mind if I borrow your phone?" Beau asked. "I need the video."

She handed it over. Now seemed like the time to leave, but she couldn't control her feet. They remained planted firmly in front of Beau's hard body. "Need anything else?"

He flashed a downright scandalous grin that answered the question, then stepped around her and left to find his brother. Alone in the security room, Devyn heard the mental echo of Beau's words from days earlier.

Knock on my door when you're ready for the real deal. I'll make you glad you came.

As if to make the decision for her, Devyn's hands

curled into fists—prepared to knock on thin air if it would bring him back to her. She didn't know how much longer she could hold out.

It was going to be a long night.

Chapter 13

They never caught Cowboy Casanova on camera, but the bastard's girlfriend sang like a diva as soon as Beau and Marc pulled her into the security office and showed her the evidence of her theft.

Jill confessed that her role in the scheme was to palm one chip at a time, then pass off the haul to her lover so he could cash them out at the end of the night. Being a high roller, the cowboy wouldn't raise any suspicions with a few hundred-dollar chips in his possession. The couple had agreed to split the earnings, and they'd done it for a cheap thrill—just like Devyn had said.

"I always knew that guy was a bubble off level," Beau told Marc while watching the police handcuff the pair of lovers. Since the *Belle* wouldn't dock in Saint Louis for another day, Marc had made an emergency stop south of the city. "Never pegged him for a thief, though."

Under the dim glow of the dock lighting, Marc nodded at the cowboy's wife as she followed the police down the bow ramp, already on her cell phone with a local attorney. "I can't believe she's gonna bail him out."

Beau had no trouble believing it. His mother would have done the same thing. Some people had more loyalty than sense.

"Anyway," Marc said, clapping Beau on the shoulder. "I'm heading back to the pilothouse. Tell Devyn thanks for me."

"Will do."

Beau imagined all the sinfully creative ways he'd like to thank Devyn for her help and they made his johnson twitch. But he kept those thoughts to himself as he returned to his suite for the night. He'd finally drawn her out of her protective shell, and the last thing he planned to do was lose ground by pushing too hard.

She would come to him when she was ready.

Once he returned to his suite, he distracted himself with a warm shower before slipping on a pair of boxer briefs and turning off the light. He was halfway to the bed when someone knocked on his door.

It was probably Marc. The police had promised to call with a case number and the name of the investigator they'd be working with. Beau swung open the door and felt his eyebrows jump. He hadn't expected to find Devyn on the other side, shifting on her socked feet and blinking at him as if she'd come to the wrong room.

She wore long pajama pants paired with a tank top, and because Beau was a red-blooded man with a functioning pair of eyes, he immediately noticed that she wasn't wearing a bra. Her pert nipples puckered beneath the white cotton top, which was so transparent she might as well not bother wearing it.

Jesus, she'd walked through the halls in this getup?

"Get in here." He ushered her inside while glancing up and down the hallway. "I hope no one saw you."

She furrowed her brow in confusion. "Why?"

"Your top," he said. "It's practically see-through. What are you doing running around in your pajamas anyway?"

Her lips parted, and she gaped at him while her cheeks darkened. "You . . . you said . . ." Abruptly, she turned and reached for the doorknob. "Never mind."

Realization struck Beau between the eyes like a hollow-point bullet, leaving his brain foggy and his heart scrambling to catch up. Had she come here for *him*? Still stunned, he slapped a palm against the door to keep her from opening it.

"Wait a minute," he said. "Did you come to spend the night?"

Still facing away, she tensed her shoulders.

"Damn it, Dev. Don't torture me." He flipped on the light so he could read her body language. "If that's why you're here, you'd better say so."

"Maybe it was a bad idea," she whispered.

Bracing his other hand on the door, he leaned in to press the length of his body against her, then bent low enough to nuzzle her ear. "There's nothing to be afraid of," he murmured. A shiver passed through her at the contact, telling him she didn't want to leave. "I promise I won't bite . . . hard."

She peeked at him and pulled her hair to one side. "What if I ask you to?"

By way of answer, he sank his teeth into the curve of her shoulder and made her gasp. He soothed the injury with his tongue while skimming both palms down the length of her bare arms. When she was pliable enough to sink to the floor, he turned her to face him.

"Do you want to be here?" he asked.

She nodded. "You know I do."

"If we get in that bed," he said, "you won't leave until the sun comes up. Understood?"

Her pale blue eyes came alive with desire, and she nodded again.

"And you'll do everything I say."

Judging by her sudden intake of breath, she seemed to like that. "Yes. Everything."

"Good," he said, jutting his chin toward the other side of the room. "Go pull back the covers. Then take off your clothes and lie down on your back." He stayed where he was, leaning a shoulder against the wall to watch her carry out his commands while he grew harder by the instant.

Her movements were slow and seductive as she tugged back the comforter and top sheet. Facing away from him, she peeled off her tank and dropped it to the floor. Her pajama bottoms and lacy panties soon followed. She stayed like that for another heartbeat before coyly glancing at him over one shoulder.

"On the bed," Beau told her. "Faceup."

With a flush of excitement on her cheeks, she crawled across the mattress and settled somewhere in the middle, then lay back, resting her head on his pillow.

Saints alive, she was breathtaking.

Beau had seen her naked before, many times. But the decade they'd spent apart had rounded her hips and thickened her thighs, making her painfully feminine in a way no eighteen-year-old could compete. The teenage Devyn had been sexy—no doubt about it—but the grown-up Devyn would bring any man to his knees.

This was a woman, not a girl.

"Raise your arms." His voice had darkened with lust. "Grab the headboard and stretch out so I can see all of you."

When she did as she was told, Devyn arched her back like a cat, lifting her exposed breasts in a tantalizing offer he couldn't refuse. Beau left his place by the wall and stretched out on the bed beside her, propping on one elbow to admire the view. The scent of vanilla lotion carried on her flushed olive skin, so warm and smooth and tempting. He longed to strip off his briefs and lower himself onto her, but Beau had waited ten years for this moment. Even if it killed him, he would take his time and savor each sensation.

"Close your eyes," he whispered, and she obeyed.

Starting at her throat, he trailed a worshipful hand down her chest until he reached the outside swell of her breast. There, he skimmed his knuckles over her velvet skin and then took her fully into his palm, lightly squeezing, testing the delicious weight of her. A growl of appreciation rumbled in his throat.

"You're beautiful, Devyn." So beautiful that he almost couldn't stand it. Looking at her was like trying to stare at the sun. He bent his mouth to her ear and breathed, "Even more spectacular than I remember."

The last time he'd tasted her pink nipples, he was too young to appreciate their unmatchable texture—smooth enough to shame silk—or how instantly they'd bead inside his mouth. Now he knew what he'd been missing, and he took one between his lips to reacquaint himself.

At the gentle tug of suction, she gasped and bowed back for more. Beau gave it to her, sucking hard and deep before using his teeth to scrape each pebbled tip. When he raised his head to admire the wet peaks of her swollen breasts, Devyn's eyes were clenched shut, and a deep patch of color stained her cheeks. Still holding to the headboard, she pressed her thighs together and murmured, "*Beau.*"

He'd taken some hard blows to the chest during his time with the marines, but nothing rocked him like the sound of his name on Devyn's tongue. Nothing on earth. He watched her writhe in need, and it fed his own desire. He didn't want to tease Devyn or make her beg. Tonight was different. He wanted to give her everything he had, to make her climax until she drowned with pleasure.

"Open your legs," he ordered. When her thighs trembled slowly apart, he ordered, "All the way."

She spread wide open for him, and Beau sat up to appreciate the thatch of dark curls between her thighs. He turned his gaze lower, to the delicate folds where she glistened with arousal.

"I love making you wet," he said. "When I see how badly you want me, it makes me so hot I can't think straight."

Gently, he stroked the core of her, letting his fingers slip and slide over her heated cleft until she mewled and opened even wider for him. He slid a finger inside, groaning at the satiny resistance of her entrance, so hot and tight. He couldn't wait to feel it clenching around his erection. He pulled out and added a second finger, then pumped her slowly, purposely avoiding her swollen bundle of nerves while he watched her chest heave with ragged breaths. Only when she'd soaked the sheet beneath her bottom did he press his thumb to her clitoris.

Devyn cried out. So he did it again.

"Do you want to come now?" he asked.

She licked her lips and nodded furiously.

He sat between her thighs and used both hands in tandem, one spreading her folds and massaging her stiff bud while with the other, he plunged his fingers deep inside, stretching and twisting and driving her toward the edge. When her orgasm hit, she tensed her thighs, lifting her hips off the mattress and giving him an erotic view of the whole thing. Beau could see the muscles of her sex contracting around his drenched fingers, and he damned near lost his mind.

"Fuck," he muttered. It was the hottest experience of his life.

He couldn't wait to feel it again, this time on his tongue. As soon as her inner walls stopped pulsing, he positioned himself flat on the bed with his face between her thighs. Then without hesitation, he lapped at her sensitive flesh.

Devyn drew a sharp breath, but she didn't ask him to stop. After a few moments, she relaxed again and gave a sigh of contentment. "I can't believe how good that feels," she said on a strained breath. "Please don't stop."

There was no chance of that happening. He couldn't believe how good she tasted, like salted caramel and raw sex, and he wouldn't have stopped for all the secrets of the universe. He used his tongue to delve deep before tracing the outline of her swollen bud, then repeated the pattern until she moaned and arched her hips against his willing mouth. When her throaty cries grew pleading, he sucked her hard while pushing his fingers inside her, and she climaxed again in a burst of wet heat. He kept going until the very last shudder passed through her. Only then did he consider his own needs.

Panting, Beau pushed onto all fours and looked down at her damp thighs. Devyn was primed and dripping, more than ready to take all of him in one hard thrust. His jock throbbed, and he tugged off his briefs. He had to be inside her—now.

But when he lowered himself between her legs, she

released the headboard and pushed a weak hand to his chest. "Just a minute," she said.

"Honey, unless the room's on fire"—and probably not even then—"I can't wait any longer."

Understanding dawned in her eyes, and she wrapped her fingers around his erection. She stroked him from tip to base, easing his agony with a firm grip. "It's my turn. I want to taste you."

Beau shook his head. It was too late for that.

"Please," she asked while squeezing him. "We've got all night. Let me get on my knees for you." She licked her lips and whittled away at his resolve. "Then tell me what to do. I liked that."

"Shit," he hissed. She wasn't making it easy to say no. The idea of Devyn's lips wrapped around him, his commands turning her on as she slid her mouth up and down his shaft, was too tempting to resist. He drew a deep breath to regain control, then sat on the edge of the bed with his feet resting on the floor. Pointing to the carpet, he told her, "Down here."

In the languid movements of a highly satisfied woman, she slipped off the bed and knelt on the floor with her little feet tucked beneath her. When she peeked up at him through her lashes and awaited instructions, she was the perfect combination of innocence and siren. It was like a scene ripped straight from his fantasies.

"Grab me at the base," he told her in a husky voice he barely recognized as his own. She curled a palm around him, and he ordered, "Tighter."

She strengthened her grip, and a bead of arousal rose to the surface. She glanced at it and back to him with a question in her eyes, so he gave her permission with a nod.

Her tongue swept a hot trail over the head, and then she sucked his tip hard enough to tear a groan from Beau's throat. He had no patience for taunting licks, so he told her to take him fully into her mouth, and she did—with gusto.

The blazing, liquid glide of her lips was perfection. With each dip, she took him so deeply that he bumped the back of her throat. Then she rose, inch by inch, up the length of him using fierce suction. The tight press of her mouth sated the ache between his legs, and for the next several minutes, he threaded a hand in her hair to guide her movements, keeping the rhythm slow and the pressure hard because he had no intention of coming in her mouth tonight.

"That's enough," Beau eventually told her. "Get back on the bed." He wanted more than simple pleasure. He wanted everything.

A renewed desire shone in Devyn's gaze when she settled on the mattress and held out her arms. Beau didn't have to tell her to look at him. Her eyes remained fixed on his as he lowered between her dampened thighs and settled atop her, supporting his weight on one elbow. He kissed her swollen lips and whispered, "Wrap your legs around me."

Her smooth calves locked around his waist, and he cupped her cheek, waiting for the emotional connection she'd denied him over the past week. It came gradually, a softening behind her gaze that deepened with each of their shared heartbeats, until she laced both arms around his neck and regarded him with a familiar tenderness he hadn't seen in years. It shook him, down to his very foundation.

"There you are," he whispered against her lips, and thrust into her.

She gasped, lashes lowering to her cheeks.

Beau clenched his jaw to trap a groan.

God, the pleasure. There was no comparison.

She was a liquid furnace, gripping him inside and out as he pulled back and rocked into her. Each slippery stroke drove him halfway to insanity, but then she opened her eyes again and grounded him. Surrendered to him. Their breathing mingled, and their bodies moved together in flawless synchronization while she gazed at him in awe.

"I missed this," he told her. "God, I missed it so much."

Her eyes went misty, and she finally admitted, "I did, too. I missed you, Beau."

Just like that, he was a goner. If there was any piece of his heart he'd set aside for safekeeping, she owned it now. She owned all of him, destroyed him with nothing more than a few words and a soft gaze.

He drove into her with a new fury, as if he could join them forever if he plunged deep enough. She matched his every thrust, rolling her hips and squeezing him with her inner muscles as the tension built to the point of no return. Her moans grew strangled in a way that told him she'd climax at any moment.

"Stay with me," he panted. "Look at me when I make you come."

Half delirious, she nodded and kept their eyes locked. When her inner walls began to spasm, he slammed into her and let go, and they flew over the edge with a mingled cry of release. In that moment of shared ecstasy, Beau could swear that he saw into her soul.

He'd never felt anything like it.

When they came back down, he refused to release her—not even to turn off the bedroom light. If he had his way, he'd never let her go again. Rotating them to the side, he held her tightly in his arms, and they lay like that until sleep took them.

At several points during the night, they awoke to make love again—first in the bed, and then in the shower, and finally on the plush armchair before returning to the bed. Each time, Beau had demanded real intimacy from Devyn, and to his surprise, she didn't object. She gave herself to him freely, and by the sun's first rays, they were so tangled up in each other that Beau couldn't tell where she ended and he began.

The faint glow emanating from the window told Beau it was nearly time to get up, and a glance at the bedside alarm clock confirmed it. He muttered a curse and buried his nose in Devyn's curls, which smelled of his shampoo. It made him smile. He enjoyed the lingering evidence that she'd stayed here and used his things.

Used *him* in every way imaginable.

But that wasn't really true. She hadn't used him, not like before. What they'd shared last night was more than sex, and he couldn't wait to do it again. He loved waking up with her sleepy head resting on his chest and her faint snuffles punctuating the silence. And taking her whenever he wanted was pretty damned sweet, too. He'd had a perpetual woody since she'd knocked on his door in those flimsy pajamas.

Even now, after a night of erotic gluttony, he was stiff and growing more engorged by the second. To relieve the pressure, he thrust against Devyn's thigh, but it wasn't enough. Luckily for both of them, they had a little time to play.

Careful not to wake her, he teased her nipple through the bed sheet—a light circling of his thumb that puckered her to a tight point—while he bent to kiss her ear. When she woke up, he wanted her already wet and throbbing. It didn't take long before he got his wish. Devyn came to with a soft moan and rocked against his hip.

"Mornin'," he said against her temple.

"Mmm." Her greeting was more of a purr. She propped her chin on his chest and blinked at him with a smile that melted every organ inside his body. "What time is it?"

Beau turned her to the side and settled close behind,

then reached between her legs to stroke her with nothing but his fingertips. He was greeted with slick heat, and his chest rumbled in response. "Early enough," he said, thrusting against her gorgeous ass.

She made a lusty noise and guided his other hand to her breast. "You're a machine, Dumont."

He nibbled her shoulder and asked around his teeth, "Is that a problem?"

"There are no problems," she said while grinding her bottom against him. "Only opportunities."

Beau chuckled to himself. He'd said that to her during the first trying days in the education center. But he didn't want to think about work right now, not when he had a raging hard-on and Devyn's writhing body begging to take it all in.

"Open your legs for me," he murmured, tugging her outside knee.

When she parted her thighs, he nudged the tip of his erection inside and played at her entrance, feeding her desire with shallow strokes while he tickled her clitoris. He imagined she'd be tender this morning, and he didn't want to slam into her like an animal. So he let her set the pace, holding still while she backed onto his shaft one gentle inch at a time. When she was nearly seated at the base, he wrapped an arm around her and thrust deep.

Beau grunted as every nerve ending between his legs crackled alive. The sensations were almost too much to bear—the silken texture of Devyn's sex, her luscious scent, the breathy sounds of arousal rising from her throat. He held her closer and rode her faster, working her with his fingers because he wasn't going to last.

Her whimpers built to a cry of ecstasy as her secret muscles quaked around him. He followed her over the edge in a heart-stopping climax that left him slick with sweat and heaving for breath.

"God damn," he whispered once his voice had returned. "I swear it gets better every time."

Unable to speak, Devyn moaned in agreement.

The alarm beeped from the bedside table, and Beau silenced it with the side of his fist. He didn't want to leave the haven of this bed, but they'd never make it out of his suite if they didn't hit the shower soon. If past events were any indication, he'd be hard again in five minutes.

"Come on." He pushed to a sitting position and glanced down at her. She was sprawled on her back with a blush on her cheeks and a sheen of satisfaction in her eyes, her curly hair fanning across his pillow. It was a damned fine sight. "Let's get cleaned up, then grab some coffee."

Devyn groaned with a pouty lower lip, then broke into a stretch that arched her back off the mattress. Her nipples tightened, and Beau felt the hitch low in his gut. Jesus, she was too sexy for her own good. Maybe they had time for one more round. . . .

"Oh, no you don't." She must have read the desire

on his face, because she held up a finger and scooted to the opposite side of the bed. "You'll make us late." She winced as she stood from the mattress. "Plus, I'm sore in places I swear didn't exist before last night."

Beau couldn't stop a prideful grin from curving his mouth. He held up both hands in surrender. "I'll be on my best behavior."

"Liar." Devyn scanned the floor for her clothes, then gathered them up. "I'm not showering with you."

"Aw, come on, Kitten. Don't you want to conserve water? It's the environmentally responsible thing to do. . . ."

"Nice try," she said while stepping into her panties. "But I don't have a toothbrush or a change of clothes. It makes more sense to go back to my room while the halls are still quiet."

She was right, but Beau didn't like it. "Fine. But bring some things with you when you come back tonight."

Devyn paused with her tank top slung around her neck. She arched one brow. "Who said I was coming back tonight?"

Smiling, he darted up from the bed and captured her waist. He dragged her back and sank onto the mattress with her straddling his lap. Before she had a chance to wriggle free, he closed his mouth over one nipple and drew it in with gentle suction. He tugged her hips downward until her most sensitive spot brushed his, and within seconds, she was at his mercy.

"God, you're good," she whispered. When he released her nipple, she tipped their foreheads together and trailed her fingers through his hair. Her blue gaze was on fire with far more than simple lust—she glowed with the possibility of second chances. "Yes, Dumont. I'll be back."

Chapter 14

Just as Devyn rounded the corner and reached her room, Ella-Claire strode out the door looking bright-eyed, bushy-tailed, and ready for the day in her crisp white purser's uniform. The instant her gaze met Devyn's, she gripped one hip and smiled.

"Well, well, well," Ella said, purposely blocking the doorway. "There's my long lost roomie." With a teasing shake of her head, she assessed Devyn's wrinkled pajamas. "You naughty girl. I know the Walk of Shame when I see it. Do I even need to ask whose bed you shared last night? Or will Beau be wearing the same goofy smile as you?"

Devyn glanced up and down the hall, relieved to find it empty. "Say it a little louder, why don't you?" Despite her critical words, she couldn't stop herself from laughing. A night of nonstop orgasms tended to have that effect on a girl. "I don't think the people on the third floor heard all the dirty details."

All teasing stopped, and Ella-Claire pressed a heart-felt hand to her chest. "Look at you. You're glowing."

Devyn didn't doubt it. Only minutes ago, Beau'd had her nipple in his mouth while she straddled yet another one of his impressive erections. She touched her fingers to her cheeks, feeling the heat that infused them. "I need a cool shower."

"That won't help," Ella said. "You're in love with him."

Devyn's jaw dropped.

"Go ahead and deny it," Ella added in challenge. "But I won't believe a word. You've got it bad—both of you."

"Do me a favor and keep that talk to yourself. There's no reason to start throwing around labels," Devyn said as she nudged aside her nosy roommate and opened the door. "I need a shower."

Ella waggled her brows. "I'll bet you do." She waved and strode down the hall, calling over her shoulder, "I'd say *see you later*, but we both know you won't be sleeping here tonight."

Devyn didn't bother arguing. It was true—she would spend the night in Beau's bed. And the night after that, and probably all foreseeable nights to come. Beau had put a force on her, stronger than a jolt of electricity and twice as hot.

Was it love?

Devyn didn't know, and she didn't particularly care. Whatever this was, she wanted more of it—for however long it lasted. Which likely wouldn't be long, considering a Dumont man was involved. But she banished those thoughts, refusing to let them harsh her glow. She liked feeling giddy for a change, so she held on to her happiness tightly as she hopped into the shower, where she sang off-key without a care for who might overhear.

An hour later, she was styled to perfection, though the effects of her under-eye concealer could go only so far. She strode to the lower dining hall for a much-needed cup of coffee and stopped short at the entrance. Beau stood there waiting for her with a smile on his face and two cardboard cups in hand. His eyelids seemed heavier than usual, but the drowsy effect heightened his rugged, masculine appeal. Only he could look this hot after a night of sleep deprivation.

It wasn't fair.

Beau raised one cup. "Already got you covered. I thought we could drink our coffee on the deck."

Though touched by the gesture, Devyn eyed the cup with skepticism. She was picky about how she took her coffee. "Two creamers, three—"

"Three sugars, and a dash of vanilla syrup," he finished. "I know."

"Wow," she said, taking the cup and inhaling the heavenly scent of roasted beans and sweet vanilla. Based on the smell, he'd totally nailed it. "Impressive."

He wrapped an arm around her shoulder and guided her down the hall. "I've been paying attention."

That made her smile. She'd paid attention, too. "You

mostly drink yours black, but sometimes you dump in a random amount of sweetened creamer. Sometimes sugar, but not always." There was no rhyme or reason to his method.

"What can I say?" he asked while pushing open the door to the main deck. "I'm a man of mystery."

She laughed and preceded him outside, where a crisp morning breeze greeted her. The riverbank smelled of wood smoke and fallen leaves, a unique scent of autumn that got her pulse hitching in anticipation of football games and roasting turkeys. She rested a hand on the railing and gazed out at the churning water behind the paddle wheel.

"Trying to keep the ladies guessing?" she asked when Beau settled close beside her.

"Nope." He sipped his coffee and added, "Just one lady."

Devyn used her cup to hide a grin. "Oh, yeah? Is she special?"

Beau didn't answer right away, but then he used a large finger to tilt her face toward his. He kissed her in a light brush of lips and pulled back to offer that lopsided grin—the one that turned her insides to pudding every single time. "*Special* doesn't begin to describe her. She's spectacular."

Devyn's heart quivered. That's when she knew she was hooked far beyond the force of physical attraction. Scarier still, she didn't want to retreat. Beau had replaced her center of gravity, making it impossible to escape his pull, so she nestled into his embrace and they sipped their coffee in contented silence.

For the first time in over a decade, she felt truly at home.

"I want to talk about something," Devyn said that night as she crushed a bag of gingersnaps for her sister's apple streusel topping. She pointed the heavy wooden rolling pin at Allie. "But you have to promise not to give me any shit."

Allie held up a paring knife in oath, her fingers damp from slicing apples. "Consider this a Zero Shit Zone."

"Okay." Devyn blew out a breath. "I want to learn everything I can about Memère's curse on the Dumonts."

Allie rolled her eyes so hard she might have viewed her own brain. "Not this again."

"Hey! You promised."

With a resigned nod, Allie went back to chopping apples. "All right. We can talk about Memère's curse," then mumbled, "even though it's just superstition that snowballed into a multigenerational pattern of dysfunction."

Devyn snickered. "It's cute how you can't contain your psychobabble. Is there a name for that? Probably some kind of compulsive disorder . . ."

"Yeah, yeah," Allie said. "What do you want to know?"

"Everything you can tell me." All that Devyn recalled about the curse was that Edward Dumont had ditched Memère at the altar. In a fit of rage, Memère had hexed him with the words *Fickle love rots your family tree. None but purest faith shall set you free.* Beyond that, the woman left no instructions for breaking the curse.

Allie shrugged. "You read the old letter to Edward Dumont. Everything I know about the hex is in there."

"But what about Memère?" Devyn asked. "I want to know more about her—anything that will help me understand what she was thinking that day. Didn't you find her journal during the move to Marc's place?"

"Mmm-hmm."

"What was in it?"

Allie shivered as if someone had walked over her grave. "Scary stuff. Our great-great-grandma was *not* a nice lady."

"So what did Edward Dumont see in her?"

A wry smile lifted Allie's lips as she took a bite of apple. "He was a man. What do you think?"

"Ah." Devyn should have known. Some things never changed, like the power of mind-blowing sex. "It was hot between them?"

"Not just hot," Allie said. "According to her journal, she and Edward were *combustible beyond measure.*"

Devyn wolf-whistled. "You go, Memère!"

"From there," Allie continued, "it turned to love. But Edward's family didn't approve of the match. They came from old money, and I guess Memère wasn't pedigreed enough for them. She didn't write a lot about it, but from what I gather, it took a while for her to convince Edward that they could be happy without his family's blessing."

"Let me guess," Devyn said. "Edward's family threatened to cut him out of the will."

Allie shook her head. "She didn't say. All she wrote was that they agreed to marry in secret, and after the wedding day, she never wrote about him again. Not a single word." Allie gave a sad sigh. "But I noticed a difference in the tone of her entries. After that, she was just so . . ."

"Angry?"

"More like bitter. She stopped making love charms for a while. The only reason she started again was because it was her biggest moneymaker. I'm surprised she ever got married."

While Devyn rolled her wooden pin over another bag of gingersnaps, she processed what she'd learned about Memère, stretching out the scant information like saltwater taffy to gain more insight into the hex. One detail stood out to Devyn—Memère had to convince Edward that they didn't need his family's blessing. It implied that their approval meant a lot to him, or perhaps it was their money he cared about. Either way, he'd turned his back on love because he feared it wasn't enough.

Purest faith shall set you free.

Edward Dumont had lacked faith in love.

But how was that knowledge going to help Beau?

When it came to matters of the heart, he was fearless. He'd held nothing back. In fact, he'd been pushing for more since he came back to town. He seemed to genuinely want a future with her.

For now, Devyn thought. *There's no telling what he'll do in the end.*

She'd never expected him to bolt after graduation, and he had claimed to love her then. Maybe his faith wasn't as strong as she assumed.

"Does any of that help?" Allie asked, drawing Devyn back to present company.

Devyn gave her bag of gingersnaps one final whack before tossing it aside and releasing a long sigh. "Not really."

"You're overthinking this." Allie offered an apple slice, but Devyn waved it off. "Beau's a changed man, and he's obviously crazy about you. Why not give him another chance and see where it goes?"

That was easy for Allie to say—she didn't believe in the curse. "Because that'd just be a temporary fix. Why should I get more attached to him if he decides to cut and run again?"

If she wanted to be with him in the long term—and that was a big *if*—then they had to break the hex.

"Hon, listen." Allie rested a sticky hand on Devyn's shoulder, then realized what she'd done and pulled it back. "I know you want to control the outcome, but you can't. There's no curse—and there's no mystical cure-all that will make your fears disappear. You've got to trust Beau. He might hurt you again, or he might make you deliriously happy. You'll never know unless you try."

"But—"

Allie flashed a palm. "No *buts*. Love's always a risk."

Devyn didn't care what Allie said; the curse was real. Just look at Beau's mama—for nearly three decades, she'd been risking her heart for his father. And what good did it do? She was alone, pining after him while he shacked up with a woman half his age—a woman pregnant with his sixth child. Allie was definitely right about one thing: Devyn couldn't control the outcome.

And she hated that.

She finished the streusel topping, then wrapped up a few cookies and tucked them in her pocket to take to Beau. After swinging by her room for her backpack— which she'd stuffed with clean clothes and toiletries— she set off for his suite. If she couldn't control forever, she'd enjoy the here and now.

Halfway to the stairwell, she passed Alex, who she imagined was headed for her room. To save him the effort she said, "Ella's not in there."

Alex came to a slow halt, his shoulders hunched as he exhaled a long breath. "Of course she's not. She's avoiding me like I'm a case of herpes."

Devyn took a step toward the stairwell, but the dejection in his voice stopped her. The last thing she wanted to do was get in the middle of someone else's drama—she had enough of her own—and yet she couldn't leave him. Not like this.

"Want to talk about it?" she asked.

"No," he said, then immediately contradicted himself. "But has she told you anything? Like what I did to make her so mad? I don't know how to fix this, because she won't talk to me. I don't even pass her in the hall anymore. It's like she's invisible."

Figuring they should keep their voices low, Devyn joined him and leaned against the wall. "Well, you know she wants more than friendship, right?"

Another sigh. "Yeah."

"I can tell you're attracted to her," Devyn said. "But does it go any deeper than that? Do you love her?"

Alex looked at her with those deep blue eyes, and for a moment, his face transformed. His gaze turned soft. A half smile formed on his lips, tugging a dimple into view. It was easy to see how Ella-Claire had fallen for him.

"She means the world to me," he said.

"That doesn't answer my question," Devyn pointed out. "Ella-Claire wants to hear those three magical words."

No longer the lovesick puppy dog, Alex sniffed a laugh, his eyes dancing with mischief. "*Put it anywhere*? Those are my three favorite words."

Devyn shook her head at the pervert, doing her best not to laugh because she didn't want to encourage him. "You're such a Dumont."

"Thanks."

"It wasn't a compliment." Folding her arms, she delivered a stern look. "Let's get back on track."

"Okay," he said with an apologetic wave. "Go ahead."

"Ella told me all the reasons you want to stay in the Friend Zone, and believe me, I understand. You made some good points. I actually agree with you."

Alex's blond brows jumped. "Finally, someone who gets it!"

"I do," she assured him with a pat on the arm. "But none of that matters, because love isn't logical. Ella-Claire can't just turn off her feelings and be your best friend again. She can't watch you move on with someone else. It's too painful."

He fell silent for a few beats. "But I'm not dating anyone."

"For now," she said. Seeing how young and attractive Alex was, Devyn knew he wouldn't stay single for long. And neither would Ella. "Put yourself in her shoes. Do you want to think about her in bed with another man?"

Alex thrust forward a palm as if to block the image. "Don't put those kinds of thoughts in my head!"

"Maybe that's part of the problem. You think she'll always stick around because you don't see her as a grown woman with needs and desires." While he processed that, she added, "Bottom line: the two of you can't be friends. Either you're in, or you're out, so figure out what you want and make peace with the consequences. Because no matter what you choose, there will be consequences."

Alex stared at the carpet between his feet. Since he

clearly had some soul-searching to do, she gave him one of Beau's cookies and left him alone with his thoughts.

She jogged up the stairs two at a time and found herself bouncing on her toes when she reached Beau's door. A surge of butterflies tickled her chest when he answered, and she saw her excitement reflected in his honest smile. He was still in uniform, but he'd removed his tie and unbuttoned his dress shirt to midchest. She'd never seen anyone more handsome, even with those ridiculous sunglasses resting atop his head.

"It's about time," he said, glancing at his watch. "I think you enjoy torturing me."

In consolation, she handed over the remaining cookie— white chocolate macadamia nut, his favorite. "I came as fast as I could."

He took the cookie and devoured it in two bites. "You're forgiven," he said with his mouth full, then ushered her inside his suite.

Devyn stood on tiptoe and pulled the sunglasses off his head. "What is it with you and these things? Was the glare inside the casino too blinding?"

After washing down his cookie with a swig of bottled water, he shrugged out of his dress jacket and slung it onto the nearest chair. "I covered the afternoon shift in the pilothouse. Marc's backup guy got sick, and until we know whether it's contagious, we're quarantining him to his room."

"Ah. Good thinking." In such close quarters, stomach bugs ran rampant on ships like this one. She tossed his sunglasses onto his discarded dress jacket and asked, "Do you like piloting the boat?"

He shrugged. "It's a nice change, but I don't really—"

"Care what the job is," Devyn finished. "You just like being here with your family."

Beau grinned. "You probably think that's cheesy."

She closed the distance between them and threaded her fingers behind his broad neck. Beau didn't have any wild career ambitions or a hunger for power. He'd made the people he loved the priority in his life, and she thought that was sexy as hell.

"There's nothing cheesy about you, Dumont." She rose up to kiss him and then said, "*Saucy*, maybe. But not cheesy."

From somewhere in the distance, a woman's voice crooned, smooth and slow, and the sounds of jazz filtered into the room. Devyn rested a cheek on Beau's chest and listened to the song for a few sultry beats.

"Live music from the main deck," Beau said.

"Mmm."

He took her hand in his and wrapped an arm around her waist, drawing her nearer. Then he led her in a dance—a lazy sway with their feet barely moving across the floor. It was more of a caress than anything else, but Devyn didn't mind. In fact, she liked it. Any excuse to be close to Beau was good enough for her.

When the song ended, he kissed her forehead and murmured, "I've been thinking about the curse."

She tipped back her head to study him, but he stared

across the room, his expression blank. "About what, specifically?"

"I still want you to help me break it." He met her gaze, and there was no mistaking the concern etched onto his striking features. "It took a long time to get another chance with you. I don't want anything driving us apart again."

The old Devyn would have said Beau was getting ahead of himself, that she hadn't promised him anything beyond a full night in his bedroom. But he'd changed her. Now she shared his hope. She didn't want their time together to end.

"I'm doing my best," she said, then told him what she'd learned about Edward Dumont. "Love wasn't enough for him. That's where the *purest faith* line came from. But I don't know how else I can help. I can't make you believe, not deep down, the way it counts."

He didn't say anything after that, just gathered her to his chest and smoothed a hand over her hair while they finished their dance. The music stopped, and he wordlessly peeled off her clothes.

When he took her to bed, he loved her stronger than before. Not hard enough to hurt her, but with a passion that took her by surprise. He withheld his own climax for what seemed like hours as he made her come again and again. It wasn't until she was too weak to wrap her legs around his waist that he finally let go. After, he held her tightly throughout the night. Devyn wasn't sure what to make of his behavior.

Either Beau had absolutely no faith in their future, or enough to last a lifetime.

Chapter 15

"Here you go." Devyn signed the elementary school vacation form and handed it to Will, then scrawled her signature on the middle school version and slid it across the table to his older brother, Jason. "I can honestly say that you two learned a lot on this trip." She winked. "And that you were a pleasure to have in class. I'm going to miss you guys."

"Me, too," Will said with an adorable gap-toothed grin. "Since it's our last day, can we play *Super Mario World*?"

"I want to crush some more Coke cans," Jason added. "Can we do that, too?"

"Anything you want," she said. "It's your party."

Devyn poured the contents of two soda cans into paper cups for the brothers, then invited them to dig into the pizza she'd special-ordered from the galley. Since the boat would dock in New Orleans in a few hours, most parents had elected to keep their children.

Which meant Devyn and the boys had the education center to themselves to celebrate in style.

Well, in twelve-year-old-boy style.

But she'd come to appreciate the *beep beep bwoop* noises of *Mario World* and the laughter of her two favorite students. She had forgotten how much fun children could be, and she hated for the trip to end.

While sinking her teeth into a slice of pepperoni pizza, she darted a glance at the front of the room, where rows of windows looked out into the hallway. Beau had promised to eat lunch with them, but he was twenty minutes late. She pulled out her cell phone and sent him a quick text.

The pizza was getting cold, so we started without you. There's still plenty left, and I'm wearing that lace-up corset dress you like . . .

A few minutes later, he replied. *Sorry, can't make it. It's madness at the purser's desk. I'm stuck here for a while, but have an extra slice for me.*

Devyn's heart sank. In the grand scheme of things, lunch in the education center was no biggie, but she couldn't shake the feeling that something was wrong. A shadow of unease had gradually crept over her all day, similar to the heaviness in the air before a storm. Her instincts told her trouble was brewing, and she was rarely wrong.

She and Beau had discussed what would happen when the *Belle* docked. They would continue to see each other. In fact, they'd scheduled a date tomorrow night to listen to a jazz band at Beau's favorite bar.

They'd even had the big exclusivity talk—no easy feat for any couple. There was no reason to worry.

But Devyn couldn't help it. She was worried.

She forced the prickle of anxiety to the back of her mind and gave the brothers her full attention. After stuffing themselves with pizza and ice cream sundaes, the boys parked in front of the Nintendo, and she cheered them on through a dozen levels. Then she let Jason hold the tongs during the steam-powered can-crushing experiment.

The afternoon passed in a whirlwind of games, crafts, and dress-up, and the next thing Devyn knew, the boys' mother came to sign them out. One quick hug from Will and a wave from Jason, and then they were gone.

Devyn stood facing the door for a few beats, stunned by the abrupt quiet.

Slowly, she turned and surveyed the center, starting with the empty travel cribs on the far wall and ending on the opposite side of the room, where a pile of historic dress-up clothes rested beside two decimated Coke cans.

Her stomach grew heavy, and she found herself hesitating to clean up the mess. It wasn't until the boat came to a stop that she tossed Jason's soda cans into the recycling bin and put away Will's silk top hat and vest. She disposed of their leftover food and dishes, then tidied the room until there was no choice but to leave.

With a sigh, she closed the door and returned to her room to pack.

Now that all the passengers had left, an eerie silence

descended over the *Belle* like fog creeping across a graveyard. Gone were the constant footsteps and the rumble of the steam engine, the sounds of laughter and the paddle wheel's steady whir. It was strange how quickly she'd grown accustomed to the motion and noise. Her room key seemed unnaturally loud when she slid it into the lock and opened the door.

She stopped short.

A travel suitcase rested on the bottom cot, and Ella-Claire bent over it, punching handfuls of dirty clothes inside with enough force to shake the bunk bed. She snatched a toiletry bag from the dresser and threw it on top of the laundry, where it bounced off and tumbled to the floor.

"Shit," the girl muttered, then simply stood and hung her head.

Devyn had never known her roommate to swear . . . or abuse cosmetics. It looked like Alex had come to a decision, but not the one Ella-Claire had hoped for. Devyn picked up the cosmetics bag and tucked it inside the suitcase. "What did he say?"

Ella drew a hitched breath and blew it out, clearly hanging on by a thread. "Exactly what I expected him to say. He cares for me, but we can only be friends."

"Aw, hon." Devyn held out her arms and Ella rushed inside, promptly breaking down in sobs. While Ella's shoulders shook, Devyn rubbed her back and made gentle shushing noises. "I'm so sorry. Love sucks."

Ella nodded, then drew back and used a shirtsleeve to dab at her eyes. "I'll drink to that."

"If it makes you feel any better, I can tell from the way Alex talks about you that he's completely smitten."

"It doesn't help," Ella said. "If anything, that makes it worse. He knows we could be happy together, but he won't try because he doesn't want to upset his family. It means I'm not enough for him."

Chills broke out at the base of Devyn's neck. She'd heard this story before—from the pages of her great-great-grandmother's journal. Devyn had originally sympathized with Alex's concerns, but now she saw the real problem.

"He doesn't have faith in love," Devyn said blankly. She couldn't believe she hadn't seen it before. "And you can't fix that."

Ella braced both palms on the dresser and stared at her reflection in the mirror. "What am I going to do?" Her voice was a thick whisper, so devoid of hope that it put a lump in Devyn's throat. "I love this job, but how can I stay here? Seeing him every day is going to kill me."

"Hey, now," Devyn said. She gripped her friend's hand and gave it a fortifying squeeze. "I know it hurts, but a broken heart never killed anyone."

Ella laughed without humor. "Yet."

"This is what you're going to do." Meeting Ella's gaze in the mirror, Devyn kept her tone firm in an unspoken message of strength. "Call your very best friends to come over, and tell them to bring chocolate and booze. Then take the weekend to wallow. Lock yourself inside your apartment and eat Ben & Jerry's for breakfast.

Watch sad movies. Sing Alanis Morissette songs. Yell, cry, draw mustaches on Alex's pictures—whatever makes you feel better. But when the weekend is over, it's time to suck it up and rejoin the living."

Ella nodded, and another tear spilled free.

"You're such a sweet girl." Devyn gave her friend's ponytail a light tug. "Don't let this change you."

"Thanks for the support," Ella said with a sniffle. "But maybe a change is exactly what I need."

Devyn asked what she meant by that, but Ella smoothly switched the subject to Beau, so they packed their bags while swapping old stories about him. When Devyn had finished clearing out her things, she hugged Ella one more time.

"Stay strong," Devyn said. "And call me. In fact, let's meet for drinks next week."

"It's a date."

"I know you're not a hardcore believer," Devyn said, "but if you want me to read the bones for you or mix a special gris-gris bag, just say the word."

"I might take you up on that." She smiled weakly. "Thanks, Devyn. I'm glad we got to know each other."

"Me, too," Devyn said, and meant it.

After donning a pair of sunglasses to hide her puffy eyes, Ella wheeled her suitcase out the door. Then she was gone, too.

Devyn's shoulders slumped.

This was like graduation day all over again, her favorite people parting ways. Sure, many of them were local, but how often would their paths cross once life interfered? She was lucky if she saw her own sister once a week.

At least she had an evening with Beau to look forward to. And since he'd promised her a ride home, she grabbed her backpack and duffel and set off to find him.

Twenty minutes later—after a wasted trip to his suite, the casino, the purser's office, and the pilothouse—she took a seat on one of the main deck rocking chairs and texted for him to meet her there.

Lulled by the warm breeze and the sounds of water slapping against the boat, Devyn lost track of time. A while later, she recognized the heavy clomp of Beau's shoes coming down the outside staircase and she glanced over her shoulder to wave at him.

He looked a little worse for wear with his tie crooked and his hair mussed. A pen was tucked precariously behind one ear, competing for space beside the sunglasses perched on top of his head, and he had a yellow Post-it note stuck to his sleeve. But despite the obvious rough day, his eyes shone bright with excitement when he spotted her.

Devyn returned his infectious smile, relieved by his reaction. "Either you had a great day," she told him, "or you're really glad it's over. Which one?"

Chuckling, Beau pulled the pen from behind his ear. "Neither," he said as his gaze landed on the laces of her corset dress. He used his pen to point at her. "But it's getting better by the second."

Devyn teasingly dragged an index finger down the

length of her laces. "Take me home, and you can finally undo these with your teeth."

He sucked in an apologetic breath. "I'll have to take a rain check. There's an avalanche of paperwork, time sheets, and accounting reports to deal with. As soon as I drop you off, I've got to come right back. I'll probably spend the next couple of nights here, too." He lowered to her height and cupped her cheek. "Sorry, Kitten."

"No, it's fine." That familiar sensation of worry crept over her again, but she forced it back. Beau wasn't making excuses. There was work to be done. "Are we still on for tomorrow night?" When he blinked in confusion, she reminded him, "The jazz band."

"Oh, right." He smacked his forehead. "Yeah, we're good. I can get away for a few hours."

"We can cancel, if you want."

"No," he insisted. "I wouldn't miss it."

"If you're sure . . ."

"One thousand percent."

There was just one thing Devyn didn't understand. If Beau's chaotic day was about to stretch into the week from hell, why was he smiling? He wasn't getting laid for at least forty-eight hours. If anything, he should be in tears.

"Not that I'm complaining, but why the happy face?" she asked. "When you came down here, it looked like you had good news."

"I do." He slung her backpack over one shoulder and grabbed her duffel, then laced their fingers together and led her toward the bow ramp. "Awesome news. This is going to change everything."

Devyn wasn't sure she liked the sound of that, but she tried to match his excitement. "Don't keep me in suspense."

"I just finished talking to Allie."

"Oh, yeah? About what?"

"About you."

When she slid him a wary glance, he explained, "You know, your issues with going back to college."

Devyn resisted the urge to roll her eyes. "Yes, and as you pointed out, they're *my* issues. I appreciate your concern, but you and my sister need to mind your own—"

"You haven't heard the best part," he interrupted. "I was thinking of ways I could help, and then I realized that since Allie moved in with Marc, her old apartment above the bakery is empty."

"I could have told you that. She's going to rent it to the—"

"No, she's not." Beau squeezed their linked hands. "I talked her into letting you stay there for free."

Devyn stumbled and came to a clumsy halt. "You did what?"

"Think about it," he said. "You're part owner of the shop, so it makes sense to let you crash there. Now you can move out of your place and use that money for tuition." He grinned so widely it crinkled the skin around his eyes. "You don't have to worry about rent until after you graduate."

Like she'd taken a soccer ball to the stomach, Devyn struggled to draw breath. She'd hidden her money problems from Allie for good reason, and it was mortifying to think that Beau had disclosed something so sensitive behind her back. Her cheeks flushed hot when she imagined what he'd probably said—how her car had been repossessed and the rent was a month overdue. That she could barely support herself, even though she was pushing thirty.

Did Beau and Allie think she needed a handout?

"I can't believe you did that," she finally said.

Beau beamed, clearly pleased with himself. "It was no big deal."

"No." She jerked free from his grasp. "I can't believe you went to my sister and begged for charity. Do you have any idea how that makes me feel?"

His smile disappeared.

"If I'd wanted to stay at the bakery," she continued, her voice rising a notch, "I would have asked Allie myself. But I didn't. And there's a reason for that." Living in her own rental house, even with its sagging front porch and a back door that didn't lock, gave her some semblance of integrity. Of independence. She had no intention of giving that up. "Who the hell do you think you are?"

"Dev." Still dazed, Beau shook his head. "I had no idea that—"

"I might not have a car," she ground out. "Or nice furniture or fancy clothes. And yes, I'm a little behind on the bills. But that doesn't mean I want a knight in shining armor to ride to my rescue. I don't need a hero!"

"I wasn't trying to be a—"

"Bullshit!" She held an index finger an inch from his nose. "That's exactly what you're trying to do—fix all my problems. I'm not a child."

How could he see this as anything other than an act of betrayal? Beau should have come to her with his idea instead of going over her head. Besides, she'd told him in no uncertain terms that she wasn't returning to college. "Damn it, I don't want to go back to school, and that's my decision to make. Not yours. Mine!"

He dropped her duffel bag and splayed both hands. "But you were happy in the education center. I can tell you don't want to lead cemetery tours for that Warren guy."

"So what?" she demanded. "The decision is still mine."

"But part of that decision had to do with money. I thought if we removed that obstacle . . ."

"No. There is no *we* in this choice." The longer she stood there watching his dumbfounded expression, the higher her blood pressure climbed. He still had no clue what he'd done wrong, so she said, "Don't think that because we're sleeping together, you get to make life decisions for me."

"I don't think that!"

"You know what? Forget it." She sighed, holding out her hand. "Give me my backpack."

He furrowed his brow, thumbing toward the parking lot. "Stop it, Dev. Let me drive you home."

When he didn't surrender the backpack, she wrestled it away from him. It took a few tries, but he eventually gave up the fight and let her jerk it from his shoulder. "I'm taking a cab."

"Don't be ridiculous. You know how far Cedar Bayou—"

She cut him off with a fierce glare and said, "I swear to God, if you say that I don't have money to waste on a taxi, I will turn you from a bull to a heifer with one kick." The corset dress didn't allow much range of motion, but she could work around that. "Don't test me, Dumont!"

Wisely, Beau shut his mouth and handed her the duffel bag. He didn't say a word or chase after her when she stormed off the boat, another smart move on his part.

Without looking back, Devyn continued across the dock parking lot and crossed the street toward the French Quarter. She would never admit it, but Beau was right—she couldn't afford a taxi ride to Cedar Bayou. As soon as she was out of sight of the *Belle*, she pulled out her cell phone and sent a text to her sister.

DON'T MENTION THIS TO BEAU, but I need a ride home. I'll be at the Sweet Spot. Meet me there as soon as you can. PS: Thanks, but I'm not taking the apartment.

Devyn pocketed her phone and set off for the bakery, hoping the staff had plenty of freshly baked brown sugar pecan scones. She was going to need one. Or a dozen.

Beau scrubbed a hand over his face and checked the clock on the purser's office wall. He felt like he'd been running accounts for a week, but only two hours had passed since Devyn's explosive tirade. He couldn't focus on profits and losses while the image of her icy-blue glare burned behind his retinas. Groaning, he pushed away a stack of paperwork and rotated his neck to disperse the tension that had his muscles tangled in knots.

Marc glanced up from his laptop, then studied Beau with a shit-eating grin. "I heard you got your ass handed to you by your girlfriend. Do you need a hug?"

Beau flashed a hand gesture that told his little brother exactly what he could do with that hug. "Who told you that?"

"Let's see . . ." Marc peered at the ceiling in contemplation. "I heard it from Alex, who heard it from Nicky, who heard it from a housekeeper he's probably banging, who heard it from a server, who heard it from the porter that saw the whole thing."

"Jesus," Beau muttered while pinching his temples. "This place is worse than high school."

"That's not the best part," Marc said with a smirk that was going to get his ass kicked if he didn't knock it off. "According to the entertainment staff, the whole thing was your fault."

"Mine?" Beau asked, pointing at himself. Unbelievable. That old saying was true: no good deed went unpunished. "How do they figure I'm the bad guy?"

"Well, that's where the story breaks down. One version says you got busted sweet-talking a dancer from the stage show, and another claims it was a guest," he said, his grin widening. "But I know you better than that. I think you opened that big trap of yours, and something moronic tumbled out. How close am I?"

Folding his arms, Beau leaned back in his chair and returned his brother's sneer. "You're off by a mile, as usual."

Marc swept a permissive hand over his laptop. "Then enlighten me."

"You know what my big crime was?" Beau asked, secretly glad for the opportunity to talk through his frustrations. He'd tried tracking down Allie, but she'd left an hour ago to run an errand. "I tried to help Dev achieve her dream." He released a humorless laugh while holding up both palms like a robbery victim. "Get a rope and call the lynch mob."

"Mmm-hmm." The twist of Marc's lips said he wasn't convinced. "What would she say if I asked for her side of the story?"

Beau could still hear the fury in Devyn's voice. Tension began clawing a ragged trail into his head, and he reminded himself to unclench his jaw. "She's stubborn."

"You didn't answer my question."

Beau puffed a sigh. "She'd say it's none of my business." Which, if you asked him, was ass backward. He cared for Devyn, so of course her happiness was his business—it was at the top of his priority list. As it should be.

"Why don't you tell me exactly what you did to *help?*" Marc said. "Then I'll tell you where you went wrong."

"Fine." Beau supposed it couldn't hurt to get an outside opinion. So he told his brother everything, starting with what happened at the Cedar Bayou reunion, where he learned how much financial trouble Devyn had fallen into.

"That's why I offered her a job in the education center," he said, then went on to explain her transformation working with the kids.

Everything was going fine until he told Marc, "Money's the biggest problem in getting her back to college, so I started thinking of ways to handle her expenses. . . ."

But when he said the words out loud, it kind of sounded like he'd overstepped his boundaries. That's when Beau felt the first pinprick of awareness in the gut, a needling sensation that told him he might have made a mistake. Money was a touchy subject. If he were the one with no cash, would he want Devyn brainstorming solutions for him—and talking to other people about it?

"And?" Marc prompted.

"Uh," Beau stammered. "So I talked with Allie. . . ."

Suddenly a new image of Devyn flashed in his mind, not the furious diva who'd threatened his manhood before stomping off the boat, but the wide-eyed beauty blinking up at him in shock. *I can't believe you went to my sister and begged for charity. Do you have any idea how that makes me feel?*

"Aaaaand?" Marc prompted again.

"Shit," Beau said, letting his head drop into his hands. For the first time, he saw how clearly he'd missed the mark. He'd gone to Allie with the purest of intentions, but in doing so, he'd taken the power from Devyn and had embarrassed her in the process. Of course she was angry. She had every right to be. "I'm an idiot."

Marc nodded and said, "Glad I could help you reach that conclusion." He tapped his cell phone and held it forward to display the red RECORD button. "Can you say that again? I'm sure you'll give me a reason to replay this soon enough."

The teasing words flew to the periphery of Beau's mind. He looked back and forth from the piles of paperwork to Marc. "Think you can handle this? I've got to go find her and apologize."

His brother considered the request for a few silent beats. "You know that private booking we've got in a couple weeks?"

"The big wedding?"

"Yeah," Marc said, pointing at the ledgers. "I'll run these reports if you'll pilot the boat during the charter. Allie and I are overdue for some time off."

For a fleeting moment, it occurred to Beau that trading one night of work for an entire weekend of nonstop responsibility wasn't a fair shake, but he wasn't exactly in a position to negotiate. "It's a deal."

"Sweet." Marc rubbed his palms together, then pointed a finger at Beau. "You're off the hook tonight. Have fun groveling."

Beau speared his brother with a glare. "Real helpful. I don't remember giving you this much shit when you mucked it up with Allie. In fact, I called in a bunch of favors to track her down in Vegas."

"You know I'm just yanking your chain," Marc said. "Good luck, man. How hard did you screw the pooch?"

Well, he'd wounded Devyn's pride, so . . . "DEF-CON one."

Marc winced. "Might want to swing by the jeweler's on your way to Devyn's place. Richman's stays open late. Tell them to show you the estate pieces—Allie's crazy about that stuff."

That wasn't a bad idea. "Thanks. I'll do that."

"See you tomorrow," Marc said, his tone growing serious. "And don't sweat this. Anyone with eyes can tell Devyn's crazy about you. Whatever you did, I'm sure the damage isn't as bad as you think."

Beau grabbed his phone and wallet, nodding in agreement. He'd worked too hard for a second chance with Devyn to give up now. One way or another, he'd fix this.

Chapter 16

Before Devyn even unlocked the front door, she dropped her duffel bag and used her bare hands to pry the MAUVAISVOODOO.COM sign off the outside wall. Her grunts and swears drew a few curious gazes from the sidewalk, but she didn't care. With an extra tug, most of the sign tore free, leaving the plastic corners firmly nailed to the siding. That was good enough for her. She marched to the side of the porch and chucked the sign into the recycling bin.

Once she let herself inside, she leaned against the door and stared blankly into the living area, where nothing but the faint drone of the refrigerator greeted her. If she thought the *Belle* was quiet, that was nothing compared to the void she faced in her own home. The scents of sacred oils and herbs from the dressed candles nearby brought a moment's relief, but a wave of loneliness soon swept it away.

She missed Beau.

Make no mistake, he still wasn't forgiven. But she

and Allie had stopped for drinks on the long drive home, which had given her time to cool off. She couldn't forget Allie's parting words: *Go easy on him, okay? He went about it the wrong way, but his heart was in the right place. He's not happy unless you're happy. When you think about it, the whole thing is actually kind of sweet.*

Devyn disagreed on the last point—there was nothing *sweet* about humiliation—but honestly, she knew she'd overreacted. And now that she'd had time to think about it, she understood that Beau had touched a nerve. He was right; she didn't want to lead graveyard tours, and bringing it up had triggered an eruption of negative emotions. But no matter what he said, college wasn't in the cards for her. The haunted tour was her best option.

Maybe she should call Warren Larabee to ask for a raise. Since she was going to debase herself for a living, she might as well make decent money doing it.

She was halfway to the coffee table to retrieve his business card when a knock sounded from the front porch. Figuring it was Allie, she swiveled on her heel and threw open the door.

But it wasn't her sister.

Beau held forward a bundle of orange gerbera daisies, her favorite. He wore an apology on his face—written in the creases between his eyes and the downward pull of his mouth. Even his broad shoulders slouched in contrition. He couldn't have looked more regretful if he'd tried, but he spoke the words anyway. "I'm awful sorry, Dev."

Just like that, all of Devyn's residual anger melted. She met him on the porch and stood on tiptoe to wrap both arms around his neck. The crinkle of cellophane warned she was crushing the flowers, but neither of them minded. Beau embraced her with enough force to lift her feet off the planks. He carried her inside the house, then kicked the door shut and held her close, his nose buried deep in her curls as if they'd been apart for a century instead of a few hours.

They clung to each other for a while, until Beau apologized again and told her what an idiot he'd been. Devyn pulled back to look at him, taking his face between her hands.

"I'm sorry, too," she said. "I shouldn't have blown up at you like that."

He lowered her feet to the floor and tossed the flowers onto the end table. "I can't believe I went to Allie without talking to you first. Baby, I swear I didn't—"

"I know." She held a finger to his lips. "You didn't mean any harm."

"That's not an excuse."

No, it wasn't. But Devyn needed to put the scuffle behind them. She couldn't stand it when she and Beau were at odds. "Let's forget it, okay? I don't want to fight."

"Me neither." Beau took her by the hand and led her to the sofa, where he settled as close to her as he could get. He kept her hand and pressed it between both of his, peering at her with a new intensity that made her tummy flutter. "I've been thinking. . . ."

When he trailed off, she nodded for him to continue.

"About us." He licked his lips nervously. "About our past, and more important, our future."

"Okaaay," she said, drawing out the word because she didn't know where he was going with this.

"Dev, this is going to sound crazy, but bear with me." Drawing a deep breath, he reached into his coat pocket and produced a black felt jewelry box. He opened it, and then time stood still. Because nestled in the box was a gleaming platinum ring. And not just any ring. A round diamond solitaire—at least two carats with the chunky facets of an old miner cut. It caught the meager light from the window and sprayed prisms onto Devyn's lap.

She stared at the ring and stopped breathing. Beau was right; he'd lost his mind.

"I want to get married," he told her. He must have noticed the lack of movement in her chest, because he squeezed her hand and ordered, "Inhale."

She filled her lungs, but she couldn't manage to blink. Her gaze remained fixed on the sparkling stone that had just turned her world upside down. Like the oleander blossom, it was beautiful but dangerous. A commitment like this—and at such an early stage in their relationship—could ruin everything. What was Beau thinking? They'd been together for only a week, and a tumultuous one at that.

"Just hear me out." He set the ring box on the coffee table. When her gaze followed it, he cupped her chin and turned her to face him. His eyes warmed with a sincerity she couldn't ignore, so she laced their fingers together and gave him the benefit of the doubt.

"I'm listening," she said.

"Devyn, I love you." His announcement was firm and clear, so full of certainty that it made her pulse jump. "I didn't always do a good job of showing it, but I'm not that boy anymore." He brought their linked hands to his chest, where his heart pounded every bit as fiercely as hers. "We spent a lot of time apart, and in all those years, I never loved anyone but you. I couldn't hide from my feelings. Every night, it was your face I saw when I closed my eyes. You haunted me."

Devyn's bottom lip trembled and her vision went blurry. She had never admitted it, but he'd haunted her, too. She'd spent their decade apart with a steady rotation of filler boyfriends, but none of them could make her forget Beau. No matter how hard she'd tried to exorcise his memory, the image of his crooked smile and the echo of his laughter had lingered like a stain on her soul.

"Do you love me?" he asked.

A tear spilled free when she nodded, her voice a wet whisper. "Yes."

He smiled as if he'd glimpsed heaven. "I want to hear it."

She cleared the thickness from her throat. "I love you, Beau. That's not the problem. I never stopped."

"Then marry me." In one brisk motion, he dropped to one knee. His grasp on her hand was warm and strong, full of promise. "I already know you're the one

I want. If you feel the same way, then why should we wait? Let's start our life together, right now."

"Right now?" A sudden dizziness swirled at her temples. She'd barely walked in the front door—hadn't even changed out of her costume—and Beau was proposing that they elope?

"Well, not right now," he corrected with a laugh. "We'll have to get a marriage license, and then I imagine there's a few days' waiting period, but still . . ."

A sobering thought occurred to Devyn. She'd seen this same light in Beau's eyes after graduation, when they'd planned their future together and sealed it with a night of wild lovemaking. She'd believed him then, and his change of heart had come with no warning—an abrupt shift that had knocked the wind out of her for years to come. She couldn't let that happen again. It would kill her.

"Maybe we should slow down," she said. "I don't want you to wake up tomorrow and regret anything. If we're right for each other, there's no reason to—"

He cut her off with a soft kiss. When he broke away, he delivered a sober look that said he understood her fears. "I won't run away again, Dev. I'm not a naïve kid who's excited about playing house with his girlfriend. I'm a grown man who wants you for my life partner." He squeezed her hand tightly. "The curse won't stop me this time, because I have all the faith in the world that we're meant to be."

Devyn hesitated. She wanted to trust him, and yet . . .

"Baby, I give you my word," he said. "I'll never leave. I'd sooner cut off my right arm than hurt you."

"I don't know." She glanced at the glittering diamond tucked into its velvet bed and then back to Beau, searching for something she couldn't name.

He placed her palm above his heart. "If there's one perfect truth in this world, it's that we were made for each other. Let me show you. Please marry me."

Devyn's blood chilled with doubt, but she couldn't say no. She wanted to believe him more than she wanted the sun to rise. Extending her left hand, she told him, "All right. I'll marry you."

"Really?" His face broke into a smile of sheer joy, and in the span of a few heartbeats, he had the ring on her finger. The platinum felt surprisingly cold and heavy, but Devyn told herself she'd get used to it. "I'm going to make you so happy," he promised. "Starting right now."

Before she had a chance to ask how long he could stay, he delivered a slow, drugging kiss that had her skin flushing with fever. Still kneeling, he parted her thighs and situated himself in between, then his fingers went to work on the corset laces of her bodice.

She broke from the kiss and helped him out of his jacket. "What about your paperwork?"

"Forget it," he said, admiring the line of cleavage displayed beneath the first loose stays. "I'm yours for the whole night." Then he bent to her ear, whispering, "And every night after that for the rest of my life."

Or at least until he gets bored with me.

No! Devyn clenched her eyes shut, silencing her inner skeptic. Beau loved her, and he had purest faith. That was enough to break the hex. "I like the sound of that," she told him, and bent her neck to welcome the hot slide of his mouth.

"Mmm," he agreed while biting her shoulder. "Me, too."

In seconds, the sultry rush of sensations made it impossible to think about anything but pleasure. When using his teeth proved too slow, Beau attacked the rest of her laces with his fingers until he had her exposed.

Groaning in appreciation, he kneaded one breast with his palm while drawing her opposite nipple into his mouth. Devyn barely had time to tip back her head before his hand disappeared beneath her dress and skimmed the inside of her thigh. She opened for him, and he stroked her into a panting, moaning frenzy.

Still kneeling, he shucked her panties to the floor and unzipped his fly. "Sorry, hon," he said while he tugged her to the edge of the sofa cushion. "We'll take it slow the next round."

Devyn didn't mind; she was more than ready for him. She spread herself wide and fisted the fabric at her sides while Beau slid gently to the hilt. Then something shifted in his gaze, and he slammed into her with fury. He made love to her hard and fast, until they came together in violent spasms of release.

As promised, the next round lasted for hours. He carried her upstairs and undressed them both before laying her on the bed and cherishing her body with his mouth. Sometime after midnight, Beau held her close and rested her newly adorned left hand over his chest. Devyn watched the diamond glimmer with the rhythmic rise and fall of his rib cage. *Beautiful and dangerous, like white oleander.* When her eyelids grew heavy and drifted shut, she promised herself that nothing was wrong.

Devyn knew she was dreaming because her mama sat on the edge of the mattress and smoothed the hair back from her forehead. The only time she saw her mother was in dreams, and she cherished each fleeting moment, even if it was nothing but a subconscious fantasy.

"Time to get up, baby," Mama said, her amber-colored eyes smiling beneath the dark riot of curls she'd never been able to tame. "You overslept."

Devyn pushed to her elbows and glanced at the bedside alarm clock, but it was missing. Her entire bedroom had undergone a snowy transformation, furnished with whitewashed pine and decorated in white linen. Even the walls were painted stark white. The room looked vacant and sterile, nothing like her style.

"What time is it?" she asked.

"Almost eight." Mama stood and backed toward the door, beckoning for Devyn to follow. "The school bus will be here in five minutes, and you haven't packed anyone's lunch."

In an instant flood of realization, Devyn remembered that she had four children. Her pulse hitched, and she threw back the covers, then grabbed her bathrobe and rushed downstairs to the kitchen.

Four lunch boxes rested on the counter beside an industrial-sized tub of Skippy and a loaf of bread. Devyn flew into action, spreading peanut butter over the first slice, but the bread tore with each sweep of the butter knife. She grabbed another slice, but no matter how many times she tried, she couldn't make a single sandwich.

"Hurry," Mama urged. "We don't have much time."

Devyn sensed her children scurrying behind her in the kitchen. She couldn't see their faces, but their rapid-fire cries filled the room.

"I can't find my backpack!"

"Did you see my planner?"

"I need help double-knotting my shoes!"

"Where's my library book?"

Devyn's heart thumped in panic. She couldn't worry about any of that until she knew her children would be fed. She ran to the pantry, finding it empty. Why didn't they have any food?

"You'll have to buy your lunches at school," she told them.

"They can't," Mama said. "Their accounts are overdrawn, don't you remember?"

Suddenly, Devyn recalled the overdue notice that had come in yesterday's mail. She owed the cafeteria fifty dollars, and she didn't have the money to pay the charges. From somewhere outside, a bus honked its horn, and chaos erupted in the kitchen as the children pleaded with her to finish their sandwiches.

In desperation, Devyn looked around. "Where's Beau?" she asked her mother. "Why isn't he helping me?"

Mama tipped her head in sympathy, her mouth pulling into a frown. "Oh, honey." She pointed at the refrigerator, where a note was taped beside a rainbow finger painting. "He left that for you."

As if moving underwater, Devyn struggled to reach the note. When she pulled it free, it was identical to the letter he'd sent after graduation. *Sorry, Dev. I joined the Marines.*

"No," she whispered. "He promised he'd never leave."

Mama rested a hand on her shoulder, though it brought no comfort. "I'm sure he meant it at the time. But things change, baby. People change. Nothing lasts forever."

An ache opened up inside Devyn's chest, quickly turning into a vacuum of suffering unlike anything she'd ever known. Tears flooded her vision, and she doubled over while sobs racked her body. She never imagined she could hurt this badly. She cried and cried, but the grief never ceased. Because deep down, she knew Beau wasn't coming back this time—and that she'd never be whole again.

Mercifully, the dream ended and she awoke with a gasp. She bolted upright in bed, still clutching the spot above her breast where an imaginary ache threatened to tear her in half.

The movement startled Beau awake. "What's wrong?" He blinked against the early-morning rays and scanned the room for signs of trouble.

"Bad dream," she said, panting.

He released a sleepy chuckle. "Lord, honey. You almost gave me a heart attack."

It was hard to feel sorry for him with this unholy pressure tightening around her ribs. She couldn't shake off the ghost of sadness that had followed her into reality.

"Come here." Beau wrapped her in his strong embrace. She was still irrationally mad at him for abandoning their family that didn't even exist, but she rested her head on his shoulder and let him rub her back until the fear subsided. "Want to tell me about it?" he asked.

"No," she said firmly. If she discussed the nightmare, it might cement into a memory. The only thing she could do was hope the images would fade, like many of her other dreams.

"Then we should probably get up," Beau said, leaning aside to check the clock. "I want to apply for our marriage license before I head back to the *Belle*. How does that sound?"

"Sounds perfect," Devyn said. She took a deep breath and blew it out. Maybe holding the license in her hands would make their engagement seem more real. "I'll get the coffee started."

"Wait," he said, catching her by the wrist. "Just let me bring this up one more time, and then I promise I'll drop it."

"*Beau.*" She wasn't in the mood for another fight. "I'm not going back to school."

"I know," he said. "But you'll be a Dumont soon. I thought you might want a permanent job in the education center. If you don't, that's fine. I'll support you in whatever—"

"Yes!" The offer sent Devyn bouncing in place, and she didn't need another instant to think about it. This was just the boost she needed after her horrible dream. She couldn't imagine anything better than doing what she loved alongside her favorite people. "I'll call Warren and tell him the deal's off."

She was halfway to the door when Beau called out and stopped her again.

"I love you," he said with a grin that lit her up inside.

Devyn returned his smile. "Love you, too."

As she padded down the stairs, she inwardly scolded herself. *See? I told you everything would be fine.*

She reminded herself of that two days later when the simple act of picking out a wedding cake made her hyperventilate. The bakery walls spun around her like a carnival fun house. Only it wasn't fun at all. She sat down and put her head between her knees, willing herself not to vomit inside her sister's shop.

"Here." Allie shoved an empty piping bag over Devyn's nose and mouth. It smelled like butter cream frosting. "Now relax and breathe, nice and slow."

Devyn did as she was told, and in a few minutes,

her lips stopped tingling. She handed back the bag. "Thanks. I don't know what came over me."

Allie watched her for a few moments, then closed the photo album of cake designs and squatted down to meet Devyn's eyes. "I'm going to ask you a question, and I want you to be honest with me." To show how serious she was, she extended a pinkie.

Devyn hooked their little fingers in a silent oath. "Promise."

"Is this what you really want?" Allie asked, nodding at a catalog of cake toppers. "You haven't been yourself the last couple days, and you don't seem very happy for a woman who's about to marry the love of her life."

"I do want to marry Beau," Devyn said. "I swear. I love him so much it hurts."

"Then what's the problem?"

"I think it's the dreams." Devyn pressed two fingers against her temples to drive out the negativity that had invaded her sleep since the night of Beau's proposal. "I keep having nightmares that he's going to skip out on me. I know it's not real, but it's messing with my head."

"Dreams can be a manifestation of your fears," Allie said. "Deep down, maybe you don't trust him."

"I should have known you'd go all *psychoanalyst* on me," Devyn said as she narrowed her eyes at her sister. Secretly, she wondered if Allie had a point though. "Beau's given me every reason to believe he can break the hex. He's got way more faith than Marc did."

"This has nothing to do with hexes," Allie said. "You haven't let go of the past."

"Of course I have," Devyn said. Satisfied that she wouldn't faint, she stood up from her chair and grabbed her purse. "Prewedding jitters are normal. I just need to power through it." She reached for her sister's hand and said, "Come on. Let's go look at wedding dresses." If that didn't warm her cold feet, nothing would.

Allie glanced down at the pastry bag. "Are you sure you're up to it?"

"Up to it?" Devyn asked, scoffing. "I've been waiting for this my whole life."

"All right, but I'm bringing the bag." Allie stuffed it in her pocket. "Just in case."

Twenty minutes later, they strode through the front door of New Orleans's swankiest bridal shop, not that Devyn could afford anything in there. But she knew she'd feel better after trying on a few designer gowns—all she needed was Gucci, her drug of choice.

As they waded through a sea of fluffy white tulle and delicate lace, a tiny spark of excitement flared to life inside Devyn's tummy. But right on the heels of excitement came a flashback from her first nightmare. Then she wasn't in the bridal shop anymore. She was inside her vacant bedroom, surrounded by white linens, white furniture, bare white walls. A sudden crush of emptiness gripped her in its icy fingers, and she struggled to catch her breath.

"No," Devyn whispered, blindly reaching out for something stable. "Not again."

Allie guided her to a cushioned loveseat. "It's okay.

Breathe," she said, pushing the icing bag to Devyn's mouth. "Nice and slow, just like before."

A middle-aged sales clerk appeared and offered a bottle of water, but Devyn waved her off. "Thanks, but I'll be fi—"

"Oh, my God!" Allie screeched. "Your hands!"

Devyn glanced down at her hands and gasped in horror. A scattering of pink welts had risen on her skin, and her fingers had begun to swell. She dropped the icing bag like it was on fire and cried, "What's happening to me?"

"Is your ring platinum?" the sales clerk asked. When Devyn nodded, the woman urged, "Take it off. Hurry!"

At first, Devyn didn't understand. But then she remembered that it was nearly impossible to cut through platinum. If her hands swelled any bigger, she might lose her ring finger. She tugged at the band, but it wouldn't budge.

"Here," Allie said, producing a tube of lip balm from her purse. She squeezed a dollop of petroleum jelly onto Devyn's finger, and together, they worked the lubricated band back and forth until it finally slipped free and plunked to the floor.

"Thank God," Devyn said as she released a shaky breath, pressing a hand to her chest. "That was close."

Allie wrapped the greasy engagement ring in a tissue and tucked it inside Devyn's purse. Then she took Devyn's swollen hands and turned them over, inspecting them. "You still don't have any allergies, right?"

"Not a single one."

Allie looked up, her gaze serious. "This is psychosomatic, Dev."

"Psycho what?"

"The swelling, the hives, the dizziness and nightmares," Allie said. "You're doing this to yourself. The wedding is stressing you out to the point that it's making you sick."

More than anything, Devyn wanted to argue that it wasn't true. But the lump rising in her throat warned that her sister was dead-on. Then, like a sign from beyond, the blotches disappeared from her skin and the swelling receded. She'd removed Beau's ring, and her body had quit rebelling against her.

No matter how hard Devyn tried to pretend otherwise, this engagement wasn't right. She loved Beau, and she wanted to be with him, but she couldn't marry him—at least not now. Tears burned behind her eyes, and she pressed her lips together to contain a sob. She didn't want to fall apart in public.

Allie tugged her to standing and led her to the car, then drove to the last place on earth Devyn wanted to show her face—the *Belle*.

"You have to tell him," Allie said when she put the car in park and turned off the engine.

Devyn hung her head. She understood what had to happen, but she didn't know if she had the strength to go through with it. This was going to break Beau's heart.

And hers, too.

Chapter 17

Beau knew something was wrong the instant Allie walked into the purser's office and locked her mismatched eyes on him. Her skin had paled a shade or two, and she gnawed on her bottom lip like it was a strip of beef jerky.

"What's the matter?" he asked. "It's not the gaming board, is it? Because I faxed over those pages from the ledger."

Her gaze dropped to the floor. "You need to talk to Devyn. She's in the parking lot."

Stomach dipping, he pushed away from the desk. "Is she okay?"

Allie nodded, but she wouldn't look at him. "She's not hurt or anything."

Interesting choice of words.

Beau had a bad feeling about this, but he swallowed his dread and jogged outside to the main deck. He spotted Devyn sitting on the hood of an old sedan, but much like her sister, she wouldn't meet his gaze. He made his way down the bow ramp, and when he strode near enough to see her folded hands, he noticed she wasn't wearing her engagement ring.

His already leaden stomach sank another inch.

The remaining few steps between them seemed to last a thousand years, because deep in his gut, Beau knew what she'd come here to say. But he refused to think the words because he was afraid that would make them true. Maybe there was a logical explanation for the slump of her shoulders and the way she stared at the ground. Perhaps she'd lost the ring and was afraid to tell him. He held on to that hope and joined her at the car, choosing to remain standing because his instincts warned him to maintain some distance.

"What's going on?" he asked. "Allie said you wanted to talk."

Devyn nodded and lifted her face. That's when any last shreds of hope drifted away on the breeze. Her pale blue eyes were bloodshot from crying, her lids puffy and smudged with mascara. But even more daunting was the expression behind those eyes: shame mingled with sorrow. She looked like she wanted to crawl into a hidey-hole and stay there forever.

Beau's extremities went numb. She was breaking up with him.

The realization must have shown on his features, because Devyn wrapped both arms around herself and tipped her head to the side while fresh tears welled beneath her lashes. He wanted to plead with her, but the mere act of pulling air into his lungs was all he could manage.

"I'm so sorry; I can't do it," she told him in a strangled whisper. She reached into her pocket and pulled out his ring—wrapped in a Kleenex, as if it were something filthy that she couldn't bear to touch. Her hand trembled as she held it forward. "But I do love you."

Beau made no move to take the ring. He didn't want it. "Then what's the problem?"

Sniffling, she unwrapped the bundle and used the tissue to dab at her nose. When she finally spoke, it was to the diamond instead of him. "Love's not enough."

He didn't understand. Of course it was enough. "What more do you need?"

Devyn covered her face with both hands, muffling her voice when she shook her head and said, "I don't even know."

Beau hesitated twice to touch her, afraid that if he did, whatever remained of their relationship would pop like a soap bubble. He steeled himself and pulled her palms away from her eyes. "Dev, none of this makes sense. You have to tell me what's wrong—that's the only way I can fix it."

"But that's the thing," she said, splaying one hand in helplessness. "You can't fix this. Nobody can."

"Is it the curse? Is that what's got you so wound up?"

"It used to be." She rested both elbows on her knees and stared out at the water, a shadow passing over her countenance. "But then I realized we're not safe, even if we break Memère's hex. Breaking her spell would let us get married, but it doesn't guarantee anything beyond that. There's no promise of forever. We can still grow apart." Another tear slipped down her cheek, and she scrubbed it away with her fist. "You can still leave me."

"But I won't."

She whipped her head toward him. "You don't know that."

"Damn it, Devyn," he said. "Yes I do!"

"How?" she demanded. "You can't see the future. Maybe this is what you want now, but people change. What guarantee do I have that you won't get the itch to run again?"

Beau couldn't believe they were having this conversation. "Have I given you any reason to believe I'm not in this for the long haul?"

Biting her lip, she shook her head.

"Have I so much as *looked* at another woman since I came back to town?"

"No, but—"

"But nothing," he interrupted, a flicker of anger rising inside him. "I've done everything I can to prove that I'm serious. For God's sake, Devyn, I asked you to be my wife! It doesn't get any more serious than that. At some point you're going to have to trust me."

She took a sudden interest in the pavement.

"Can you do that?" he asked.

A full minute of charged silence hung between them, providing her answer.

Beau pinched the bridge of his nose and expelled a long breath. He wanted to shake Devyn's shoulders until she felt the certainty of his commitment, but he couldn't force her to believe in him any more than he could stop the earth from turning. Faith had to come from within, and he didn't have enough for the both of them.

"If you can't trust me," he said, "then we don't have a future. I don't know what else to say."

Apparently, neither did Devyn.

She pushed off the car hood and stood before him, then pressed the ring into his palm. Her fingers were cool and stiff, with no hint of the affection that had once filled her touch. She closed his hand around the metal and left him with one last apology before she strode across the parking lot.

And then she was gone.

Beau didn't know how long he stood there—maybe five minutes, maybe ten—blinking back the heat that expanded behind his eyes. He'd awoken that morning halfway to being married to the woman of his dreams. Now he was alone. He couldn't believe how quickly he'd lost it all. His rib cage felt like a jack-o'-lantern, scooped out of everything that had once made him complete. Worst of all was the knowledge that he couldn't do a damned thing about it.

At some point, he put one foot in front of the other

and blankly made his way back onto the boat, seeing nothing, hearing nothing.

Feeling nothing.

Devyn's cell phone rang from beside her at the kitchen table. The screen read *Belle of the Bayou*, so she continued sipping her coffee and let the call go to voice mail.

It wasn't Beau on the other end of the line, she was confident of that. In the week that had passed since the breakup, he'd made no effort to contact her. Not that she blamed him. But she didn't want to talk to anyone on the *Belle*. The association hit too close to home, too near her bruised heart for comfort. Even cashing her paycheck had brought tears to her eyes, because giving up that simple piece of paper had severed her last ties to the boat . . . and to Beau.

No, she corrected. *Not to him.* As long as her sister was a Dumont, Devyn would be tethered to Beau in that way. Surely their paths would cross on occasion; there was no preventing it. And she couldn't expect him to stay single forever. Someday she'd have to watch him move on with another woman.

A sudden coldness overtook Devyn, and she tugged the lapels of her robe together. She eyed her steaming mug, but she knew that all the coffee in the world wouldn't thaw the chill inside her.

She'd lost her sun.

The phone rang again, but this time it showed *Warren Larabee* calling. Figuring her day couldn't get any worse, Devyn swiped the screen and answered.

"Miss Mauvais," he said, sounding surprised. "I'm glad I caught you."

The way he spoke to her, you'd think she had a life. Little did he know she hadn't left the house—or her bathrobe, for that matter—in days. "You barely did," she lied. "I was on my way out the door. What can I do for you?"

"I'll make this quick, since we're both on the run." In the background, his car shifted gears. "I know you said you're not interested in graveyard tours, but I couldn't leave town without trying to change your mind one last time."

She opened her mouth to speak, but he beat her to it.

"If you'll reconsider," he said, "I'd be willing to offer you a partnership."

Devyn almost dropped the phone in her coffee. "Come again?"

"Just for the Cedar Bayou location, mind you," he clarified. "But this would mean more creative control. And certainly more money."

"But I can't invest anything. All my funds are tied up in my sister's bakery."

"You don't have to spend a cent," he told her. "Your last name is what you'd bring to the table. What do you say?"

For a few beats, she couldn't say anything. Then she stammered, "Uh . . . I'm sorry. You caught me off guard. It sounds like a generous offer, but I'm in shock."

He laughed as if he liked the sound of that. "Listen, I'm on my way to the airport. But I left a signed con-

tract with my New Orleans attorney. If you're interested, all you have to do is swing by his office and
countersign it. There's a clause that voids the agreement if it's not executed within three days, so you have
until then to think it over."

Devyn thanked him and took down the name of his
attorney, then said good-bye. She sat there and stared
at the phone in her hand, still unable to believe he'd
offered her a full partnership—with no investment. A
smile pushed up the corners of her mouth.

Maybe her luck had finally changed.

It took every bit of her inner strength to wait twenty-
four hours, but Devyn forced herself to think through
all the implications of signing Warren's contract. The
only thing holding her back was pride, but self-respect
wouldn't pay the rent. When she couldn't come up
with a logical reason not to go through with the deal,
she dressed in her finest—and only—business suit and
called a taxi to shuttle her to the lawyer's office in New
Orleans.

Twenty minutes later, she strode through the front
door of Rylon & Associates and checked in with the
receptionist, a pretty young brunette wearing a pant-
suit and a bun that made her look more like a granny
than a recent college graduate.

You're one to criticize, Devyn thought. *Once you take
this deal, you'll have to dress up like your great-great-
grandmother every night.*

She shook off the observation and forced a grin.

"Make yourself comfortable," the receptionist said, sweeping a hand toward a cluster of cushioned armchairs. "Mr. Rylon's last appointment ran a bit longer than expected, but he'll be with you shortly. Can I get you anything to drink? Some coffee, maybe?"

"Coffee would be great. Thanks."

"How do you take it?"

"Two creamers, three sugars, and a dash of—" Devyn cut off, not wanting to sound like a prima donna. "You know what? Never mind. Water will be fine."

"Coming right up."

Devyn settled in the middle seat and tried to ignore the nervous flutters in her belly. The contract waiting for her in the next room was legally binding, which meant she couldn't change her mind again. On the one hand, Warren had offered her a lot more money than she felt she deserved. She'd be crazy to turn him down. But once she signed on the dotted line, her fate was sealed, and that scared her more than she wanted to admit.

"Here you go." The receptionist placed a chilled bottle of water on the table, along with the newest copy of *People*. "Thought you might like something to read while you wait."

That was exactly the kind of distraction Devyn needed. She reached for the magazine but paused when a uniformed delivery man walked in the door, carrying the most exquisite floral arrangement she'd ever seen—tall and elegant with a sampling of orchids ranging in color from pale pink to rich fuchsia.

The receptionist's face broke into a smile as if she already knew the flowers were for her. "Delivery for Angie?" she asked the man.

He checked the envelope secured to the vase, then handed her the arrangement. "Yes, ma'am."

When the receptionist—Angie, presumably—carried the vase to her desk, Devyn followed to admire the orchids. She lovingly touched one delicate petal and told the woman, "They're gorgeous."

Angie beamed. "My fiancé has excellent taste in flowers."

"Congrats on the engagement." A prickle of envy stabbed at Devyn, but she ignored it. "When's the big day?"

"Tomorrow," the woman said. "But it's a weekend destination wedding, and we leave this afternoon. In fact, I'm slipping out in a few minutes."

Devyn leaned in to smell the orchids. "Well, this arrangement is spectacular. Either your fiancé did something very naughty, or you did something very nice."

Grinning, Angie blushed and averted her gaze. "No, it's nothing like that. Today's his last radiation treatment." She shrugged. "It might not sound very romantic, but we celebrate every milestone we can."

"Radiation?" Devyn asked, drawing back a bit. "Does he have cancer?"

"Hodgkin's lymphoma." Angie's smile faltered and returned to her lips with a little less brightness. "The prognosis isn't good—he's got about six months. That's why we moved up the wedding date."

Devyn's hand flew to her chest. "I'm so sorry." She felt awful for bringing it up, and even worse for the young woman and her fiancé. "I shouldn't have said anything."

"It's all right. I don't mind talking about it." Studying the floral arrangement, Angie separated a few stems and seemed to recover a fraction of her earlier cheer. "We get a lot of questions, especially from our families. They don't understand why we're having such a lavish ceremony." She rolled her eyes, and for a moment, she resembled a typical bride. "I know what they're thinking: why spend so much money on a marriage that can't last? But look at all the divorces around here. Nobody faults *them* for having the wedding of their dreams. At least I'll mean it when I say *till death do us part*."

In awe, Devyn studied the young receptionist. Angie was quite possibly the bravest person she'd ever met. This woman would be a widow before her first anniversary, and yet here she was, planning her nuptials and celebrating the little time they had left. If Devyn were in the same position, she'd probably distance herself from her partner so his death wouldn't hurt as badly when it happened.

How did Angie cope with the knowledge that her husband would be gone so soon? Devyn remembered the grief from her dreams. She couldn't imagine facing that agony. Though it was none of her business, she had to ask, "Are you scared?"

Angie didn't hesitate. "Terrified."

"Then why are you doing this?"

A soft grin curved Angie's lips. Tears pooled in her eyes, but they looked like the happy kind. "Because he's my other half. I'd rather have six amazing months with him than a lifetime of mediocrity with any other man."

Devyn was moved by the love in that statement. Her gaze had grown misty, so she dabbed at the corners of her eyes. "Then I'm happy for you. I know the wedding will be perfect."

"Thanks," Angie said. "I'm trying really hard to protect my joy. And that means focusing on the present, not the future."

The desk phone rang, and she paused to answer it. When she hung up, she nodded toward the hallway and said, "Mr. Rylon is ready. I'll walk you to his office."

"Oh." Devyn had nearly forgotten why she was here. "Right."

Angie led the way down the hall to a corner office, where a bespectacled gentleman sat behind a mahogany desk and a mountain of paperwork. "Unless you need anything," Angie told the man, "I'm going to head out now."

He glanced up and smiled. "Have a wonderful wedding. Take plenty of pictures, and don't hurry back. We'll hold down the fort for as long as you need."

Angie waved good-bye and shut the door, and then the mood shifted from tear-jerking poignancy to business as usual. Devyn reached across the desk to shake the attorney's hand. He had a warm grip and a friendly face that reminded her of Mr. Rogers, but the transition was too abrupt. She couldn't stop thinking about the receptionist, and more specifically, what she'd said about living in the present and—

"Miss Mauvais?" Mr. Rylon said. "Did you hear me?"

"Pardon?"

"Have you had a chance to review the contract?" he asked. "Warren said he was going to e-mail it to you."

"Uh . . ." Devyn had lost her Internet access when the trailer park across the street finally wised up and changed their Wi-Fi password. "No, I never got it. Must've gone to my spam folder."

"Not a problem." He opened a manila file and pulled out a stack of papers, then handed them across the desk. "Go ahead and look this over. Let me know if you have any questions."

They both took their seats, and Devyn began reading the first page of the contract. But she didn't make it past the third paragraph before her mind started drifting back to her conversation in the lobby.

He's my other half. I'd rather have six amazing months with him than a lifetime of mediocrity with any other man.

Devyn had never thought about it that way. But the more she turned the words over in her mind, the more she felt the truth behind them—a warm certainty that spread all the way to the bottom of her heart.

She'd never loved another man besides Beau, and she doubted she ever would. Assuming she met someone else and married him, would her life partner be nothing more than a cardboard stand-in for the one she truly wanted? And if so, how was that fair to anyone involved?

Devyn had always considered herself fearless, never hesitating to stand up to the schoolyard bullies of the world, but maybe she wasn't so brave after all. Was she really willing to settle for less than the love of her life simply because it might crush her if the relationship ended?

By breaking the engagement, that was exactly what she had done—refused to give Beau her whole heart for fear that he'd break it again. But what was the point of playing it safe if she spent the rest of her life unfulfilled, trapped in a prison of fear?

"Oh, my God," she whispered, staring through the words on the page. "Purest faith shall set you free." Beau hadn't lacked faith—she had. "I'm a coward."

"Beg your pardon?" Mr. Rylon peered at her from above the rim of his glasses. "Did you have a question?"

"No," she murmured. "Just talking to myself."

She buried her nose in the contract and pretended to scan its pages while her mind reeled with the power of her discovery. Beau was her other half, and more important, he was worth the risk. If they married, their union might last fifty years, or it might crumble after six months. But she would rather completely share her soul with him and risk the pain than hide and stay safe.

So now that she knew she'd made a mistake in letting him go, how was she going to repair the damage? She'd broken his heart, and she'd done a dirty job of it.

Devyn set her jaw. She wasn't sure what to do next,

but she wouldn't earn another chance with Beau by sitting in this office. She slapped the contract on the attorney's desk and abruptly stood from her chair. "I have to go."

Mr. Rylon scrunched his forehead and studied the unsigned pages. "Is there a problem?"

"Yes," she called while throwing open the office door. "And I'm going to fix it or die trying."

As she jogged down the hallway, the attorney called out to her, warning her that the contract would expire in less than forty-eight hours. Devyn couldn't bring herself to care. All that mattered was reaching Beau. She would figure out what to say to him when the time came. She had faith—for the first time in over a decade—that he was her future.

She rushed outside and glanced up and down the street for a taxi, but there were none in sight. So she set off on foot toward the dock, never mind that it was over a mile away. Devyn was powered by determination, and she'd crawl to the *Belle* if she had to.

However, three blocks later, her feet cramped inside their four-inch patent leather bindings. She'd picked the wrong shoes for a trek across the city. Taking a seat on the nearest bench, she pulled out her cell phone and called a taxi . . . praying she had enough remaining credit on her MasterCard to cover the fare.

When the cab pulled up to the curb, she practically flung herself into the backseat and said, "To the riverboat dock, and lay rubber."

The driver nodded and they took off like a shot. He

ran every yellow light—and even a few red ones—but they still arrived at the dock parking lot a few minutes too late. The *Belle* had already pulled away from the ramp and churned downriver.

"Damn it," she swore. "A dinner cruise."

"No," the driver said. "It's a wedding party—they won't be back until Sunday afternoon. I just drove a few of the groomsmen here about half an hour ago."

Devyn muttered another curse and paid the driver. She had enough credit for the fare, but not for a trip to Cedar Bayou, so she stepped onto the parking lot and watched him drive away. There was only one thing to do.

Hey, she texted Allie. *I need another ride home.*

While waiting for her sister to arrive, Devyn sat at the curb and considered her next move. She could call Beau and apologize, but that didn't seem adequate for what she'd done. What she needed was to make a grand gesture—something that would *show* him the depth of her faith.

She bit her lip and brainstormed for the next several minutes. By the time her sister's car turned onto the lot, Devyn had an idea. It was a move so daring that she'd never be able to show her face in Cedar Bayou again if it didn't work. But if this didn't prove her faith, nothing would. Devyn gulped a breath and prepared to set her plan in motion.

It was time to be brave.

Chapter 18

"Of all the private charters," Beau grumbled to himself while increasing the engine speed to seven knots, "it had to be a wedding."

He wasn't one to begrudge another man his happiness, but *damn*. The wound was still fresh, for crying out loud. Walking aboard the boat—its deck rails wrapped in twinkling lights and floral garlands—was like immersing his lacerated heart in a bucket of salt water.

At least he didn't have to participate in the ceremony, or worse, perform it. Part of his upgrade to cocaptain had meant becoming a licensed officiate. In his current mood, he'd need a fifth of scotch to join anyone in holy matrimony, and he doubted the couple would appreciate him slurring their vows or calling them by the wrong name.

Two decks below, the rehearsal dinner was in full swing. Beau tried not to imagine the scene, but he could almost hear the tinkling laughter and the clink of crystal champagne flutes as family and friends toasted the happy couple. His temples ached, and he reminded himself to unclench his jaw. It should be *him* down there with Devyn tucked by his side, surrounded by his idiot brothers while they delivered good-natured jeers over aged whiskey.

But it wasn't him, and that left a bitter taste on his tongue.

The setting sun sliced through the pilothouse window, momentarily distracting him from his troubles. Beau slid his Ray-Bans in place and calculated what time he'd reach the first port and dock for the night. Not for another two hours. Until then, he was stuck in here with no one to talk to, no radio, no television . . . no distractions from Devyn's ghost.

Lord have mercy, it was going to be a long weekend.

His cell phone buzzed from his breast pocket. It was a text from Ella-Claire, who'd landed the unfortunate job of head party planner for the festivities. When they'd crossed paths in the purser's office earlier that afternoon, she hadn't looked any happier to be here than he was. By now, Beau recognized the mask of heartbreak, and she'd worn it well. He didn't know which bastard had put that sadness in her gaze, but he intended to find out and pay that man a visit.

Take a break for a few minutes, she messaged. *You should be here to toast the bride and groom.*

Beau groaned so loud he expected the windows to rattle.

As if she'd heard him, Ella added, *You're the acting captain. It's your duty.*

"Shit," he muttered. This was the last thing he needed right now, but Ella was right. He had to sack up and do his job. *I'll be there as soon as we dock,* he told her. *Remind me to kick Marc's ass for talking me into this.*

I'll hold him down for you, she said. *As long as I get in some good swings, too.*

It's a deal.

When Beau strode inside the formal dining hall, it was to the tune of "The Way You Look Tonight," played by a live band the couple had hired for the weekend. He didn't know what these people did for a living, but they'd spared no expense. Pink linens and elaborate orchid centerpieces adorned each table, with at least a hundred guests dining on bourbon-grilled salmon and filet mignon. The wait staff darted smoothly between clusters of partygoers, ensuring that each guest had a flute of custom-made strawberry champagne in hand. Even the small parquet dance floor was transformed beneath the sparkle of a disco ball affixed to the ceiling.

Must be nice to have that much cash to burn. *And a willing woman to burn it on,* he thought. Wiping all traces of envy from his face, he scanned the room for Ella-Claire until he spotted her arranging punch glasses at the dessert table.

He nodded a few polite hellos, intentionally taking the long way around the room to avoid interacting with more guests than he had to. Ella glanced up and met his gaze, then ladled out a serving of punch for him.

"Here," she said, keeping her voice low. "I wish you were off duty, so I could give you something stronger. This can't be easy for you."

Beau didn't want to talk about his short-lived engagement. He had one mission: get in, make his toast, and get the hell out. "Where are the bride and groom?"

Ella linked an arm through his and rotated him toward the center of the room. As discreetly as possible, she pointed to a lone couple swaying on the dance floor. "Right there. Michael and Angela, but they go by Mike and Angie."

One glance at the couple, and all the envy Beau had once felt for them slid down his throat and settled in his stomach like a bowling ball. Clearly the groom was sick. Not the kind of sick that landed a man in bed for a few days, but the kind that would send him to his maker—and soon, judging by the look of him. The man's head was clean-shaven, his skin dull. And while his tuxedo jacket might've concealed his emaciated frame, he couldn't hide the hollows in his cheeks. Beau didn't know how much time the young lovers had left, but the bride clung to her fiancé's shoulders as if a stiff breeze might carry him away.

The pair couldn't be a day over twenty-two, barely old enough to drink and certainly too young for anything this heavy. They should be buying a fixer-upper and clipping coupons, not facing the end of their journey together.

"Aw, shit," he muttered. "Life isn't fair."

Ella rested her cheek on his arm and gave a sad sigh.

"No, it sure isn't. I heard he's got six months, best-case scenario."

"Damn." Beau shook his head and watched the bride and groom gaze soulfully into each other's eyes. He couldn't change the young couple's fate, but he could do his part to make this the best weekend of their lives. "Tell the staff to double their efforts—more smiles, more Southern hospitality. There's a bonus for whoever goes above and beyond. And I'm comping the fare for this trip as a wedding gift from all of us. If Marc has a problem with it, I'll cover the expense myself."

"I think that's a great idea," Ella said. "Want me to dim the lights so you can make a toast?"

"Not yet. Let them finish their dance." The closeness they shared was more important than a few token words from a stranger. "They won't get nearly as many as they deserve."

There wasn't a dry eye on the boat the next day when Mike and Angie exchanged rings and said *I do*. During the minister's pronouncement, even Beau had to face the breeze and blink a few times to clear his vision. The ceremony had put his troubles in perspective, and though he still ached for Devyn, he'd let go of his bitterness.

And that helped, a little.

While the wedding guests celebrated in the formal dining hall, Beau piloted the *Belle* upriver at a leisurely pace, occasionally blowing the steam whistle in an unspoken signal for the bride and groom to kiss. He sent texts back and forth to Ella-Claire to make sure the reception was going smoothly, and instructed the maids to deck out the honeymoon suite with every romantic weapon in their arsenal.

All in all, it was a good day.

Soon after the autumn sun slipped over the horizon, Ella peeked inside the pilothouse wearing the first genuine smile he'd seen on her in weeks. He couldn't help grinning back.

"What?" he asked.

She held up a single sheet of paper. "A fax came in for you. I thought you'd like to see it right away."

Beau's smile flattened. "If it's from the gaming board—"

"Just read it," she interrupted, thrusting the paper at him. "I'll give you some privacy, but text me when you're ready to crack open a bottle of sparkling cider. I want to be the first person to toast you."

Then she backed out of the control room and shut the door, leaving him alone. Beau turned on the overhead light and read the fax.

The honor of your presence is requested
at the marriage of
Devyn Rebecca Mauvais
and
Beau Christopher Dumont
Sunday, the third of November
at eight o'clock in the evening
Saint Mary's Church
Cedar Bayou, Louisiana
RSVP by the second of November

Confused, Beau continued to a handwritten addendum at the bottom of the page, where he recognized Devyn's loopy script.

> *I'll be waiting at the altar in front of all our family and friends, wearing my mother's dress and ready to give you my whole heart. Turns out it was yours all along. No need to RSVP because I have faith—the purest kind—that you'll be there with me. I love you, and I can't wait to begin our life together.*
>
> *Yours always,*
> *Dev*

He stared at the paper for the longest time, half expecting the text to disappear, or for a celebrity to jump out from beneath the control panel and announce that he'd been pranked. But the words stayed right where they belonged, and not a creature stirred inside the pilothouse except the pilot. After a few minutes of stunned silence, Beau allowed himself to believe that the invitation was real.

And he didn't need another second to think it over.

A chortle of laughter arose from his chest while his body broke out in delicious goose bumps. Never in a million years did he expect to receive a faxed invitation to his own wedding, but he wasn't complaining. Devyn wanted him, and that was all that mattered. Besides, nothing between them had been conventional, so why would their wedding day be any different? As long as the wedding *night* went off without a hitch, he'd be a happy man.

With a face-splitting grin, Beau reached up and pulled the steam whistle, then hollered to everyone within earshot, "I'm getting married!"

"I'm getting married." Devyn sighed, using a fingernail to trace the photo of the cake she'd selected—a two-tier red velvet with cream cheese frosting. "Can you believe it?"

Giggling, Allie nodded from her spot behind the bakery sales counter. "Actually, I can. Because you keep reminding me every five minutes."

"I'm happy," Devyn said, and shimmied her hips. "Sue me."

"Not a chance. *This* is the reaction I wanted from you the last time you got engaged." Allie held up two plastic cake toppers, first a traditional bride and groom, then a pair of wedding bells. "Which one? Sorry for the lack of options, but these are all I've got in stock, and we don't have time for a special order."

"I don't know. Which is cheaper?"

Devyn was on a serious budget. She'd sold her flat-screen TV to a neighbor for a couple hundred bucks, and that was all she had to spend on the entire event: alterations for Mama's dress, secondhand wedding bands, decorations, invitations, food. Thank goodness Beau had paid for the marriage license weeks ago, or that would've taken a significant chunk out of her funds.

Narrowing her eyes, Allie chided, "They're both free, just like the cake."

Devyn pointed at the bells.

"Okay." Allie scribbled some notes on her order pad. "Did you hear back from Father Durand about the fellowship hall?"

"Yep, we can use it—no charge."

All those years of chairing the Saint Mary's fish fry had finally paid off. At first, Father Durand had refused to officiate the wedding on such short notice. But when she told him the alternative was a trip to town hall for a civil ceremony, he'd begrudgingly waived the Pre-Cana classes and offered the use of church facilities.

"And since the wedding is after dinnertime, we can get away with just cake and punch, right?"

Allie pursed her lips in consideration. "We should offer a few appetizers, too. I'm sure we can put something together on the cheap."

"What about decorations? I bought a ton of votives from the Dollar Store, but is that enough?" she asked, wishing she had enough money for flowers. Why did pretty things have to cost so much?

"With a few fall touches—like some whole pumpkins and colorful leaves—I think it'll look classy and understated."

"Good. I was hoping you'd say that."

"And the invitations?" Allie asked, pointing at her checklist.

"Got 'em to the post office first thing yesterday morning and sweet-talked Mrs. Sheen into adding them to the truck before the deliveries went out." Since most of their guests lived in town, the invitations had likely arrived that same afternoon. "I called anyone outside the bayou to let them know . . . including that jerkface, Jenny Hore."

Allie wrinkled her nose. "You want her to come?"

"You bet your sweet ass I do." Nothing said *purest faith* like inviting your high school rival to a wedding in which the groom wasn't a guaranteed participant. "Slade, too."

Allie chewed the pencil eraser and studied Devyn for a few beats. "Aren't you just the slightest bit worried that Beau won't come?"

"Nope," Devyn said. "He loves me. He'll be there."

"But how do you know he even got your fax?"

Devyn held up her cell phone. "Because Ella-Claire RSVP'd with regrets that she can't make it. She's working the same charter as Beau, so if she saw the fax, that means he did, too."

"You're gutsy," Allie said, arching an appreciative brow. "I'll give you that."

Devyn decided to take it as a compliment, though she wasn't sure it was meant that way. She checked the time on her phone and noted she was late for her appointment with the seamstress. "I'm off to my fitting. Thanks again for letting me have Mama's dress."

"Of course you should have her dress," Allie said. Moisture began to well in her eyes, and she blinked it away. "Mama would want you to wear it. That way, a part of her can be with us tomorrow."

Devyn fanned her own eyes. "Okay, enough of that. I don't want to get mascara all over her Chantilly lace."

After an over-the-counter hug and a reminder to meet at her house later for an evening of appetizer preparations, Devyn left the Sweet Spot and walked two blocks to the alterations shop. As much as she tried fighting back tears, she completely lost it when she stood before the full-length mirror in her mother's gown.

The white silk sheath with its lace overlay hugged her curves to the waist before flaring out above a hidden petticoat and continuing to the floor. Its capped sleeves had been modernized to slip off her shoulders, but the dress still brought back memories of the wedding portrait that had hung at the top of the stairs in her childhood home. She looked like her mama, and that filled her with more happiness than her body could hold. It was all she could do to keep breathing.

"Your bust is larger," the seamstress said, sweeping a wrinkled hand along the side of Devyn's chest. "So I had to pull apart the seams and add a new panel of fabric. It's not a perfect match, but I don't think anyone will notice." She lifted Devyn's elbow in demonstration. "I hid it beneath your arm, see?"

Devyn rotated in front of the mirror, pretending to inspect the lace at her sides, but all she could see was a blur of white. "It's perfect," she whispered. "Thank you."

Now she truly felt like a bride.

"Do I look like a respectable groom?"

Appraising his reflection in the pilothouse window,

Beau straightened his black bowtie and then turned to face Ella-Claire. He didn't have a tux onboard the *Belle*, and once he docked in New Orleans that afternoon, there wouldn't be time to have his suit cleaned and pressed before the wedding. So he'd opted to wear his formal captain's uniform—starched white slacks and coat paired with a matching black cummerbund and tie. He hoped it was dapper enough, but having no idea what kind of ceremony Devyn had planned, there was no way to tell.

Ella tipped her head and put her hand on her hip, scanning him before delivering a teasing wink. "Well, I don't know about *respectable*, but that's not something you can fix with a tuxedo."

"Very funny."

"You know I'm just messing with you," she said, and stood on tiptoe to kiss his cheek. "You're the handsomest Dumont groom I've ever seen."

Beau laughed. Over the last hundred years, the only other Dumont groom to make it to the altar was Marc, who'd sported one hell of a black eye at his Vegas wedding. "I'm not so sure that's a compliment."

"I've seen the way Devyn looks at you," Ella said. "You could show up in your pawpaw's ratty overalls and she wouldn't care."

Beau brushed a bit of lint off his sleeve. "I just want our wedding day to be memorable."

"Stop fidgeting." Ella-Claire lightly smacked his hand. "You look perfect. And even if you didn't, it's the marriage that counts, not the wedding. Devyn understands how rare it is when the love of your life actually loves you back. She knows how lucky—" Cutting off, Ella cleared her throat and dropped her gaze to the floor.

"Aw, hon." He held out his arms for a hug, but she waved him off with a lame excuse about not wanting to get makeup on his jacket. "At least tell me whose ass I need to beat."

Instead of answering, she changed the subject. "We're about to serve a late lunch. You want me to send up a plate of chicken or ham?"

Beau gave her a look that said he wouldn't be deterred. Whoever had hurt her was going to pay. Maybe he should ask Alex for the guy's name. If anyone knew the details of Ella's personal life, it would be him. The two had been best friends for ages. Hell, Alex would probably want to confront the asshole, too.

"Which one?" she pressed.

"Chicken."

"And we're still on schedule to dock at five thirty?"

"Yes, ma'am."

"Good," she said, and patted his chest. "I'm really happy for you, Beau."

He'd just opened his mouth to thank her when the emergency weather radio affixed to the control panel screeched an alert for a severe thunderstorm warning. "What the hell?" he muttered, glancing through the front window at the clear blue sky. He stepped around Ella to check the radar, which had shown nothing significant that morning. Now a mass of greens and reds drifted into view on the screen to show incoming rain.

"How bad is it?" Ella-Claire asked.

Tapping the keyboard, Beau zoomed out to get a feel for the size of the storm. He swallowed a curse. The system continued all the way to New Orleans, following the river's path as if it knew he was coming. There was no way he'd make it back to Cedar Bayou by eight o'clock tonight—not in this squall. In fact, if the lightning was as bad as it looked, he should probably find the nearest port and evacuate the boat.

"Really bad," he said. "Doesn't look like I'm getting married tonight."

Chapter 19

"Do me a favor," Beau said to Ella-Claire while scanning the map for the nearest docking point. As soon as he found the contact information, he pulled out his cell and dialed the port authority. "We don't have much time before this thing's right on top of us. Get on the phone and find somewhere for the guests and crew to hang out until the storm passes. See if you can hire some buses to meet us at the dock. Then call Devyn and explain what's happening. Tell her I'm sorry, and that I'll touch base with her as soon as the boat's evacuated. Maybe we can have the wedding tomorrow."

Ella nodded. "I'm on it."

Twenty minutes later, after receiving permission from the nearest port authority to dock, Beau turned on the intercom and made an announcement to the entire boat. "Attention, everyone. I'm afraid there's some nasty weather ahead, and we're going to have to stop until the worst of it passes. We should arrive at the next port in about thirty minutes. At that time, I need everyone assembled in the formal dining hall and ready to move to a secure location."

He pushed the *Belle* to full throttle and hoped like hell that the storm was moving slower than they were. The wind kicked up and dark clouds knitted together to block the sun, but at least the rain continued to hold off. He was within ten minutes of their destination when his radar flickered and went dead. The computer immediately followed, and upon closer inspection, Beau noticed that all his electronic equipment had died.

"Damn," he muttered to himself. Whatever lay ahead must be some seriously nasty shit.

A knock sounded at the door, and Ella-Claire stepped inside. "I've got good news and bad news."

"Start with the good," he said. "Then work your way down."

"The city gave us permission to use the community center, and they've agreed to send a few buses to shuttle us there. They say the power's already out, but they've got a backup generator so we won't be sitting in the dark the whole time. I've got the staff brainstorming activities to keep the guests entertained."

"Excellent." That took care of his most immediate concern. "What's the bad news?"

Ella sucked an apologetic breath through her teeth. "I wasn't able to reach Devyn. My phone died right when I was about to make the call."

"I'll do it." But when Beau pulled out his cell phone, it showed NO SIGNAL.

"No one has service," Ella said. "I checked with the

whole staff—even the guests. I can't get a connection on the *Belle*'s outgoing line either. And no fax. We're totally incommunicado."

"Just my friggin' luck." Beau heaved a sigh. "I'll have to call her from the port."

But the bad news kept coming when he docked the *Belle*.

The sky opened up on top of Beau and his passengers as they jogged down the bow ramp and onto the city buses idling at the rear of the parking lot. One guest slipped and sprained her ankle, and another had an asthma attack—a mild one, thank God, because there wasn't a working telephone with which to call nine-one-one. Even the landlines were down; Beau had checked at the port office when he'd first dropped anchor.

"Maybe there's a working phone at the rec center," Ella shouted over the howling wind while shielding her eyes from a sideways rain that seemed to defy gravity.

"Doubtful," Beau shouted back, then peeled a wet blade of grass off his forehead. He pointed at the first bus. "Go with this group and get settled in. I'm gonna stay here and see if the port authority can radio the sheriff in Cedar Bayou." Come hell or high water—and with the river rising so quickly, the second part was guaranteed—Beau had to get word to Devyn before the wedding. He couldn't let her think he'd ditched her at the altar.

Ella nodded, then boarded the first bus. The remaining staff filled the second shuttle, and when Beau saw them safely off the property, he turned and ran toward the port authority office. The sky was black as pitch, making it difficult to see fallen tree limbs and debris flying through the air. By the time he threw open the office door, Beau was soaked to the skin and wearing more leaves than the trees.

"I need to get a message to Cedar Bayou," he said to the old-timer kicked back behind his desk, reading a magazine by the light of a battery-powered lantern. "It's an emergency."

The man turned up a palm. "Sorry, son. The electrical storm knocked out everything, even my police scanner." With a shake of his head, he pointed to the heavens. "I've been here thirty years, and I've never seen anything like it."

Beau raked a hand through his soggy hair and grappled for a plan B. If he couldn't send a message to Devyn, he'd have to find a way to make it to the church on time. He hated to leave behind the *Belle*'s guests and crew, but his backup pilot could transport them home. Plus, he did have Ella-Claire there to ensure that things went smoothly. Considering he'd already comped the cruise fare, he figured that nobody would complain.

"Then I'll have to drive there," Beau said. "Where's the nearest place to rent a car?"

"Well, there's an Avis not too far from here, but that won't help you."

"Why not?"

The old man hooked a thumb toward his radio

equipment. "Because the last thing I heard before the scanner went dead was the mention of a twenty-car pileup on the interstate. The highway patrol probably shut it down by now, and I don't imagine the back roads are any better. We get a lot of flash floods around here."

Beau's stomach dipped into his boxer-briefs. "So there's no way for me to get home?"

"Not unless you can fly," the man said, then flinched when a windblown object *thunked* against the outside wall. "And I wouldn't recommend that either."

Like a scene ripped from his nightmares, Beau stood there dripping wet and helpless. The weather in Cedar Bayou was probably fine, and a squall in another state wouldn't make the news. Devyn would be waiting for him at the altar in front of half the town, oblivious to the fact that he wasn't coming.

Beau imagined how she might feel when the minutes ticked by in painfully awkward silence, their guests staring at her and whispering that history was repeating itself. Abandonment was her greatest fear, and he was about to bring it to fruition—in front of an audience. Even if Devyn forgave him, she'd never fully recover. It would take another decade to regain her trust, assuming she ever let her guard down again.

"God help me," Beau whispered to himself. "It can't happen like this."

Devyn pressed a hand to her belly, which felt like it was about to sprout wings and fly to Canada. The act caused her to drop a pair of candle tapers to the chapel floor, where they broke in half against the hardwood. She stifled a curse, not wanting to swear in the Lord's house.

Allie slanted her a glance while pushing a long white taper into the standing candleholder at the altar. "Nervous?"

"A little," Devyn admitted, bending down to pick up the pieces.

Overall, nothing was wrong. The sanctuary looked lovely, decked out in dozens of simple brass candelabra and a lacey white runner adorning the aisle. She and Allie had just finished decorating the fellowship hall and had set up the cake. Their mother's freshly steamed gown was hanging in the dressing room along with a matching veil borrowed from a friend. But despite the fact that everything had gone according to plan, Devyn couldn't shake her jitters.

"It's natural," Allie said. "All brides feel this way on their wedding day, and that's under *normal* circumstances."

Devyn propped a hand on her hip. "Are you saying my wedding's abnormal?"

Allie's eyes went wide. "No, it's beautiful. But you have more reason to feel nervous because you haven't spoken to the groom in weeks. Technically, you don't even know that he's coming. That has to be weighing on your mind."

"It's not bothering me at all," Devyn insisted, and she meant every word. She had perfect faith that he would be there. "I think I'm more worried about the guests. I haven't had much time"—or money—"to put this together. No one wants to be known for having a tacky wedding."

"Baby, you're talking to the queen of tacky weddings," Allie said with a smile. "I was married in a bikini, remember?"

Devyn snickered at the memory. As maid of honor, she'd worn a bathing suit and leopard print sarong. "Your point?"

Allie set down an armful of candles and gave Devyn's hand a hearty squeeze. "A wedding lasts for a few minutes, but a marriage lasts a lifetime. Look at the big picture."

Devyn returned the squeeze. "You're right. I've got Beau, and that's all that matters."

Allie nodded as if to get down to business. "Now let's finish up in here so I can get started on your hair and makeup."

A hopeful smile curved Devyn's lips. Once she dolled herself up and changed into Mama's gown, all of this would begin to feel real.

"There has to be a way," Beau said while staring out the window into the blackness. A bolt of lightning struck in the distance, momentarily illuminating the raging river, its surges snatching limbs and debris from the parking lot like a greedy child. "I can't stand here and do nothing."

"Once in a while," the old man said from his desk,

"Mother Nature likes to remind us who's boss. I know you want to reach your fiancée, but I'm afraid the Mississippi's got the upper hand tonight."

Beau couldn't argue with that—he'd never seen the river so angry—but his mind kept working to find a solution. Instinctively, he knew there was a way to reach Devyn, and he'd find it if he kept trying.

A few minutes later, a small searchlight pierced the darkness. Beau pressed his forehead to the window and squinted at the half-submerged parking lot, where a speedboat rocked in the current. The passenger holding the light swiveled it to and fro, probably looking for a place to tie off the boat while they sought shelter from the storm.

"There's a small craft out there," Beau said to the old-timer. "I'm going to give them a hand."

When Beau stepped outside, it was to a gust of wind that knocked the hat from his head and sent it flying. He waded through the ankle-deep water, which quickly grew more forceful as he approached the boat. By the time he found an anchor for the craft—in the form of a streetlamp—the water covered his thighs, and it took all his strength to stay on his feet.

"Ahoy!" he shouted above a crack of thunder. The driver glanced at him, and Beau yelled, "Toss me a rope, and I'll tie you off."

As soon as he had the boat secured, he helped the driver and passenger inside the port office. The lantern's glow revealed a middle-aged couple, their dark hair slicked to the sides of their faces. They said the storm had caught them off guard and ten miles from home.

"If the lightning weren't so bad," the husband said, "I'd push ahead. The *Flying Lass* is the fastest boat I've ever owned." He glanced longingly into the parking lot. "My girl's going to take a beating out there."

His wife used her hand like a squeegee to remove the water from her face. "Boats are replaceable. People aren't."

Still gazing into the darkness, the man grunted in reluctant agreement.

That's when Beau realized how he could reach Cedar Bayou—on the very river he'd fled an hour ago. "You say the *Lass* is quick?" he asked, nearly cringing at the stupidity of the plan forming in his mind.

"Quick?" The man scoffed. "She'll pass *quick* and leave it spinning in her wake."

"Is she gassed up?" Beau asked.

"Yeah, why? You think I should dump the fuel tanks in case lightning strikes?"

Beau ignored the question because he didn't have a second to waste. "I'm the pilot and co-owner of the *Belle of the Bayou*, the big steamer docked out there."

"Okay," the man said, furrowing his brow.

"I'm telling you this," Beau said, "because I need to borrow your boat."

The port authority official nearly tipped back in his chair. "*What?* Are you out of your mind?"

Again, Beau ignored the question. "Ten years ago, I almost ruined the best thing that ever happened to me when I ran out on my girlfriend. It took a long time, but I finally convinced her to give me another chance, and eventually, to be my wife. Our wedding's set to take place in a couple hours, and I've got no way to tell her about the storm. If I don't show up, there'll be no coming back from that. She'll think I aband—"

"Listen, mister. I sympathize with you," the boat owner interrupted. "I really do. But if I give you the keys to the *Lass* and you wind up getting yourself killed out there, I'd never forgive myself."

"One way or another, I'm getting home tonight." Beau thumbed toward the parking lot. "If I have to, I'll wander up and down the riverbank until I find another boat. Seems to me, the *Lass* is the safest option. If you lend her to me, you'll be giving me my best shot." He pulled in a breath and hoped for a miracle. "What do you say?"

For the longest time, the man stared out the window. When he met Beau's gaze, it was with a disbelieving shake of his head. He pulled a key float from his pocket and slapped it in Beau's palm. "Godspeed, you crazy SOB."

After ninety-seven bobby pins—yes, Devyn counted—Allie secured one final curl in place and announced, "Now for the veil."

"Can I look yet?"

"Nope," Allie said. "Let's wait until we get the dress on so you can see the full effect."

Devyn bounced one high heel against the floor, but she sat obediently while Allie pinned the veil in place at the back of her updo. The noise of mingled voices carried from the sanctuary into the dressing room, telling Devyn that the guests had begun to arrive. Her pulse kicked into high gear, and she wiped her clammy palms on her robe. She wondered if Beau was in the opposite dressing room feeling the same butterflies of nervous anticipation.

It was like Allie had read her mind. "I told Marc to text me as soon as Beau gets here. So far, no word."

Devyn checked the time on her cell phone. The ceremony was scheduled to begin soon. "He's cutting it close."

"Time for lipstick." Allie used a finger to tilt Devyn's face toward the ceiling. "I've always heard you're supposed to do this before putting on the dress, just in case you drop the tube."

"If you're trying to distract me," Devyn said, "it's not working."

"Shh. Keep your mouth still."

Devyn parted her lips long enough to receive a coat of Flaming Vixen, and then she said, "Maybe I should ask Marc to call him." Immediately, she changed her mind. "No, that doesn't show perfect faith. I just need to calm down and trust that he'll be here." She peeked up and resisted the urge to gnaw on her freshly painted bottom lip. "Right?"

"I know what you need," Allie said. She opened one of the bottles of Chardonnay they'd brought for the reception and poured a generous serving into a plastic cup. "Bottoms up."

Devyn drained the cup and held it out for a refill,

then finished that one, too. The wine did its job, allowing her shoulders to sink from her ears down to their normal position.

Allie unzipped the plastic protector around Mama's dress and lovingly lifted it from the hanger. After shedding her robe, Devyn stepped inside the gown, slipped her arms in the sleeves, and waited for her sister to fasten the back.

"Ready?" Allie asked, and rotated Devyn to face the mirror. "Now tell me that's not a radiant bride."

Devyn gasped when she caught a glimpse of the dark-haired beauty in the mirror. Raven curls spilled from her French twist, peeking out beneath a white veil of delicate lace. Her eyes were dusted with shimmery shadow, her cheeks blushing a shade lighter than her lips. She looked classic and elegant, like she'd stepped out of a copy of *Modern Bride*. Devyn barely recognized herself.

"Thank you," she whispered to her sister. "You're good."

"Psh," Allie said with a dismissive wave. "You made my job easy."

A peal of laughter rang out from the sanctuary, and Devyn glanced at the wall separating her from the guests. There was no more putting it off—it was time to face her friends. She didn't know why the prospect put a hitch in her pulse, but it did. "I should go out there," she said. "I told Beau I'd be waiting at the altar."

Allie checked her cell phone, then pursed her lips in consideration. "Still nothing from Marc."

"Maybe he forgot to text you."

"You go ahead," Allie said with a nod toward the chapel. "I'll check the other dressing room and see if the groom's here." But first, she handed over a cluster of gerbera daisies in jewel tones of burgundy and orange. "I know we said 'no flowers,' but I had this made for you. Every bride needs a fresh bouquet."

After a hug, Allie slipped into the second dressing room while Devyn followed the hallway leading to the front of the sanctuary. She peeked out at the rows of pews populated by smiling, chattering friends, and her heart lifted. These people loved her, and they'd come out tonight to show their support. There was nothing to fear. Keeping that in mind, she summoned a smile and approached the first pew.

Too bad Jenny and Slade were seated there.

"I see you went with white," Jenny said, raking a gaze over Devyn's gown. She sniffed a dry laugh. "Interesting choice."

Devyn fought the urge to smash her bouquet in Jenny's face, instead tightening her smile and keeping her voice chipper. "It was my mother's dress."

"Hmm." Jenny tipped her head and returned the fake grin. "At least it's not *my* gown. I donated it to the Goodwill along with that red Gucci, so you could have easily picked it up on your last scavenging mission."

"Bless your sweet little heart," Devyn said, when what she really wanted to do was knock that Hore into next week. "And thanks for coming."

"We wouldn't miss it." Jenny patted her husband's leg. "Would we, babe?"

Slade quit staring at his iPhone and jerked to attention. "Where's Beau?"

Devyn peered around the chapel but didn't see him. She spotted Allie talking with Marc at the rear of the room, darting frequent glances out the open doors into the parking lot. "Running a bit late," Devyn said. "He'll be here any minute."

With the throttle wide open, Beau hauled ass downriver. Each raindrop stung his face like a tiny missile, but he'd faced worse pain than that in recon training. What really kept his heart pounding was the lightning. White-hot bolts struck the trees lining the riverbank, followed by a deafening boom that rattled his teeth. One surge hit so close that he felt a charge of electricity crawl over his skin.

He damned near wet himself.

The worst part was that he knew he'd never make it to the ceremony on time, and he had no idea how long Devyn would wait for him. All he could do was keep his head down, hold on tight, and hope that the *Lass* had enough gasoline in her tanks to get him to the New Orleans dock where he'd parked his SUV . . . and that lightning didn't strike him dead before then.

Another mile into his journey, the searchlight affixed to the front of the boat illuminated a shadowy object ahead, so he slowed the engines and approached with caution. A tree had fallen into the river and lay partially submerged. If he hadn't spotted it in time, the boat would've been gutted. Carefully, he motored around it and uttered a prayer of thanks.

He kept his speed in check after that, squinting against the rain while he scanned the muddy water for obstacles. He knew it was the safe thing to do, but he couldn't stop picturing Devyn standing at the altar, staring at the chapel doors for his arrival. Every moment he hesitated was another beat of agony for her. He checked his cell phone to see if his service had been restored, but the screen was dead. Likely because the cursed thing was soaking wet.

An hour later, his fingers ached from clenching the steering wheel, and his muscles were stiff enough to crack granite. An occasional sputter from the engine warned him that he'd nearly depleted his gas supply, but the rain had lightened to a drizzle, and the *Belle*'s docking station appeared in the distance. A bubble of hope expanded inside Beau's chest. Once he reached his SUV, he could be in Cedar Bayou within twenty minutes—fifteen if the traffic cops weren't watching.

After hitching the *Lass* to the dock, Beau hit the pavement running and patted his coat pockets for his key fob. Then his footsteps came to a gradual halt as realization set in. He'd left his car keys in the captain's quarters onboard the *Belle*.

"Shit!"

He growled in frustration and slammed the heel of his hand into the driver's-side window. The glass didn't break, but it gave him an idea. Beau had two choices: either siphon the gas from his vehicle's tank, then use it to pilot the boat downriver to Cedar Bayou, or he could break the SUV window and hotwire the engine.

He knew the second option would get him to the chapel faster, so he didn't spend another second debating what to do.

Beau scanned the parking lot for a heavy object, eventually settling on a broken cinder block near the sidewalk. He'd just retrieved the block and held it above his head to smash the rear passenger window when he heard a man's voice shout, "Freeze! Throw down your weapon and get on the ground!"

Father Durand raised his wrinkled hands and announced, "Go in peace and serve the Lord," to which the congregation responded in unison, "Thanks be to God."

Devyn pretended to scratch her cheek while sneaking a covert glance over her shoulder toward the chapel's rear entrance. She'd pleaded with the priest to perform the wedding Mass first, separate from the ceremony, in order to give Beau more time, but he still wasn't here. She plucked a hymnal from beneath her pew and caught Father Durand's eye, then held up the volume in a silent message.

"Uh," Father Durand said before understanding flashed in his gaze. "Please rise and join me in singing 'Gathered in the Love of Christ.'"

The assembly obeyed, but Devyn noticed half of them peering around the sanctuary in confusion. Clearly it hadn't escaped anyone's notice that the groom was missing, and she didn't know how much longer she could keep stalling. While mouthing the words to the hymn, Devyn peeked to her left at Allie, who in turn peered around Marc's arm at his cell phone. After checking the screen, Marc shoved the phone in his pocket with a bit too much force, and Allie furrowed her brow. Their reactions told Devyn everything she needed to know: Beau hadn't checked in.

The hymn ended far too soon, and Father Durand stood at the pulpit in silence while looking to her for direction. God bless that man, she would owe him a hundred fish fries to make up for this. She cleared her throat and said, "The groom is a bit delayed. How about we sing 'A Marriage Blessing'?"

The priest nodded slowly, then led the hymn.

Allie leaned close, pressing her lips to Devyn's ear. "Baby, I know you have faith," she whispered. "But it's past nine o'clock. We can't keep singing hymns all night."

"Just a little bit longer," Devyn whispered back. "I know he'll be here."

But when "A Marriage Blessing" ended, Beau's father and his pregnant girlfriend left their pew and headed for the exit. Encouraged by the defectors, Alex and Nick ducked their heads and followed up the aisle.

"Wait!" Devyn shouted. "Sit back down! Beau's on his way. Give him a few more minutes!"

Beau's father had the decency to pause while the other guests scurried around him and out the door. He gestured at his girlfriend's bulbous belly as if to say, *She can't take these hard pews any longer,* then gave an apologetic wave and left.

"No," Devyn whispered to herself. "Let's sing one more—"

"Miss Mauvais," the priest interrupted. His eyes were round with sympathy when she faced him. "Can I speak with you, please?"

She spun toward the group and held up both palms. "Everyone stay put!" Then she hitched up her gown and jogged up the steps to the altar. "Father, I know this looks bad. But I promise that—"

"Child, I'm sorry," he said with a shake of his gray head. "I have to release the congregation. If the groom has been detained, I can marry you another day."

"Please," she began until noise from behind distracted her. Devyn turned to find that half the assembly had snuck out while her back was turned. Each time a guest left their pew, it seemed to spur two more into action, and within seconds, only a few people remained.

Ironically, Jenny and Slade were among the last to leave. They stood in unison, and when Devyn locked eyes with her nemesis, her stomach turned heavy. She'd expected Jenny to gloat or laugh—at least to deliver her signature sneer—but her expression was thick with pity. She held up a hand and mouthed the word *sorry* before turning and following the others.

That's when Devyn's vision finally blurred with tears. She could handle Jenny's cruelty—it'd always been a sign that the girl was threatened by her—but not sympathy.

Anything but that.

Soon the only people who remained were Allie, Marc, and the priest. Nobody spoke for the longest time. Devyn stood at the altar, staring at her bouquet of orange and red daisies. The logical part of her brain told her to leave—that Beau wasn't coming. But her heart begged her to stay. Even after two hours of practically holding her guests hostage, she still believed he would come.

Maybe she was a fool.

"Hon," Allie said. "Father Durand needs to lock up." She held out a hand. "Come with me. I want you to stay at our place tonight."

A tear slipped down Devyn's cheek, and her voice cracked. "But I know he's coming."

Marc's eyes turned to slits. "You two go ahead to the house. I'm gonna track down my brother. Whether or not I let him live remains to be seen."

A breath hitched inside Devyn's chest, turning to a sob when she realized there was nothing more she could do. She wasn't going to get married tonight. Nodding in defeat, she tossed her bouquet to the floor and strode away from the altar. Allie met her in the aisle and wrapped her in a hug.

Marc patted her back and started to speak, but he cut off when the noise of sirens approached. The wail grew progressively louder until red and blue lights flashed through the church's windows. Then the rear doors busted open with a *clunk* and an enormous man bolted inside the sanctuary.

"Dev!" he shouted. "Thank God you're still here!"

Devyn's jaw dropped. She never would've recognized Beau if he hadn't spoken first. He was soaked to the skin, his filthy uniform plastered to his body while mud caked his cheeks. If she looked closely, she could make out the imprint of an oak leaf stuck to his head.

She wanted to ask what'd happened, but the joy of seeing him rendered her temporarily speechless. He hadn't abandoned her—nothing else mattered.

"Big electrical storm," he panted, lumbering closer. "Knocked out all the phones. I had to evacuate the *Belle* in Mississippi. Then I borrowed a speedboat and made it to New Orleans."

A pair of young police officers followed him inside. One of them grinned and added, "We caught him trying to bust out the window in his car. It's a good thing he had ID on him, otherwise, we'd have taken him in."

"An electrical storm?" Devyn repeated, bringing a hand to her breast. "You could have been killed."

"That's what we told him," said the second officer.

Ignoring everyone but Devyn, Beau strode forward until he stood close enough for her to smell the cool, musty river on his clothes. He reached down and took her hand, his grip wet but firm. "Kitten," he said, gazing at her as if nothing else existed. "I would die a thousand times before missing my chance to marry you."

Devyn's eyes welled with fresh tears, but these were the happy kind. Careful not to ruin her mother's dress, she stood on tiptoe and kissed him lightly on the lips— the only spot not covered in mud.

"You know," Father Durand said from his place at the altar, "we have more than enough witnesses to perform the ceremony. . . ."

Beau peered at her and smiled. "What do you say? I know I'm not much to look at, but if you don't mind—"

"*But* nothing," Devyn said, matching his grin. "You're the most breathtaking groom I've ever seen, and I can't wait to be your wife. Let's get married!"

Chapter 20

With her face glowing and framed by dark curls, Devyn was so beautiful that Beau had a hard time catching his breath. A tiny smudge of mascara shadowed her eyes, proof that he'd made her cry, and he longed to wipe away the evidence with his thumb. But since his hands were muddy, he stroked her palm and gazed at her with all the love in his heart—which was nearly more than he could contain.

"If it is your intent to enter into marriage," the priest said, "declare your consent before God and His church."

That was Beau's cue. "I, Beau Christopher Dumont, take you, Devyn Rebecca Mauvais, to be my wife." No words had ever tasted as sweet. "I promise to be faithful to you in good times and bad, in sickness and in health, and to honor you for all the days of my life."

When she repeated the vow, Beau feared that the joy expanding beneath his breastbone might literally burst him at the seams. He didn't know what he'd done to deserve such happiness, but he was grateful all the same.

Minutes later, Marc reached into his breast pocket and handed over a simple band of white gold. Devyn must have picked it out on her own, because they hadn't had a chance to visit the jeweler together. The engagement ring he'd given her—the one she'd given back—was tucked beneath a stack of socks in his top dresser drawer. He couldn't wait to put it back on her hand. In the meantime, Beau slipped the dainty wedding band on her finger and said, "Take this ring as a sign of my love and fidelity."

Devyn did the same, adorning his dirty finger with a band of gleaming metal. It was a damned fine sight, and he imagined his face would be beaming if it weren't buried beneath a layer of muck.

Finally came the moment Beau had been waiting for—the pronouncement: verbal proof that he and Devyn belonged to each other.

The priest gave them a wide smile. "Insomuch as Devyn and Beau have consented to live together in holy matrimony, having promised their love for each other with these vows, I declare that they are husband and wife." Then he bent at the waist and said to Beau, "Congratulations. You may kiss your bride."

Beau's first instinct was to embrace his wife and kiss her into next week, but he didn't want to stain her dress. It was all Devyn had left of her mother. So he tipped Devyn's chin with one finger and lightly brushed her lips while applause broke out from their meager audience.

"Go change out of that gown, Mrs. Dumont," he whispered against her mouth. "Then I'll give you a proper kiss."

"It's a deal, Mr. Dumont," she whispered back. "And by the way, there's a set of clean clothes for you in the groom's dressing room."

Thank God for Devyn's meticulous planning, because Beau's uniform was beginning to feel like a wetsuit of crushed ice. "I wish I'd known that before the ceremony."

Devyn shook her head. "I wasn't letting you out of my sight until we said *I do*. Now you can change."

Marc piped up, wearing a smile that oozed mischief. "Not yet. I want photographic evidence that I wasn't the ugliest groom in Dumont family history."

Allie gasped, then smacked her husband on the arm.

"Can't argue with that," Beau said. Chuckling, he stood near Devyn and posed for a photo. "I caught a glimpse of my reflection in the car window back in New Orleans. It's a wonder the cops didn't shoot me on sight."

The officers laughed, and after they agreed to stay for cake, Beau reluctantly parted from Devyn to change clothes. He hated to be away from her, so he made it quick—scrubbing his face and hands in the sink, then shucking off his wet uniform in favor of the pressed suit she'd brought over from his place. He still didn't resemble a proper groom, but if Beau had his way, his clothes would adorn the floor of a hotel suite within the hour.

When he met Devyn in the fellowship hall, she was filling two cups of punch for the officers. She wore jeans and a pink T-shirt with BRIDE printed across her chest, and she'd removed the veil but kept her curls pinned in place so they spilled gradually around her cheeks. Beau leaned against the doorjamb for a moment and simply took her in, all smiles and warmth and laughter.

He couldn't believe she was his.

As if she sensed him watching, Devyn glanced over her shoulder. An instant smile appeared on her lips, and she ran toward him with outstretched arms. He pulled her tightly against his chest to savor her soft curves. Suddenly, something deep inside clicked into place, making him whole when he hadn't even realized he was lacking. Beau filled his lungs with her scent of honeysuckle, and then he gave her the kiss she deserved—deep and thorough with a passion that wasn't fit for polite company.

It didn't take long for objections to arise from the peanut gallery.

"Aw, come on," Marc said. "There's a priest here, for Crissakes." His wife elbowed him hard in the ribs, so he crossed himself while tipping his head in apology to Father Durand. "Sorry, Father."

The old man checked his watch. "You're forgiven, but perhaps we should cut the cake. I'm running late for an anointing at the hospital."

"Oh," Devyn said, taking Beau's hand and leading him toward the cake. "I almost forgot."

Allie snapped pictures while they fed each other a bite of red velvet cake. Beau had never liked the act of "smashing," so he slid his fork carefully between Devyn's parted lips, and she did the same. Afterward, Marc lifted his champagne flute in a toast.

"To my big brother and his beautiful bride," he said with a genuine smile. "Beau, we haven't always seen eye to eye, but I want you to know that I'm proud to call you my friend. You're a good man, and you're going to make an even better husband. Devyn, welcome to the family. We're a crazy bunch, but we love you, and I promise that life with us will never be boring."

"I can confirm that," Allie added.

Beau's heart warmed. It was hard to believe that this time last year, he hadn't been on speaking terms with his brother. So much had changed, and he was thankful for that, too.

"To Devyn and Beau," Marc said.

The rest of the group echoed his words, and the clinking of crystal followed. Allie cut a slice of cake for everyone, and within minutes, each plate was clean. The police officers were the first to go. They shook Beau's hand and kissed Devyn's cheek, then congratulated them and left to resume their patrol.

Devyn presented a small wrapped gift to the priest and promised to lock the fellowship hall. The man offered a quick prayer of benediction and said good-bye, leaving Allie and Marc as their last remaining guests.

"You two get the honeymoon started," Allie said. "We'll handle the cleanup."

"Take my car." Marc tossed his keys across the room. "We'll make do with Allie's until you guys get back."

Beau wasn't going to argue with that. After a round of hugs, he scooped Devyn into his arms and carried her to the door. Just when they reached the threshold, she stopped him and made one last request of her sister.

"Hey, do me a favor and run an announcement in the *Cedar Bayou Gazette* with our wedding picture, then mail a clipping to Jenny Hore. She'd better not be nice to me the next time our paths cross."

Beau didn't understand that last bit, but he didn't spend another second dwelling on it. He carried Devyn into the parking lot, and before you could say *Just Married*, they were on the main road leading to the highway.

"Where to?" he asked. "The airport? The moon? I'll take you anywhere you want."

Devyn leaned to the side, resting her head on his shoulder. "I made reservations for us in Baton Rouge."

"Nice." They could make the drive in a little over an hour. "I'm glad we're honeymooning on dry land. I've had my fill of the water."

"Hurry up and get us there," she whispered in his ear. "Because I want my fill of *you*."

"Yes, ma'am." Beau found the interstate and laid rubber. "My wife gets what she wants."

It was all Devyn could do to keep her hands to herself at the check-in counter and then the elevator to their suite on the third floor. During the drive to Baton Rouge, a gradual longing had settled in her bones until she couldn't think of anything except Beau inside her, making them one flesh. She'd never needed him so desperately, and the instant he opened the door, she started pulling off his suit jacket.

"Hold up," he said, extending a hand to keep her in the hallway. "I want to do this right." He swept her into his arms and carried her across the threshold, then kicked the door shut. "There," he murmured against her mouth while setting her down. "Now feel free to rip off my clothes."

She accepted his invitation, peeling off both of their shirts. When she went to work on his trousers, he stopped her.

"I need a shower," he said. "Want to join me?"

By way of answer, she stripped naked and led the way into the bathroom. Moments later, they were standing beneath a steaming spray, locked at the lips while Devyn soaped him up in all her favorite places.

She imagined how she must look, with mascara running down her face and her updo ruined, but she didn't give it a second thought. Instead, she ran her palms over her husband's chiseled chest, down his flat abdomen, over his muscular thighs, and finally to the powerful erection pressed to her belly.

She grasped him at the base and stroked him hard enough to draw a groan of pleasure from his throat. A new desire overtook her, this time to taste him. After rinsing the soap from his body, Devyn sank to her knees and took him fully into her mouth in one brisk motion that had him gasping out loud. Tipping back his head, Beau braced himself against the tile wall and let her take what she needed. She licked and sucked, working him with each long slide of her lips, savoring the sweetness of his skin and the salty beads of arousal rising to his tip until he made her stop.

"No more," he ordered, and tugged her to standing. His eyes were heavy with lust, but there was something else there: the same all-consuming need that burned her from the inside out. They'd made love many times before, but this was different.

Bigger, somehow.

He took one of her breasts in his palm, then lowered to draw her nipple deep into his mouth. She felt the pull of each wet tug directly between her legs, and he must have known it, because he used two fingers to sate the ache, slipping and sliding over her sensitive flesh before dipping inside to tease her until she throbbed.

Beau growled with desire and pushed his shaft between the slick passage of her upper thighs. "God, Dev. I want you right now, but our first time shouldn't be in the shower."

Releasing a soft laugh, she hitched a leg around his hip, then took him in her hand and guided his plump head inside her. Her toes curled at the sensation, and she strained to take him deeper. "Baby, our first time was more than a decade ago, right on the riverbank where anyone could've caught us."

"I remember," he said, and inched deeper. "I wanted

to take you somewhere private, but you were so wet, and you felt so damned good that I couldn't tell whether I was coming or going."

"Mmm." She recalled the sensation all too well. "We couldn't stop."

"Like now."

"Just like now."

Beau rocked into her one luscious inch at a time, and with a final upward glide, he filled her completely. They shared a low groan and locked eyes. In that moment, they were so connected in body and spirit that Devyn couldn't tell where her flesh ended and his began. It was a new emotion—beautiful and so strong that her rib cage hurt.

"I love you," Beau said while he held her hips between his massive palms and pulled out to the tip. She wanted to tell him the same, but when he thrust impossibly deeper, all she could do was make an embarrassing mewling sound. "And I love that noise," he added with a primal rotation of hips that sent her eyes rolling back. "Make it again, Kitten."

She didn't have to try. With each rhythmic stroke, each slow grind, a chorus of animalistic sounds arose from her lips. In desperation, she reached out blindly for traction so she could move with him, but her wet fingers slid off the tile. So she sank her fingernails into Beau's shoulders and panted while he rocked into her so slowly she feared her knees might buckle. Then he held her gaze and quickened the tempo, deepening his thrusts and driving her toward the edge. Soon her lower back was pressed against the wall as he slammed into her, one loud clap of flesh and then another filling the steamy room.

Sweet pressure built between Devyn's legs, increasing until she sobbed with mingled agony and bliss. Beau held inside her to gyrate his hips, and the pain burst into spasms of ecstasy. She came so hard that her vision went black for a moment, and when she focused again, it was to the sight of Beau's green eyes on her. She saw complete adoration there when he bucked against her one final time and let go.

As he came deep within her, Devyn told him, "I love you more."

After that, she went limp as a dishrag.

Beau took her in his powerful arms and turned off the water, then carried her to the king-size bed, where he tucked her beneath the covers and joined her. In the light streaming from the bathroom, she noticed the change in the skin above his heart for the first time.

"Your birthmark," she whispered, stroking the spot with her thumb. "It's gone."

He glanced down and grinned. "Good riddance. I never liked that thing."

"I guess we really did break the hex."

"Of course we did," he said. "Was there ever any doubt?"

They both knew the answer to that question. There *had* been doubt on Devyn's part, and it'd nearly driven them apart. A shiver rolled over her skin when she remembered how close she'd come to letting fear and insecurity keep her from a fulfilling life with her true companion.

"Yes," she answered. "But I promise it'll never happen again. Beau, I'm sorry for ever doubting—"

"Shh." He pressed a finger to her mouth and settled atop her, using a knee to part her thighs. "No apologies allowed on our wedding night." A hint of amusement danced in his gaze. "Have you forgotten what your tongue is for?"

Smiling, Devyn opened for him and slipped both hands possessively over his broad back. *This is my husband*, she thought. *Now and forever.* It seemed she didn't have room for any more happiness, but that wouldn't stop her from trying. "I might need a reminder."

"Lucky for both of us," he said, "I love making you remember."

The last thing she saw before his head dipped beneath the covers was a flash of dimples. Then he kissed a trail down her belly until he reached his destination.

After that, there was no more talking.

Epilogue

Beau spotted Devyn staggering up the bow ramp with an armload of textbooks, so he rushed to help her. He took the volumes and peered at the one on top of the stack. *Science Content for Secondary Students*. It sounded boring, but he'd never admit that and risk giving her a reason to change her mind again. "How exciting," he said instead. "You're on your way to being a licensed teacher!"

She rolled her eyes but couldn't conceal a smile. "In four years."

"Maybe three," he reminded her. "If you take a full summer schedule."

"We already talked about this." As they climbed the outside steps, she shielded her eyes and admired the sparkle of sunlight dancing on the river. The wind tossed her curls, and her lush pink lips spread into an appreciative smile. It stunned Beau into a beat of silence, and he wondered if he'd ever get his fill of looking at her. Probably not. "I'm taking summers off to work in the education center during high season," she said. "My mind's made up."

He knew better than to argue. And truthfully, he liked the idea of them spending summers together aboard the *Belle*. In their nearly three weeks as husband and wife, he'd had to leave her for only one overnight charter, and that was one night too long.

"And by the way," she added, "you don't want to know how much those textbooks cost."

A receipt peeked out from between the pages, so Beau pulled it free and scanned the total. He nearly dropped the whole stack. A hundred dollars per book? She was right—he didn't want to know. "Well," he said. "I guess you can't put a price on education."

Devyn stood on tiptoe to kiss his cheek. "Actually, you can. The university is really good at it."

They made their way to the captain's suite on the top floor, where they usually camped out when Beau was on duty. After depositing her textbooks, they linked hands and headed back down the stairs to the formal dining hall's executive bar, where a family meeting was already in progress.

At once, Beau sensed that something was wrong.

Allie sat beside Marc, dabbing her eyes with a tissue while her husband stared blankly at a piece of paper in his hand. On the other side of the table, Alex and Nicky wore dazed expressions, their twin blond brows lifted and their blue eyes wide. The only sound in the room was the steady *whir* of a refrigerator behind the bar. Not only that, but the head purser was absent.

"What's the matter?" Beau asked, glancing from person to person. "Where's Ella-Claire?" Everyone at the table avoided his gaze, so he pulled up a chair and repeated the question while Devyn settled on his lap.

Marc scrubbed a hand over his face, then slid a piece of paper across the table. At first glance, it looked like an ordinary business letter, but then Beau recognized Ella-Claire's signature at the bottom. He held it up so Devyn could read it at the same time.

Dear Marc and family,

Please accept this letter of resignation from my position as head purser aboard the Bell of the Bayou, *effective immediately. I'm sorry for not being able to give you more notice, but I have accepted another position out of town, and they requested that I start right away.*

Thank you for your support and understanding, both now and for the past decade. I have loved working alongside all of you, and I will miss you deeply. However, I'm at a point in my life where a change is needed, and I trust you to respect that.

Take care of one another while I'm away.

Much love,
Ella-Claire

Beau fisted the paper as his jaw went slack. Just days ago, he'd seen Ella when she had brought a gift to the house—a framed wedding portrait and an "Our First Christmas" ornament for the upcoming holiday. Now she was gone, just like that.

It didn't seem real.

But as the seconds passed, he recalled her behavior on the last charter, and the puzzle pieces clicked into place. Anger flushed his cheeks because he knew exactly why she'd left. He shook the letter at Marc. "This is because of that asshole she was dating."

Marc sat straighter. "What asshole?"

"I don't know," Beau admitted. "She wouldn't give me his name, but I could tell that he messed with her head." He pointed the letter at Alex, her best friend. "Did she tell you anything about this guy?"

Before Alex had a chance to answer, Devyn spoke up. "I think we should mind our own business and do what Ella asked of us: respect her choice. She's a grown woman, and she knows what she wants."

Nicky waved her off. "Screw that. If someone hurt her, I'll have his ass."

"Not before me, you won't," Marc said in a low growl.

"Let's not get ahead of ourselves," Allie said, but then the table erupted in a riot of conversation and arguments, each voice raised in an effort to be heard.

It went on for several minutes until Alex stood up from the table so quickly that his chair tipped over. His typically fair skin flushed dark when he locked eyes with Marc and yelled, "It was me. I'm the asshole. Are you happy now?"

Allie and Devyn shared a sideways glance that told Beau this wasn't news to either of them. But he sure hadn't seen it coming. "What're you talking about?" he asked.

Alex never took his gaze off Marc when he answered. "Ella wanted to be more than friends, but our brother made it perfectly clear that I couldn't touch her. So I told her no." His tone was charged with contempt when he added, "Looks like you got what you wanted."

"Don't twist my words," Marc ground out. If he clenched his jaw any harder, he'd break his face in half. "This is *not* what I wanted."

"Bullshit! You've been riding my ass for months about keeping away from her."

"Damn straight—because I don't want you *riding* my kid sister!"

Devyn held up both palms and said, "Everyone needs to calm down." But the staring match didn't end until she said, "Ella-Claire talked to me about this."

Marc whipped his head around. "And you didn't make her stay?"

"She didn't tell me she was leaving town," Devyn said. "But even if she had, I would have let her go. I know she's your little sister, but she's not a child, Marc. She knew that pursuing a relationship with Alex would have consequences, but she was willing to accept it because she's been in love with him for years. Maybe she resigned because she doesn't need a big brother to protect her from the things she wants in life. Have you considered that?"

The room fell silent and everyone went back to avoiding one another's eyes.

It was Alex who spoke first. "You can have my resignation, too." And then he strode from the table.

"Wait a minute," Marc objected. "We haven't talked about—"

"I'm done talking." Alex never slowed his steps, leaving them with one final message before he disappeared out the door. "At least to you."

Well, add that to the list of things Beau didn't see coming today.

"Wonderful." Marc threw his hands in the air. "Now we're missing our head purser and our personnel director."

"*And* your half brother and sister," Allie reminded him in a chiding voice.

His shoulders drooped an inch. "That, too."

Beau wrapped an arm around Devyn's waist and bent his mouth to her ear. "Your first day back on the job," he whispered, "and you've already caused a mutiny, Mrs. Dumont."

"It'll be all right in the end." For a while, she peered quietly out the port window. "Alex learned something today that took me a long time to figure out, too."

"What's that?"

She looked at him and her gaze turned soft. "Some things are worth the risk."

Beau placed a kiss on her nose. "I'm proud of you."

"For what?" she asked.

"For turning down Larabee's partnership and going back to school." He knew she hadn't taken the easy road, and he respected her for that. "It'll pay off in the end."

She looked confused at first, but then realization dawned in her eyes. "That's not the risk I was talking about."

"Then what was it?"

"You," she said, locking both arms around his neck. "It took me a long time to make peace with the fact that I can't control the future. We might have one year together, or fifty. But I'll cherish each moment, because it's a gift."

Her words made him go all warm inside. Just when he thought Devyn couldn't make him any happier, she outdid herself. "I'm a lucky man," he told her.

"The luckiest," she agreed, then proved it by leaning in to kiss him.

Beau brushed her lips with his and whispered, "There was never any risk, Kitten. I've been yours since our first date."

"Ditto." She grinned as if replaying the memory, and Beau could swear that he heard the chirp of bayou crickets from his old fishing hole. "Something happened that night. It was . . ."

She paused until their eyes met, and then they answered in unison, a smile on both their faces.

"Magical."

Macy Beckett

MAKE YOU MINE
The Dumont Bachelors

For ninety-nine years, every man in the Dumont family
has remained a perpetual bachelor—supposedly cursed
long ago by a voodoo witch. In truth, the Dumont men
have their own player personalities to blame, and Marc is
no exception. As captain of his family's riverboat, he's
broken hearts up and down the Mississippi.

But when his high school crush, Allie Mauvais, fills in as
the riverboat pastry chef, old feelings are rekindled. But to
reach Marc's heart, she must show him that the hex is all
in his head. Will Allie's love be enough to finally make
Marc hers?

macybeckett.com

Available wherever books are sold or at
penguin.com

facebook.com/LoveAlwaysBooks